Silver Love

Silver Love

Josette Murray

SAPPHIRE BOOKS

SALINAS, CALIFORNIA

ISBN - 978-1-948232-51-7

Editor - Heather Flournoy
Book Design - LJ Reynolds
Cover Design - Fineline Cover Design

Sapphire Books Publishing, LLC
P.O. Box 8142
Salinas, CA 93912
www.sapphirebooks.com

Printed in the United States of America
First Edition - March 2019

This and other Sapphire Books titles can be found at
www.sapphirebooks.com

Dedication

"One day an army of gray-haired women may quietly take over the Earth!"
-Gloria Steinem

This book is dedicated to all the silver-haired foxes who refuse to go quietly into our advanced years. May our love and chutzpah go on forever.

Acknowledgments

Thank you to my love and most excellent beta reader, Pascal Scott, for getting me started, urging me forward, supporting me, prodding when needed, and in general being my Muse.

Many, many thanks to my other most-excellent: my editor, Heather Flournoy, of Feather In Your Cap Editing. She is not just an editor; she's a teacher in the grand style, a thoughtful commentator on story and intent (which sometimes don't match), an eagle-eyed manuscript inspector, and funny to boot. A writer couldn't ask for anything more.

And finally, my sincere gratitude to Christine Svendsen and Sallyanne Monti for welcoming me into such a wonderfully professional publishing house and family of talented writers. I am honored.

Chapter One

"Well, I didn't *mean* to lose my bathing suit in the water! But it was nighttime and there was no one around and I just love skinny dipping. So I slipped out of it and just slung it over the side of the dock, and at some point it fell in. This happened up at my brother and sister-in-law's cabin up on Lake Burton. I was just about to come out of the water, naked or not, when their neighbor Bob chose exactly that moment to turn on the floodlights on his dock across the way, so I was stuck. I couldn't find my suit in the dark, although I dove down several times and groped in the darkness and mud, undoubtedly mooning Bob every time. And it was about then that I remembered I'd forgotten my towel, too, which hadn't bothered me much before because it was no big deal to walk back up to the cabin in a wet suit on a warm summer night."

Dory took another sip of her wine and grinned self-consciously as her friends began to laugh.

"So I just stayed in the water, hanging onto the ladder which, wouldn't you know, faced Bob's boathouse, until my eight-year-old niece, Rita, came down to tell me dinner was ready.

"'Honey, go tell Auntie Robby I need a towel, okay?' I sweetly asked her.

"'I don't want to leave you here in the dark,' she replied. 'And besides, Robby told me to bring you back.'

"'No, it's okay, really, honey, I'm fine. I just need a towel because…well, because I lost my swimsuit in the water and I can't get out without it.'

"'No, I don't want to leave you,' she replied stubbornly.

"Back and forth we went for a few minutes until I lost my temper. 'Goddammit, Rita, go tell Robby I need a towel so I *can* get out of the water and come up.'

"Off she fled, to stay away a long time. I wondered what was taking so long, and later Robby told me that she came back with a very hang-dog expression.

"'What's the matter, Rita?' she asked. 'Where's Dory?'

"Rita broke out into sniffles. 'Auntie Dory was mean to me,' she said. 'She said a bad word and that she wouldn't come out of the water until we brought her a towel.'

"Mystified, Robby turned the gas off on the stove, grabbed a towel, and came down to the dock with Rita, who was still in high dudgeon.

"'Oh, thank God,' I said as she came down the catwalk to the dock.

"'What on earth is going on? Rita said you were mean to her. Why are you still in the water?' I rose up a little. 'Oh! I see!' she said, starting to smile. 'Why are you naked?'

"'Oh, Rita, I'm sorry, honey,' I said. 'But I really, really needed a towel and you just weren't listening to me. I didn't mean to be mean to you.'

"Robby started laughing as she handed the towel down. 'I can't *wait* to hear how you got into this pickle, Dory Martin. I have a feeling you've outdone yourself.'

"Thus rescued, we walked back up to the cabin, Rita still flouncing in a little bit of self-justified outrage.

Later, she watched a movie while we relaxed on the deck with burgers and vodka gimlets, and I told my tale. Robby laughed and laughed, commenting that at least I would never be accused of being boring."

"Well, I don't wonder," Charlene said. "But that is so typical of you, Dory. They say God takes care of drunks and little children, and you weren't even drunk at the time, were you? Maybe it's fools and little children."

"It should be fools," Dory said ruefully. "And that wasn't the only time that happened to me. A couple of years before, I was on another lake boating and decided to skinny dip in broad daylight, since the lake was deserted. Same thing happened, and just as I saw it slip off the side of the boat and go under and I started desperately diving, I heard the brrr of a boat approaching. Luckily, they just went on by. I tell you, I'm hopeless."

Shaking her fresh shaker of martinis, Jill laughed. "No argument there, Dory girl, but we adore you anyway, or maybe because of it. You seem to meet disasters regularly but manage to go on coasting through life. I don't think I'd be so lucky," she commented to nods all around. "I'd probably get busted."

"Now, who's done what in the last week?" Charlene demanded. "Share time! With the election, you know, I'm living my life vicariously through you guys, so catch me up."

"Sure, as long as you share some of your old stories from the claims court."

"Oh, I've had a few good ones. One guy came before me charged with fraud and theft by taking. His name was Coupe de Ville Brown. Guess he had to support the lifestyle that his name demanded."

"Coupe de Ville!" Jill whooped. "I love it. Okay, let's see, what's happened with me. I've met someone interesting—but she's quite young, and I'm sure you'll meet her soon. I'm not going to say more than that, though. I'll just let you judge her for yourself."

"Oh, I'm sure," Charlene said, teasing. "Since when are you so reticent? Come on, dish, girl. For example, just how young is she, you cougar?"

Jill made a face. "Oh, that horrible term. Makes me sound like a ravenous cat at the least, and maybe a raggedy-coated old tabby to boot. I'm neither, although the idea of being a sleek cat isn't so bad. Anyway, to answer your impertinent question, my dear, she's in her thirties."

She flushed at the predictable round of whistles and shouts that greeted that announcement and said defensively, "Well, what of it? And she's drop-dead gorgeous to boot, and quite interesting. Enough so that I think I'm going to be exclusive for a while."

"Uh, yeah, I can imagine she's interesting," Charlene deadpanned. "But why would you want to settle down when there are so many fish in the sea?"

Jill snorted. "Oh, yeah? And where would they be? It was different in the roaring days of our youth when there were five lesbian bars in Atlanta for us to choose from. They're almost all gone now but for Girls Only, and let's be honest, we're not as young and thin and therefore simply gaw-jus as we were. Okay, so this city has about five million people in it. Say ten percent are gay—"

"More," Dory interrupted.

"Well, even so," Jill said. "So, that's five hundred thousand people, and say even twenty percent of those are lesbians. That's a hundred thousand lesbians.

And say thirty percent of them are over fifty, which is cutting it a little young, even. That's, let's see..."

Putting on her glasses, she pulled up the calculator on her phone. "Oh, duh, of course, that's thirty thousand lesbians. Wow. Where are they all? We could practically fill a stadium with them, like in the old days when women's music was thriving and people like Cris Williamson and Meg Christian were recording. No women's concert or festival is likely to happen now."

"Ugh, music festivals. Tents in the mud and bare-assed cabins with lumpy beds," Dory said. "But then there would be bare-assed women, too, not to mention the women—I mean, the music. Maybe not so bad after all."

Jill mock-glared at her. "So how do we find all these wonderful women, who are probably staying home and only going out to meet with friends like we do?"

Charlene sighed sympathetically. "I know, I know," she said. "And my history of meetings with people from online sites is littered with uncomfortable moments. Either they posted a picture taken forty pounds or twenty years ago, or both, or they're just a little weird...or they might be perfectly nice, but it's just not a match."

"You've gotta kiss a lot of frogs before you find the princess." Robby nodded in agreement. "But why don't you try the meet-up groups? They include all kinds of hobbies and interests, and it's a lot less fraught than a hookup website where everyone knows everyone else is looking for that 'certain someone.'"

"Well, but I guess it can work, though," Charlene said. "I remember after my last breakup, I posted clearly that I wasn't looking for a relationship, just companionship and, if the chemistry was right, maybe some good old-fashioned sex. The responses I got were just as clear, and some were rewarding…"

"You slut," Dory said fondly.

"Well, what's the harm?" she said.

"No offense," Dory hastened to assure her. "I was just teasing you, you know, dear."

"Well, really," Charlene insisted, "we are old enough to know what we want, and young enough to reach out and take it—if we're smart, in my opinion. Who knows how long any of us has, anyway? I'm sixty-nine, although I still don't believe it, and you're sixty-three, Robby's sixty-seven, and Jill's a young'un at fifty-eight, but still. We've gotten to the point in life that we always wished for, with the right to be downright eccentric if we want to. Who's going to gainsay us?"

"You're right, of course," Jill agreed.

"And sometimes it does work, although maybe not in ways you expect," Robby said, directing a loving look Dory's way. "Dory and I met the old-fashioned way, face-to-face, at a party in New Orleans over twenty years ago. But I know women who've met the love of their life online. You've made a number of friends online from people who didn't share a sexual spark with you, didn't you, Charlene?"

"Yup, and I love 'em all. Not in the biblical sense, of course. Worse luck. But okay, Dory, dish," she said. "Past histories can be fun, but what's happening more recently?"

"Well, you know, even though we've been together forever, Robby and I are still learning about each other…"

"Surely not in the biblical sense, as Charlene

said?" teased Jill.

"Oh, no, love, we've covered the Bible very well and are still studying seriously," she responded with a grin. "No, I mean as people, individuals. Like last week, I really hurt her feelings with a remark. I was talking about one aspect of what I'd said—how I felt about an acquaintance—but what she heard was that she was failing in comparison. I felt terrible afterward and apologized for being thoughtless. It's an ongoing adventure."

"For which I so envy you, girlfriend. To be in love and having hot sex at our age? You are one lucky girl," Jill said. "I'm happy to have the hot sex, but I miss the 'in love' part."

"I am lucky, I know," Dory admitted.

"All right, now, y'all, I have a proposal to make that should take all our worries and cares off our minds, at least temporarily," Robby said. "Are you ready?"

"Good heavens, do tell," said Jill, refreshing her glass for her second—or was it her third?—martini. "Did you buy us all winning lottery tickets and forget to tell us?"

"Ha! Like that's an issue for you, Jill," chided Dory. "Now, I for one would purely love to hear that."

"No, nothing so amazing, but still pretty wonderful," Robby replied. "I think we should all go to New Orleans's French Quarter Festival this year. It'd be nice to get out of Atlanta for a while. It's April twelfth to the fifteenth and it's the biggest free music festival in the country. Dory and I used to go all the time—first separately and then together, after we met—and we just loved it. I found a great house that would hold all of us in comfort, for cheap. What do you say?"

"Absolutely, let's do it," Dory begged. "You just

won't believe how wonderful New Orleans is. We'll have such fun!"

"Sounds good to me," said Charlene.

"Me, too," echoed Jill. "What's the house like?"

"Oh, it's great," Robby reported. "Three bedrooms and two baths with towering ceilings and windows, a porch and walled backyard with a fountain, and right near the Canal Street cable car stop to take us straight into the French Quarter."

"Air conditioned?"

"Of course," Robby reassured Jill.

"Then sold!" Jill said, and the friends began plotting their great excursion.

Chapter Two

"Welcome to NOLA, ladies," Marie, the B&B hostess, smiled warmly. "Here for the French Quarter Music Festival, are you?"

"Yes." Dory grinned back. "And excited to be here! Robby and I lived here for years and have missed it since we moved, and believe it or not, it's our friends' first visit."

"Hello, I'm Charlene," Charlene said, shaking Marie's hand.

"And I'm Jill," Jill added, doing the same. "And this is my friend Taylor."

"Robby," Robby said, the last to shake hands.

Taylor's presence caused a little bit of a stir among the friends. At only thirty-five, she was considerably younger than the others, and she was eye candy for sure. At five feet seven inches and a delightfully curvy 135 pounds, she had cascading layered black hair, vivid blue eyes, and razor-sharp Angelina Jolie cheekbones. In short, she was a knockout. While they loved and appreciated Jill's multiple charms, the three friends had to wonder what this millennial found so enchanting that she wanted to hang with a bunch of sixty-somethings, even young-at-heart ones.

The two had met at a fundraiser. Jill's curiosity had been piqued by Taylor's work. She had a Kickstarter account to raise money to produce a film based on a popular book Jill had read about women—including lesbians—of a certain age, and had raised more than $20,000 locally in addition to funds raised in Los Angeles. Jill had enjoyed the book and was interested in the movie because she was sure there was a big market out there for such work. And then lust had taken over.

Smitten, Jill asked for Taylor to come along, and the friends just rolled their eyes and made room for the newbie, however long she lasted. But while she might be part of the group for this trip, they vowed she was not part of the posse. And since Jill was paying her freight, they just couldn't resist keeping an eye on her.

"Come on in and make yourselves at home," said Marie. "I live right next door, so if there's anything you need or if I can help in any way, just knock on the door or call me. I'll be happy to steer you to some great little restaurants or groceries nearby, or help with the city's transit. Whatever, just call on me."

"Thanks, Marie," Robby said. "We probably will."

Marie took her leave and they started to move into their rental house. Online, Robby had found an unusually large three-bedroom classic New Orleans shotgun on Iberville Street. Inside they found a spacious, high-ceilinged living room leading to a long hall, off of which were two of the bedrooms and a bath, and the eat-in kitchen and screened porch were in the back. The third bedroom was luxuriously tucked under the back porch, with its own deluxe bath. From the porch, they looked down at a lovely cobblestone courtyard with a raised fountain in the center, flowers and plants in profusion, and an intricately scrolled wrought iron table with four chairs. Sophisticated, charming, and lush, it was everything one imagined New Orleans to be, and the ladies fell in love instantly.

"Lordy, I could live here, easily," said Jill, taking it all in appreciatively. "Well, this porch can be the coffee and cocktail lounge. And oh, look, there's a grill in the courtyard if we feel like cooking."

"Since I organized this trip, I call dibs on the downstairs courtyard room for me and Dory," Robby said.

"Good call," Charlene responded as Taylor looked crestfallen, and they moved back out to bring their bags to their rooms.

"We're going to take a little nap before we launch out into the wilds of New Orleans, ladies," said Jill, opening the hallway door to the first bedroom. The other three glanced knowingly at each other and proceeded to get settled in their own rooms.

"Damn, I feel like we should echo," said Jill. "These ceilings must be fourteen feet tall."

"I guess they had to be, to let the heat rise away from the people," said Taylor, admiring the décor. The windows rose to eight feet off the floor, the glass covered with lace and framed with heavy damask draperies. The sleigh bed was a queen with a high, hotel-quality mattress—she could tell—with four down pillows piled at its head and a lace canopy overhead. It was a dark wood, as was the antique dresser to the side, topped by a large mirror. Tufted Queen Anne chairs graced both sides of the night tables. The bedroom and closet doors rose a majestic seven feet and closed with a whisper.

After a quick shower, Jill closed the thick draperies and slipped into bed. She smiled appreciatively as Taylor re-entered from the bath, slipping off her silk robe to reveal a skimpy black negligee. "Darling girl, you are an artist's dream," Jill said, holding out her arms.

Taylor's lips curved as she slipped into the bed. "Oh, does this humble body please you?" she said, pressing close and nuzzling Jill's neck.

"Um-hmm, and how," said Jill, arching her neck and sighing.

Taylor's hands traveled over her naked body, dipping into the curve of her waist and tracing the swell of her hips, then rose up the other side and paused at her breasts. Tweaking a nipple to Jill's slight squeal, she said "Your breasts are still firm and round, just beautiful, darling."

"Hormone replacement therapy, honey," responded Jill. "We're all on it. It keeps me young."

"Ummm, yes it does," Taylor said, as her hands drifted through Jill's thick hair and traced the outline of her chin, kissing her harder. She slowly traced a path down to and back up from Jill's knees, caressing and kneading as her strong hands inexorably rose. Her fingers lightly brushed Jill's cleft, eliciting a groan and raised hips.

"Shhh, baby, not too loud, now. You wouldn't want to disturb Charlene next door. Be very, very still, lover," Taylor commanded as her strokes became more insistent. Jill gave another muffled groan, eyes watering with the intensity of feeling pulsing through her body, unable to give it voice. She squirmed and whimpered as Taylor stroked. "Ah, you're getting wet, sweetheart. Good girl. Be still, now," she whispered with a wicked grin as she entered her lover.

In an agony of ecstasy and frustration, Jill grasped the pillows in a death grip, lips clamped shut to muffle her keening as she came, over and over again.

"That's my hot lover," Taylor said, and settled back on her pillow, smiling into the shadowed room as her eyes narrowed in concentrated thought.

In her room, Charlene was similarly charmed by their temporary home. She brushed aside the lace curtains to look down on the street scene below, watching neighbors sitting on their porches drinking coffee and talking. An artist hurried down the street carrying an enormous portfolio, and schoolchildren meandered home in a cackling cluster. And everywhere there was green—with flowers, bushes, banana trees and palms, as well as stately old oaks. The city was simply *alive*, she thought.

What a gorgeous place. I'll have to come back sometime by myself and spend more time. Or, even better, with some engaging companion. I wish Jill hadn't invited Taylor. I can't help but feel a little bit like the odd girl out, even though we've all been friends forever, seems like. But maybe it's a good thing I'm solo, actually. Might be that someone has to keep an undistracted eye on Taylor. Something's not quite right with that girl.

Later, the group discussed their transportation options with Marie and set out for the French Quarter. They walked down the broad promenade of South Jefferson Davis Parkway, shaded by massive old oaks, to the Canal Street trolley stop, and climbed on board for the slow and charming ride through the old city's neighborhoods. Reaching the French Quarter, they cruised the multiple music performances at the three main stages of Riverfront Park, pausing to lean over the iron rail to watch the dark Mississippi roll by. They strolled down Decatur Street to Jackson Square, circling around to view the artists' displayed work. Halfway through, they came upon Rue d'Orleans, which stopped Dory dead in her tracks.

"Pirates Alley!"

"Huh?" Taylor arched her eyebrows in puzzlement. "That's not what it says."

"No, but that's what it is," Dory said gleefully. "Legend has it that this is the alley where General Andrew Jackson met with the infamous Lafitte pirates, Jean and Pierre, to discuss the defense of New Orleans in the War of 1812. Let's pop down here. I could use a drink or a good cup of coffee, and we need to celebrate our arrival."

They turned down the narrow alley, enjoying its shade after the heat of the sun. A small table was set up in the gloom halfway down, with a woman sitting by it. She looked to be in her eighties, garishly dressed in a loud, flower-print skirt, puffy yellow blouse, and an equally colorful scarf partially covering her gray hair, but her dark eyes were sharp and calculating as she took in the fivesome.

"Good afternoon, ladies. Want to know your future?" she asked.

"Oh, sure, let's do," cried Robby. "As long as you tell me I'm going to come into a fortune, that is."

"I don't know," said Taylor uneasily, taking a step back. "Sometimes I think it doesn't pay to tempt the gods, trying to find out things we have no business knowing."

"Oh, come on." Jill laughed. "Surely you're not taking this seriously. It's just fun!"

"Of course, of course," crooned the seer. "Just

good fun, what could it harm? But I can tell you all something right away. You all have a secret."

Taylor started and looked away, flushing. Charlene frowned at the reaction and looked to her friends, only to discover that she seemed the only one to notice.

After a second's silence, Dory started to laugh.

"Ooh, a secret!" She whooped. "Aren't we the dark ladies?"

The others joined in the uneasy laughter as the crone smiled, eyes glittering.

The group continued walking.

"Come on," said Jill. "I see a neon sign further down, and that usually means alcohol. It's after five, so let's start the evening off right."

After fortifying themselves with a cool glass of wine, they strolled over to Muriel's Restaurant on Jackson Square.

"It's an indulgence," Dory said, rationalizing. "I'm not used to the prices, but this is our first night and we have celebrating to do. I have my new book, Robby's short stories are already widely published, Charlene may be our next State House representative, and Jill is finally retired. Let's blow it out!" Nonetheless, the four friends ordered the prix fixe three-course meal. Taylor, on the other hand, went a la carte, sparing no expense. Glances were exchanged and Jill flushed a bit, but did not demur.

The wine flowed and toasts were offered until finally, groaning and filled to the gullet with Coq au Vin, shrimp and grits, double-cut pork chops, and wood-grilled filet of beef, the five departed with lighter wallets and hearts. Charlene chatted with her seatmate on the trolley back home, pleasantly hearing all kinds of things about New Orleans, including its long tradition of voodoo, Santeria, ghosts, and fortune tellers. That brought the old woman back to mind, as well as Taylor's reaction, and she frowned again while the two couples quietly snuggled together. Walking through the warm night back to the house, she thought about secrets. Yes, just about everyone had them, she thought, herself included, but surely the posse was beyond all that?

A cloud scudded across the full moon and she shivered. Maybe not.

Suddenly tired from the travel and walking, the five sought out their rooms. Robby and Dory opened the French doors to the courtyard and stood arm in arm for a moment, looking at the rising moon.

"What do you think, lover?" asked Dory. "Feel up to some loving tonight?"

"No, afraid not," Robby replied. "I'm pretty tired."

"Yeah. Me, too," Dory said, then paused. "But honey, you've been tired a lot lately. Is there something you'd like to tell me? Some secret, that you've been hiding?" she asked, trying to joke.

Robby turned to look at her, sighed, and paused long, looking around the courtyard and at the moon. "Okay, honey. I have been thinking about something, I confess. And you're right, something hasn't been right with me and for quite some time I couldn't put my finger on it. Then I finally did, but couldn't figure out how to broach the subject. And we share everything honestly with each other, so hiding something from you disturbed me even more."

Dory looked away, then back at Robby.

"I know, you're probably shocked. I'm sorry. But I did finally figure it out; it's your book. It's a big success and I'm so proud of you, but at the same time it's like a seismic shift in our relationship. I'm the butch here, right? I'm supposed to be the strong one, and all along I've been the one in the lead, including writing-wise. And now you're gaining notoriety and fame and I'm still stuck in the little path I've been following. It makes me feel a little inadequate all of a sudden, and I don't like that feeling. And to tell even more of the truth, I feel a little threatened in our relationship's roles. I'm not proud of the way I've been feeling, but I can't seem to help it. I didn't want to tell you because I feel ashamed of it, but you asked. I guess that makes me a little bit of a shit."

Dory took her hand and led her over to the wrought iron chairs, where they both sank down. The fountain splashed gently as she leaned forward and took her lover's hands in her own. "Darling, you are my guide, and you always will be. That will never change, nor the way I feel about you. I love you more than I've ever loved anyone. You are absolutely essential to my life, both as Robby the person and as my North Star. I depend on you, sweetheart. I rely on knowing that you're with me, the solid rock of my life, and the strength that supports me and guides me when I veer off course. Which I do a lot, as you know."

Robby smiled at that and stood, pulling Dory to her feet and into her arms. "So you're not hurt or mad at me?"

"Good grief, no. Well, maybe a little. I wasn't jealous of your successes, was I?"

"No, you weren't." Robby sounded a little sheepish. "But I'm the butch, and I'm supposed to be the successful tide that raises all the boats. Or just two, in this case. But you're right, which is partly why I've been a little ashamed of how I've been feeling. You didn't go there and I shouldn't either. But it's how I feel, and I can't seem to control that."

"No, you can't control feelings, lover, and I understand that. But I hope it passes soon. We have so much together, you and I, and I don't want to waste even a single moment to jealousy or doubt or shame. After all, we're not kids anymore. Who knows how long we've got?" She raised her face and stretched up on tiptoe to kiss Robby's lips.

Softly at first, and then with increasing urgency, Robby kissed her in return. "I adore you, you know that? I'll try to bring my ego into control, my love. It might take time for me to get used to the shift. I'm not used to thinking of you as a powerhouse in your own right, just as my girl and my woman, as well as the complete person who just enchants me. I've always admired you and loved you, but this is a new persona that I have to adjust to. You understand?"

"Yes, sweetheart," Dory replied, brushing her lips to Robby's as her hands roved over the body she loved. "I adore you, too. And I think I'm feeling a lot more energized than I was before. Want to go to bed?"

"Oh, honey, honey, honey. I'm always ready to go to bed with you, sweetheart. Lead on. What's a big strong butch for, anyway?" Robby took her lover in her arms and planted kiss after kiss on her lips, deepening the kiss each time.

Dory melted into her arms. "Oh, baby." She sighed. "Is this not perfect? In a lush, walled New

Orleans garden, fountain splashing, moon above?"

"Yes, it is." Robby ran her hand through Dory's salt-and-pepper hair and then suddenly grabbed and pulled it, to Dory's gasp. "Your silver is glinting in the moonlight," she said, leaning close to her petite lover. "And your scent is filling my mind with the unspeakable things I'd like to do to your luscious body. Interested?"

Dory was weak at the knees. She could never resist Robby anyway, but especially when she pulled her hair and went all domineering on her. "Yes, my love," she said in her lowest, sexiest voice. "Please do come into my parlor, said the spider to the fly."

"Ha! We'll see who the spider is." Robby laughed, and then shocked Dory by sweeping her up in her arms and carrying her into their room.

"Ooh, honey, your workouts have really paid off," Dory said after being summarily dumped on the lace-canopied bed. She looked on with appreciation as her lover stripped, her strong arm and leg muscles products of hours in the gym and the pool. She sighed a little bit as she pictured herself, the relatively soft dumpling that she was. She thanked her lucky stars that Robby didn't seem to mind her very non-athletic status. In fact, she liked her curves and told her so repeatedly, so she chose to believe it.

Robby hovered over her, pulling at her top, but rather than sitting up Dory jumped out of bed. "Why don't you lie down, baby, and I'll give you a little preview entertainment?" Robby smiled and settled on the down pillows, eyes shining as she watched her lover slowly disrobe. Dory inched up her silk top, pulling it over her head and offering it to Robby, who breathed her scent in deeply and then dropped it to the floor.

She rose up on one elbow, watching as Dory wriggled out of her shorts, turning around to step out of them and giving Robby a good view of her rounded ass, which produced a low whistle of appreciation. Turning again, she unsnapped her bra and slowly draped one strap off her shoulder, then the other, and looked down demurely as she slipped it off to free her "girls." Robby sat up at that and slipped off the bed.

"Let me," she said, and began to ease Dory's lace panty down. Ever so slowly, she pulled it, leaving kisses in its wake on the exposed skin over which it traveled. She began on her abdomen, moving down to her smooth cleft, kissing the juncture of hip and leg on both sides. Dory gasped as Robby's nose nudged her cleft, and felt her body moisten in response.

Robby worked her way down, kissing her inner thighs, the tender spot behind her knee, and down her calves. "Sit down," she commanded hoarsely, and Dory complied, perching on the soft bed. Robby slipped the lace off and, standing over Dory, dropped it to the floor. She put her hands on Dory's shoulders and gently but firmly pressed her down onto the bed, reaching over as she did so to grab a small hand towel from the antique stand by the bed. Tucking the towel beneath Dory's hips, she climbed above her and slipped between her legs. Looking deep into her eyes, she said "Love, we've been together for twenty years now, and still you take my breath away. I simply adore you."

Dory breathed deeply as Robby caressed her body, but her breaths soon shortened as her need grew. She moaned softly when Dory massaged her breasts, circling her nipples and then squeezing them. The delightfully soft pain caused her juices to flow even harder. Robby began to brush her clit, and it wasn't long before Dory was pleading. "Please, baby, please."

"Please what, lover?"

"Oh, please baby, give me your fingers," she begged, squirming and hips rising. "Please, please, please…"

"Okay, soft and gentle." Robby inserted one finger. Dory moaned as the tickle increasingly aroused her vaginal nerve endings, her volume increasing with her rising need to be filled.

"Please, please, honey," she begged again, and was rewarded with two, then three fingers. As her orgasm approached, she had to concentrate to keep her voice down, finally burying her head in the pillow as her muscles contracted and she screamed out her pleasure. "Oh my God, Robby, please fist me," she said faintly when she could speak again.

She felt Robby pause, then remove her hand. Hearing the pop of the lube container lid, she smiled in anticipation, her body still on high alert. She felt her lover's hand again, slowly filling her deeper and deeper. Her pussy began to stretch to accommodate the larger object, to the point of pain. No stranger to pleasurable pain, she pushed down to receive Robby's fist, feeling like a woman in loving labor, a conflicted mass of pleasure and pain. At last Robby was deep inside her, and she exulted in the feeling of fullness. She wished Robby would pump, but this was still a relatively new practice of theirs and, being still a little nervous, she didn't ask for it. But Robby gently moved her hand inside, and Dory buried her head in the pillow again to stifle her loud moans of pleasure, lifting her hips in joyous welcome.

After a few moments, Robby withdrew, tenderly wiping her pussy with the towel. She slipped into the bathroom to wash the lube off her hands and came back to hold her lover tightly in her arms. Dory snuggled into her embrace, endorphins flowing so freely in her brain that she began to giggle. Robby, used to this, held her still tighter, smiling.

"You amaze me, you know?" she said softly. "You have the body, and certainly the pussy, of a much younger woman. Many women our age have a problem with dryness—"

"Not me, that's for sure," said Dory.

"—and cannot open enough to be fisted. You are the perfect woman for me."

"And you for me." Dory sighed, snuggling even closer, draping her leg over her lover's. "Most people seem to write off women our age for sex. But I wonder if that's true, especially in the age of HRT? I'm having the best sex of my life with you, darling, and I just can't believe that others aren't, too. It's just not discussed… except for the complaints about the absence of sex."

"You're right," Robby responded thoughtfully. "I mean, consider the number of single lesbians out there. It's enormous. Why do people have such trouble finding each other?"

"I know. But think about us. It was an unimaginable stroke of luck that we encountered each other when we did at that party. Maybe luck has an awful lot to do with it."

"Yeah, maybe it does. Or Fate. I'd just wish this for all our friends, for everybody, actually. Although, you know, an awful lot of people would find us unbearably kinky, with me enjoying tying you up and you enjoying some pain. Maybe we should just wish this kind of contentment for everybody, whatever they enjoy."

Dory smiled sleepily. "Yeah, contentment, definitely."

And with that, nestled in each other's arms, they drifted off to sleep.

Upstairs, Jill relaxed in the tufted armchair, wearing a long white sleeveless silk gown that perfectly complemented her long, thick blond hair and cornflower blue eyes, breasts seductively swelling from the plunging neckline. As she filed her nails, she looked up as Taylor came in from her bedtime prep. Dressed in a lace-trimmed blue silk babydoll set, she crossed to Jill. Hands resting on the chair arms, Taylor stood quietly, waiting.

With a raised eyebrow, Jill looked up at the younger woman. "Something on your mind, lover?" she asked, a smile ghosting her lips.

"A few things, actually," replied Taylor. "One will require some...*time* to cover, but the other is shorter. What can you tell me about Robby and Dory? They interest me."

"Ah, really?" Jill put her file down. "What would you like to know?"

"Well, I'm curious. Robby seems to run the show somewhat. You've known them a long time, right? What makes them tick? How do they complement each other? Are they in some kind of D/s relationship?"

"Yes, I have. And I might be able to tell you, as soon as you tell me what a D/s relationship is," Jill answered, laughing.

"Dominant-submissive, where one is the stronger personality in the relationship than the other.

In BDSM—oh, do you know what that is?" She sat back, resting on her heels.

"Umm, like S&M?"

"Yeah, S&M plus. The B and D are bondage and discipline, the S is submission or sadism, and the M is masochism."

"Goodness," Jill said. "That's a lot wrapped up in one little acronym."

"Yup. And the relationships can go from mild, like just the titillation of being tied up or held down during sex—to extreme, where the Dominant actually runs every aspect of the submissive's life in a complete power exchange."

"Really. Huh. And what does the submissive get out of this arrangement?"

"Well, for one thing, she or he is free to live their life without any worries. They have no responsibility other than what the Dominant requires of them, and the Dominant usually takes care of every detail of day-to-day life."

"Wow, who wouldn't want that? And what does the Dominant get out of it?"

"Well, the Dominant controls everything. And if you take it to the extreme, where the submissive wants to be a slave, the last decision she makes is to agree to this relationship. After that everything is essentially controlled by the Dom: who she sees, where she lives, what she eats or drinks, when and where she sleeps or wakes. Her chores. If she works, she turns her salary over to her Dom. Everything she does is with the Dom's permission, or not done at all, even the music she listens to. And of course, she is submissive to her Dom's sexual desires, whatever they are, within the parameters of their agreement or contract."

"Boy, doesn't sound like much of an exchange to me," Jill exclaimed. "The Dom gets it all, and she gets what? No free will at all."

"Not quite true. She can always say no, although that risks her losing the relationship. And many people crave this kind of thing, especially, surprisingly, people in very powerful and responsible positions. For them, it's a relief to simply let go when they get home."

Jill looked thoughtful, but still a little dubious. "Wow, is all I can say. I can't see any of that in Robby and Dory's relationship, at all. They just complement each other. Dory's a little harebrained and Robby's more logical. And they operate at different speeds; you might say Dory's the second hand of a clock and Robby's the hour. See? Complementary."

"I see. Well, I was just interested. Now, lover," Taylor said, rising to her knees and tracing the lines of Jill's exposed arms and décolletage. "At what speed would you like to move tonight?"

"Oh, lordy," Jill said, shivering in delight. "You're going to have to take it slow on this old girl tonight, baby. It's been a big day."

"Don't say 'old girl.'" Taylor caressed Jill's face with ghost kisses, then nibbled on her ear. "You're just about the youngest-spirited person I've ever met, Jill. Sometimes I have trouble keeping up with you."

"Thank you, sweetie. I do still feel like I'm thirty-five, I confess. And you," she continued as she rose, pulling Taylor up close in an embrace. "You make me feel every bit that young. Come to bed, darling, and let's be wild and young together. Wait, what are you doing?"

"Wild it will be." Taylor practically purred as she held Jill's hands above her head. "Keep your arms up, lover," she commanded as she kissed her hard.

"Oh, baby." Jill breathed a satisfied sigh as Taylor's lips descended from her face to her breasts. "Oh, my," she said, squirming as her lover's hands explored her body and pulled up her gown. "Yes, baby, yes," she said, the lacey canopy disappearing as her eyes closed.

Next door, Charlene tossed in her bed. She was charmed when they checked in, and she loved the French Quarter. *Ah, to have someone to share it with.* She adored her friends and reveled in their adventures, but it wasn't the same as having a lover to intimately connect with.

Charlene was as sensible a woman as a jurist should be and she often served as counselor to her friends, but she had her own secrets.

She grew up in Atlanta, in a lower-middle-class family that emphasized education but had little money for her college. She went through college and law school on loans, work, and scholarships. In college, she made extra money as a "party girl," dancing and semi-stripping but never prostituting herself. The secretaries and desk clerks would tip her off about the keggers, parties, and platonic escort opportunities. All this history she kept to herself, along with her occasional anonymous sex with high-priced lesbian escorts. The irony of now being the client instead of the service provider was not lost on her.

But between her public and private life, Charlene knew what was what, which was why she was concerned about Taylor. Jill was impelled to follow where her enthusiasms led her, and lord knew she was currently enthusiastic about Taylor. There was something off about Taylor, but Charlene didn't know what—yet. As a former judge, she had the contacts to find out, and she intended to. Given Jill's generous inheritance, Charlene's radar was on high alert for her friend.

In the meantime, here she was in a romantic, lace-canopied, top-quality bed, surrounded by antiques and flowers, and...alone again, naturally. She thought about calling her contacts in Atlanta to arrange for some companionship in New Orleans, as she could always generate some story about a long-lost college friend's niece. But then she nixed the thought; it was too risky, even if appealing. Her girlfriends might not mind if they found out—hell, they might even applaud her—but the media had a way of finding out the most well-disguised foibles. But still. She opened her laptop and pulled up hearts.com, typing in New Orleans as her location.

Like classical music? she typed. *I'm in NOLA for the weekend festival and will be at the chamber music concert at the Ursuline convent tomorrow afternoon. Care to join me? I'm a very young 60-ish lesbian, not bad to look at, who loves good conversation and intimate sharing with other lesbians. I'll be wearing a magenta scarf and white floppy hat.*

"Well, a shot in the dark. Who knows?" After closing her laptop and putting it on the bedside table, she opened the drawer and took out her vibrator. "Hello, old friend," she said with a sigh. "Here we are again, but at least in more romantic surroundings."

Ten miles away, the door swung open to Sappho's

Dream, New Orleans's lone lesbian club, and Lee Childs entered. Carefully wiping her size ten cowboy boots on the rug, she smiled at the greetings called out to her and ambled up to the bar. Sporting a light brown crew-cut hair and a big smile, she was undoubtedly butch, but her swagger belied the shy, almost courtly nature that was the bedrock of her personality. Lee had been looking for a wife for some time.

Behind the bar, Krista pulled her favorite brew from the chiller and placed it before her. "How's it going, Lee?" she asked.

"Still shoveling, Kris," Lee replied with a smile. "Anything happening with you?"

"Nah, nothin' much ever happens in my life." Krista laughed. "I'm just an old married woman."

"Well, count your blessings, girl. I wouldn't mind being in your shoes at all."

"Still no luck on the internet? You'd think with the millions of people on it, someone would pop up eventually."

"Wouldn't you, though? I haven't checked tonight, but if it's anything like the last few months, it's more really old pictures and wishful profiles that don't match the reality. Well, let's see, why not?"

Pulling out her phone, she opened the usual website and scanned it desultorily. Yadda, yadda, yadda; same, same, same. Why wasn't there ever anything new? *Wait a minute.* She scrolled back up. What did that say? Classical music?

Lee was a country and jazz aficionado, but she had grown up with classical music and still had a soft spot for chamber music. *Hmm, that's different. This could be interesting.*

She lifted the cold bottle to her lips and considered.

The French Quarter Festival was sure to be jammed with crowds, which she abhorred, but this invitation was intriguing. Good conversation was always fine and not always available, and "intimate sharing," well, that just left a world of possibilities. The age didn't bother her; she was closing in on that herself.

Hmm.

She finished off her beer and reached for her wallet in her back pocket.

"Leaving already, Lee? You just got here," Krista exclaimed.

"Yeah, think I'll hit the sack early," she replied. "I might have a hankering to go to the fest tomorrow and hear some music."

Chapter Three

The following morning dawned bright and clear, and the pajama-clad group assembled on the porch for morning coffee and day planning. Robby spread out the big multicolored chart of events as the others looked over her shoulder. "There are only five stages today—"

"Only!" hooted Dory.

"—but there are eight the next three days, and those are only the big stages. There are little stages scattered all over the streets of the Quarter. Okay, nine o'clock is the kickoff parade, but we probably won't make that in time."

"Omigod, there's so much to choose from," Jill said. "But I think I'm interested in Raw Oyster Cult, Honey Island Swamp Band, Los Po-Boy Citos, and Rockin' Dopsie and the Zydeco Hellraisers, if only for their names. I think I'm going to be haunting the Bienville stage for zydeco, to tell you the truth. It's just so much fun!"

"I'm going to go to the Ursuline convent this afternoon to hear classical music, and until then I think I'd like to roam a bit," Charlene said. "Anyone with wanderlust want to join me?"

"That's part of the festival's magic," Dory said. "You just walk down the street and you can hear any kind of music for free. Well, it's all for free. Maybe the largest free festival in the country, in fact. But I remember a lot of street performers who weren't even on a stage who just knocked my socks off with their talent. I dispensed a lot of ones and fives into their buckets."

"I like the idea of wandering, both together and singly," Robby said.

Charlene nodded. "Me, too. How about we wander singly tomorrow morning and be our own little crowd today as we get used to the lay of the land and the bands? Tomorrow we could meet at one o'clock at Muriel's again. But let's not stay there, my budget just won't take it. We can go somewhere else to eat lunch. I absolutely must have an oyster po'boy before I leave. But first, we need breakfast today."

"Gumbo for me," said Robby. "But yes, breakfast. Last one ready is a rotten egg! Get it? Breakfast, egg?"

"Darling, your puns are getting worse," said Dory, joining in the others' groans.

"Okay, okay, that wasn't a great one. But Marie told me about a sweet little restaurant a few blocks away, Mimi B's, with a killer-sounding menu. Let's go there."

With that agreed, everyone dispersed to get dressed.

As they were making the bed, Taylor said to Jill, "You know, I'd like to talk to you and your friends about investing in the movie. When do you think would be a good time?"

"I don't know that any time would be good on this trip. We're on vacation, honey. Let's let that lie until we're home. And even then, I'm not sure how I feel about you soliciting my friends. I'd have to think about it."

Taylor frowned but refrained from further

comment as they moved to meet the others in the living room.

Heading out the door, Jill asked, "Now, which way do we go again?" Dory suggested left, which of course was wrong, and they turned back.

"Well, we're getting a good start on our exercise for the day already," Robby joked.

"I know," said Jill. "And I'm a little worried about it, to tell you the truth. I don't know that I'll be up for the whole day. I may have to come back and take a nap."

"Why don't we go to Riverfront Park and start with the three big stages there?" practical Charlene suggested. "And then we can go straight across Decatur Street to the Jackson Square stage. By that time, it'll probably be time for lunch and we'll likely be ready to sit down for a spell."

"Good idea," Dory agreed. "And I might want to go back to one artist I saw on the Square yesterday and look at her work again, too, afterward."

Mimi B's was everything that Marie had promised and more. After feasting on coffee, cinnamon waffles, eggs and grits, mile-high biscuits with gravy, bacon, and fruit, the group launched into the day. They strolled to the trolley stop, hats shading them from the bright sun, and idly passed the time chatting with each other and their fellow passengers. While they gathered the local lore and good advice from the natives, Dory's phone rang. She answered and, with a frown, stepped aside to take the call. When she returned, her usually placid face was marred by what sure looked like worry.

"What's up, Dor?" asked Robby, concerned.

"Oh, nothing, really," said Dory. "Just some follow-up questions from the reporter who's including me in an article about the book for the gay newspaper. It's nothing."

Sure doesn't look like nothing to me, Robby thought, but let the matter drop.

The trolley ride delivered them to the French Quarter at 10:00, when it was coming alive, the new arrivals converging with the parade spectators. But the air was still cool under the bright sun, and the streets were still pretty clear so the friends could walk five abreast from the trolley stop. Overhead, shutters were being flung open to greet the day, and the smell of brewing coffee was tantalizing.

"Oh, you know, breakfast was terrific, but tomorrow maybe we should start off at the Café du Monde and begin the day sinfully, with fabulous coffee and freshly made beignets," Dory suggested. "You just haven't lived until you've had one of their beignets, smothered with confectioner's sugar."

"I may need that this afternoon as a pick-me-up," said Charlene. "Your comment about a nap is well taken, Jill. We're not the spring chickens we used to be, and I may have to do the same. Maybe we could just Uber or Lyft home instead of wasting a lot of time on the trolleys. As charming as they are, it takes a long time to get anywhere."

As they walked, Jill heard a "hello!" from above and looked up to see a little girl tossing her a string of Mardi Gras beads from her balcony. "Thank you!" She laughed, thoroughly charmed as she caught them and put them on.

They happily wandered from stage to stage at Riverfront Park, enjoying all kinds of music: zydeco, blues, jazz, classic rock, gospel, country, brass band. Charlene had brought a portable lawn chair, and

Robby and Dory had small fold-up tripod stools. Jill and Taylor just sat on the grass, enjoying the breeze, the sun, and the music as the majestic Mississippi River rolled on by. Small Coast Guard craft plied their way up and down, patrolling the water's edge. A loud horn sounded and they turned to see a paddle wheeler putting away from its dock. "Oh, let's do that tomorrow," said Dory. "It'll be a great way to see the sights and rest our bones mid-day, too."

By noon, they were ready to collapse into real chairs and headed for the restaurants.

The first stop had to be Killer Po-Boys, an altar to the sandwich that resided in the back of the hole-in-the-wall Erin Rose bar on Conti Street. The po'boys were made with fresh and inventive flair by Chef Camille, whose similarly hirsute dad handled the ordering and serving. Charlene munched happily on her fried oysters, while the others explored the Dark and Stormy pork belly and the coriander lime Gulf shrimp sandwiches. They ate perched on the bar seats and washed it all down with frosty beer that well countered the growing heat of the day.

"Now I might be ready for a nap," Jill said, but Taylor shook her head.

"You can if you want to," she said. "But I'm going shopping today."

"And I think I have just two performances left, energy-wise," said Charlene. "I think I'll do the Cajun band at the Bienville stage and then head to the Ursuline convent for some nice, quiet classical, and then head home."

"The Cajun sounds perfect," said Dory. "Mind if we tag along?"

"Not at all."

"Well, me too, then," said Jill.

After they made their way through the growing masses, Charlene lamented, "Oh, lord, they only allow chairs at the tiny strip in front of the stage. Guess this will be an SRO concert." The band started up its enthusiastic drum, accordion, guitars, and fiddle, and they all danced in place until Robby had had enough.

She sat on the curb, placed the festival map carefully behind her head, and half-lay down on the sidewalk. "Don't let anybody step on my head, okay?" she asked Dory.

A few moments later, Jill looked down and was shocked to find her fast asleep. "She's amazing!" she said to Dory, who laughingly agreed.

A man walking by, festooned in Mardi Gras beads and a stovepipe hat, looked down at her and burst out laughing, too. "Guess she's done some *real* partying!" he said, and walked on, chuckling.

After a while, Robby awoke, observed that "a little Cajun can go a long way," and declared herself ready to move on. They continued to the little stages on Royal Street, where Taylor split off to peruse the wares of all the little shops along the way. They stopped in the shade of the buildings to watch a woman wow the spectators with her clarinet, again to watch a small quartet of drum, violin and guitars, and finally a young Asian woman playing beautiful classical music on her violin.

"Oh my goodness, most of them are so young," commented Jill, stuffing more dollar bills in her pocket. "It's nice to know that talent can still blossom in the world."

"I agree. Okay, this is where I leave you guys," Charlene said. "The convent is down this way. Have a nice nap."

She made her way down the street, dodging people coming down the sidewalk and weaving her way to the old building. The chapel door was two steps up right on the sidewalk and she slipped into the quiet sanctuary, where she sank gratefully into a pew near the back. *I'd forgotten how enervating crowds can be*, she thought, fanning herself with the program. *This is just what I need.* As the harpist and violinist tuned up, she looked around the church, admiring the beautiful stained glass and statuary. Sighing with contentment, she relaxed and abandoned herself to the music soaring to the height of the nave.

The church was full of music lovers whom she watched with fascination. There was one couple with a clearly bored young wife, she guessed, while her older husband listened raptly. They left early. There was a young family, little girl standing on the pew and charming all around her as she swayed to the music and smiled at everyone, her doting young parents looking on. There was a young man who didn't fit the classical music "look," dressed all in black with spiky hair and multiple piercings, but clearly transported as well. *Just goes to show*, Charlene mused to herself with a little smile. *You really can't tell a book by its cover.* There was a good mix of ages present, she was glad to see. She would hate to think of a world where classical music had disappeared due to lack of interest.

She had sat near the end of the row on the center aisle, and someone suddenly appeared beside her. A little irritated—*why couldn't she have sat in the empty row in front?*—she moved to her right and glanced over to see a very well-dressed butch woman smiling at her. Her heart jumped a bit, remembering her post of the night before, and she smiled faintly in return.

Her seatmate leaned over slightly and whispered, "Thank you for letting me know about this concert. I love chamber music." Charlene's heart began to pound as "be careful what you ask for" flashed through her mind. She surreptitiously looked again at the woman, now looking forward and concentrating on the music filling the space. She had rosy cheeks, a strong chin, and light brown crew-cut hair. Her crisp shirt was black, her impeccably knotted tie a medium blue, and her pants were a razor-pleated gray above expensive-looking boots. A small diamond glinted in her ear and, as she caught Charlene's glance again, her eyes were a merry brown above a somewhat prominent nose and even, white teeth. Charlene flushed and looked away hastily.

Well, well. Where do I go from here? This woman was not quite what she was expecting, used to more feminine lesbians of a certain class. But then, she couldn't tell her class—only conversation would reveal that. She liked classical music; that was a plus. The selection ended and, distracted, she was late in applauding. "Don't you like Hummel?" came the whisper from her left as she hastily clapped her hands. "I prefer Vivaldi myself."

Charlene turned and looked her companion full in the face, whose eyes crinkled in an amused smile as she looked back. Defensively, Charlene coolly replied, "I like them both, immensely. My mind was just elsewhere for a moment."

"Oh, was it? Actually, mine was, too. It often is when I find myself sitting next to the woman who invited me, and who turned out to be quite lovely, not just 'not bad looking.'"

Charlene could feel her face redden again—*why can't I stop doing that?*—but she smiled in return. "Thank you," she said, looking back forward.

The concert continued and she relaxed as she focused on the music, which ended with a rousing rendition of Vivaldi's *Four Seasons* "Summer" movement. The performance brought the audience to their feet with applause as the musicians took their bows and left the sanctuary.

Strike while the iron's hot; best defense is a good offense. She turned, extending her hand. "Hello, I'm Charlene," she said.

"And I'm Lee," her companion said. "I enjoyed that very much. Thank you for turning me on to it. The festivals are generally so crowded that I don't attend, but I'm very glad that I came to this one. And, I'm glad to meet you. Can I persuade you to join me in something to drink? Some good New Orleans coffee? Or something cold?"

"Well…yes, okay, sure," stammered Charlene. *What is wrong with me?* "I have some time before my friends are expecting me."

"Ah, you're here with friends. That must be fun. Where do you live?"

"Atlanta. This is my first visit to New Orleans, actually. I'm loving it, although all I've seen so far is the festival and a peek at the neighborhoods from the trolley car."

"I'd be happy to show you some of the sights," Lee replied. "But right now, would you prefer to go to a little bistro around the corner, or walk a few blocks over to our local gay establishment?"

"Around the corner sounds fine," said Charlene as they walked to the door. Lee leaned forward and opened the door for her and, when they got to the bistro, repeated the performance. "Thank you again," Charlene said as she thought, *Goodness, she's so polite! I like that.*

They settled in at a small table by the window and ordered two espressos. "It's my guilty pleasure," Lee confessed, smiling. "I'm addicted. My doctor actually told me I should cut down my intake because my adrenal glands were exhausted. Too much fight-or-flight prompting, I guess."

"Well, that's a new one to me." Charlene laughed. "Although, now having had coffee here, I can understand your passion. What is it about New Orleans coffee that makes it so special?"

"It's chicory, cher. It started in the Civil War, when coffee was scarce and the enterprising natives found that adding chicory added body and flavor to the brew. It's also added to soften the bitter edge of dark roasted coffee. It makes the Café du Monde's coffee almost a chocolate flavor. Have you been there yet?"

"No, but two of my friends lived here and absolutely refuse to leave unless we go, for the coffee and the beignets."

"Oh, my heart, the beignets! Yes, you certainly must sample them before you go."

"And you? Are you a native of New Orleans?"

"Yes, born and bred. We went through some terrible times with Katrina, but you know, I don't think I'd live anywhere else. It's such a rich city in its history, music, and civic pride. People here are passionate about their hometown. You won't find a more fun, giving people anywhere, I don't believe.

"And you? Are you a native Atlantan?"

"Believe it or not, yes, I am, which makes me

a rarity in my own city. I've watched it grow from a small-town feel to the metropolis it is now. I'm sometimes nostalgic for the old days, to tell you the truth, although it has so much more to offer now. I guess growth always involves a trade-off. So, what do you like to do? Do you work? What do you do to play?"

And so they passed the time, learning about each other with an ease that Charlene had rarely encountered. She felt as if she knew this woman from another time, perhaps, as the conversation flowed from one thing to another. She was a reserved person, but she found herself sharing things that she normally would never dream of saying to a stranger, or even to an acquaintance.

Eventually, she glanced out the window and was startled to see that it was getting dark. Looking at her watch, she exclaimed, "Oh my goodness! I have to go. It'll take me forever to trolley back home and my friends must be wondering what on earth happened to me."

"No problem, I'll drive you home," Lee said, signaling for the waiter.

"Oh, no, I wouldn't want you to go out of your way."

"Not out of my way. And put your purse away, cher. The gentlebutch always pays."

"What? Oh, no, that's too much." Charlene tried to protest again, beginning to argue.

"No, sorry, it's a rule," Lee said firmly. "And besides, you're a guest in my city. I insist. Come on, I'm parked in a garage not far from here."

As they walked out, Lee skirted around Charlene to be on the street side, changing sides to ensure that again when they crossed the street. When they got to the garage, she rushed forward to open the passenger door of her shiny F250 and helped her into the seat of the gleaming interior. And when they arrived at the house, she said firmly, "Now, you sit right there for a minute, ma'am." Charlene watched bemused as she hastened to open her door and took her hand to help her out.

Her hand lingered in Charlene's, who was astonished to see a blush start to flush her cheeks. "I had a wonderful time with you, Charlene, and I surely would like to see you again. Can I serve as your escort around town tomorrow and show you the sights? There's so much to see and learn about New Orleans, and you can glean a lot more from someone in the know."

"Oh, that's very kind of you."

"Not kind, not at all. You'd be doing me the favor of sharing your time with me. I'd very much enjoy that."

Somewhat flustered by the realization that she really *would* like to see Lee again, Charlene was furious to find herself stammering yet again. "Oh, thank you, that's...that's very nice of you. It would be lovely, I'm sure, but I am here with my friends and we'd already planned on lunching together tomorrow, although I'm not sure of the day's itinerary. We had talked about wandering solo in the morning..."

"Perfect. Let me be your solo guide, then. I'll deliver you to your lunch and you can share all the legends and lore I've imparted to you and be the envy of your friends...as long as you'll do me the honor of going out to dinner with me tomorrow night?"

"Oh, gracious. Well, I don't know about dinner, but...okay, let's do tour a bit tomorrow morning,"

Charlene found herself saying.

"Excellent!" Lee beamed. "I'll pick you up at eight-thirty or nine, let's say? And we can go sample the Café du Monde's legendary coffee and beignets."

"You are most persuasive, friend Lee." Charlene laughed. "Okay, I'll see you in the morning, then."

Lee walked Charlene to the front door where, as she opened it, she found two of her housemates lined up behind the lace curtains, ready to pounce.

"Well, helloo there," Robby said, grinning.

"Had a good afternoon?" asked Dory, arching an eyebrow.

Charlene looked at her friends and noticed one was missing. "Where's Jill?" she asked.

"Oh, she and Taylor decided to go back down to the Quarter to have some fun at Harrah's Casino," said Dory. "They'll probably be back soon. So, oh-kayy? Spill, girl! Where have you been? And just who is that impressive-looking and remarkably courteous butch woman who just drove off?"

Charlene rolled her eyes and prepared to be grilled.

Chapter Four

"Well, I'm dragging a little this morning, I confess it." Charlene sipped her coffee. "I don't really get in much walking at home and I'm not used to it. I do the gym and that's a challenge, but a different kind of exercise can take a toll, too."

"Yeah, me, too," Dory said. "Not a walker. My brain always figures out what I'm doing and calls a halt to it."

"Ha ha," said Jill. "Seriously, Dory, you should go to the gym with me sometime. Morning walks are fine, but I think you'd be surprised at what fun some of the classes can be, and you'd love the rewards to your figure."

"I know." Dory sighed. "I can use all the help I can get. Maybe I will. I'll have to think about it."

"Well, you know the old saying, Dory: there is no 'try,' there is just 'do' or 'don't do.' But you're always welcome to come with me."

"So what are we all doing today?" asked Robby. "Yesterday we were talking about solo wandering today but meeting for lunch."

"Still sounds good to me," Charlene said. "Actually, Lee is picking me up for breakfast at the Café du Monde this morning and then showing me the city a little bit."

Jill's eyebrows arched. "Ah-ha! The plot thickens. You didn't happen to mention that last night. Are you holding out on us, girlfriend?"

"I have to admit, I did think at first, why? What could come of it? But then I thought, why not? We shared espressos after the concert yesterday and she was just delightful. Why should I deny myself some great company and good conversation just because she and I live in different places? How self-defeating is that?"

Robby nodded, leaning forward. "Well, tell us more about her."

"Not much to tell, gleaned from a cup of coffee, other than that we're about the same age and love classical music," Charlene replied cagily. "But I have to admit, it was the easiest conversation I've had with, well, anybody but you guys, in a very long time. Boy, if we were home, I'd be a little excited about this. But what the hell, fun's fun."

"Go for it! Well, that leaves us," Robby said. "I'd be up for an Uber today. I want to do a little shopping and Dory wants to hear a couple of bands I'm not interested in. We three could share the ride. Jill and Taylor, what are you going to do?"

"We'll hang out here for a while." Taylor smiled at Jill, who actually blushed.

"Oh, I see," said Dory. "Well, don't do anything I wouldn't do," she said meaningfully, and Jill turned scarlet again.

Jill and Taylor relaxed in comfort on the sunny porch while the hustle and bustle of preparation and departure echoed from the rest of the house. Jill read the *Times-Picayune's* editorial and financial pages while Taylor caught up on social media on her tablet. Finally, when the house was peaceful and they were alone, Taylor rose to stand by Jill's recliner.

"Yes?" Jill smiled, dropping the paper into her lap.

Taylor picked up the paper between two dainty fingers and dropped it on the floor, bending down to brush Jill's lips with her own. "I thought they'd never leave," she said breathily.

"Baby girl, are you ready again?" Jill laughed. "You're voracious, my dear."

"Only because you're luscious, lover," Taylor replied, dark tresses half hiding her face. Her blue eyes gleamed above her smiling lips. "I wonder if I could distract you from your stocks and bonds and politics for a while?"

"Oh, I'll just bet you could," Jill answered. "Okay, you firecracker, let me go get refreshed for play and the day, and I'll meet you in bed. Just leave me some strength to get through the day." She left the room as Taylor idly picked up her tablet again. After a while, Jill's phone rang. Taylor glanced toward the bedroom and, hearing the shower still running, answered the phone.

"Hello, is this Jill Hunt?" a male voice inquired.

"No, she's not here at the moment. Can I take a message?"

"Not your monkey, not your circus. No, thanks."

"Oh-kay," Taylor said slowly. She hung up the phone and stared at it thoughtfully for a long moment.

Jill entered, clad only in her white silk dressing gown, and raised her eyebrows at seeing Taylor holding her phone. "What's going on?" she asked.

"Oh, nothing. Your phone rang when you were

in the shower and I thought I'd be helpful and take a message for you," Taylor replied smoothly.

"Well, please don't henceforth," snapped Jill. "I prefer to keep my communications private, baby, okay? Well, who was it?"

"Don't know, he wouldn't say," Taylor replied curtly, turning away.

"Oh, please don't take it personally, sweetheart," Jill said, crossing to her. "It's just that I get a lot of calls from brokers and others that I just don't want to risk signals getting crossed. Okay?" She put her arms around Taylor and gave her a hug. "Okay, baby? Nothing personal, God knows."

"Okay," Taylor murmured as she gazed out the window. But her eyes narrowed and she pursed her lips. *I've never heard of a broker who would talk like that. What else is going on here?*

Pulling back to face Jill again, she smiled as she unfastened the robe's belt. "Now, where were we again? Oh, yes..." Slipping the robe off Jill's shoulders, she stepped back and gazed admiringly. "Honestly, honey, I'd never know your age if you hadn't told me. You're just beautiful."

Clearly pleased, Jill smiled. "We can thank the cosmetics and workout industries for that, my love. So, shall we repair to the boudoir?" she said in an extremely false Southern accent. "Oh, we are in the boudoir. Voulez-vous coucher avec moi?"

"Your wish is my command, oh goddess," Taylor replied, her smile hiding her thoughts. *Yeah, and a whole lot of money to spend on those good looks, huh? And, we'll see, maybe on other things.*

The young woman playing her saxophone on Decatur Street had won a large crowd of fans who stood transfixed by her performance. Robby stood in the front and to the side, alternately studying her with open admiration, and then scanning the crowd. *Old detective's habit: know your environment,* she thought. *And God knows, that's hectic at best in the French Quarter, but inundated with thousands of music-loving tourists? Wow, ripe pickins.* She smiled when she noticed someone else looking everywhere but at the artist, easily identifying a fellow brother of the blue.

She shifted her gaze a little farther along the front of the crowd and then was arrested by the sight of a woman looking directly at her. Her heart fluttered as she recognized her, swearing softly to herself. "Goddamn. What are the chances?" She began moving to that side of the circle and the woman did likewise, heading to her. They met in the middle of the street behind the crowd, eyeing each other with grins.

"Old habits die hard, don't they Robby? I saw you casing out the crowd," the woman said.

"Well, hello, Jessie, imagine meeting you here. What brings you to New Orleans?"

"Same as you, I imagine," Jessie replied. "The festival. Never could resist a good free party, as you might recall."

Robby's grin widened. "Oh, yeah, I do recall some good parties, for sure. We were young and wild back then, weren't we? I'm still kind of amazed we didn't end up in the lockup ourselves sometimes."

"I prefer to think of it as living life to the fullest, rather than being wild." Jessie's eyes twinkled.

"You're looking good, Jess," Robby said, taking

her in appreciatively. "You're not still on the force, are you?"

"Thanks. No, I retired a few years back. Got tired of running after dirtbags in alleys and keeping up with the politics. But I got bored pretty quick and now I'm a part-time PI, if you can believe that, if the case interests me."

"No shit. Really? That's amazing. How is it? Do you get cooperation or resistance from the force?"

"Both, actually. Still have enough friends that I can get information fast when I need to. And I have to say, being of the—ahem—senior generation is a big help. Absolutely no one expects a grandmother-aged woman to be a threat, or even worthy of attention, generally speaking."

"Yeah, I know what you mean. It really bothered me for a while, suddenly becoming invisible. I swear, no one under the age of thirty-five would be able to identify me even if I murdered someone on the sidewalk right in front of them. Clerks in stores? Forget about it; the sweet young thing next to me gets the first attention. And if they do notice me, well, then I'm just this little old lady, sort of an object rather than a person. It's very odd. I don't see myself that way. Don't get me started. It hurt my pride for a while, and then I just thought, 'Oh, fuck it,' and rode with it. But yeah, I can see how that could be very helpful to you. Whaddya know, I know Miss Marple!"

Jessie bellowed a laugh at that. "Never thought of myself that way. Tell you what, though, I still don't like steaming in the sun. How about joining me for a cold beverage and talking over old times? Are you by yourself?"

"Yes, at the moment I am. That sounds like

a great idea. One thing the Quarter isn't short of is places to drink and eat. How about this one?" she said, gesturing toward the Crescent City Brewhouse. "It's eleven, a little early, but I'll bet we could find some fine ales in here."

"Let's do it."

They went into the cool recesses of the bar, ordered a local microbrew, and grabbed a corner table by the front window.

"So, how are you, really, Robby?" Jessie asked, hand touching her arm. "Still with Dory? Still writing? Are you happy? I worried about you and thought about you for a long time, you know. Still do, sometimes. You leave quite an impression."

Robby shifted in her seat, feeling her face redden. "Well, thank you for that, Jess. We do have a lot of good memories, don't we? But yes, I'm still writing and still with Dory, who's doing great. As a matter of fact, she's become a writer, too. Just had a book published that's doing great on Amazon. We're fine, a couple of old ladies joined at the hip."

"Ah," Jessie said, dropping her eyes to the table. "Well, I'm glad for you."

"What about you? Are you still with Darlene?"

"No, Darlene died a few years ago," Jessie said softly.

"Oh, I'm so sorry, Jess. I didn't know."

"Yeah, well. No one in my life now, I'm afraid. I'd like to have someone to share it with, but I'm not much on the internet meet-up scene. And you know, you have a circle of friends that you stick with, and that doesn't often present an opportunity to meet someone new. But my life is okay, I'm not complaining."

"I know what you mean. Funny, I was just talking

to my friends about that recently. It's not easy. Not like the old days, when there were a bunch of lesbian bars in town that everyone went to and we had the energy to stay out half the night socializing. We had to be careful, of course, with our jobs, but those were good times."

An awkward pause was filled by the waiter bringing their brews. "So, tell me about your cases," Robby said, breaking the silence.

The two old friends bent their heads together, each understanding every nuance of what the other said. Their conversation continued until Jessie said, "Gee, I'm getting hungry. Want to order some food?"

Robby sat up with a start. "Oh, my God! I'm supposed to meet Dory and my friends for lunch at—well, right about now. Thank you for noticing the time. It was wonderful seeing you again. Let's do this again when we're back home and if I can be of any help with your cases, feel free to let me know."

"Sure. Go on, don't be late. But first, can I give you a hug?"

"Absolutely," said Robby, smiling. She left Jessie, feeling an old and familiar twinge of guilt. She knew it was unearned, but she also knew that her partner had always had a soft spot for her. But surely after all this time it was gone? She shook her head slightly as she walked on. Let sleeping dogs lie.

"So this is the famous Café du Monde," Charlene said. "Great place for people watching, with the crowded café and probably one of the busiest streets in the Quarter in the front."

"Yes, siree," Lee said, smiling. "But I think I'll be focusing on the lovely face before me, thank you."

Charlene took a sip of her coffee and a generous bite of the sugar-drenched beignet before her. Embarrassed to feel herself blush, she thought, *Oh, really now, aren't you a bit old for a flirtation? Or are we ever too old for that? What's the saying? Something about "never being too old to play, but getting old when you stop playing"? And besides, why did you post that ad on the internet in the first place?* It took her a millisecond to make up her mind and she put down her coffee cup and smiled right back. "Then I'll do the same with the handsome face before me. This is delicious, by the way. No wonder it's so famous. So, where are we off to this morning?"

Lee rubbed her hands together with delight. "Well! You've already seen the Ursuline Convent. Did you know the Ursulines conducted the first Catholic, Indian, and Negro schools and the first orphanage here? Good folk. But I thought we should start with the closest place first and stroll through the French Market, home of a million tchotchkes and a few good buys, and the St. Louis Cathedral, the oldest one in the country. You said you'd already done Jackson Square, right?"

"Yes. I'm eyeing a piece of art down there, but I'm not in buying mode yet."

"Okay. Well, we certainly should see one the Cities of the Dead, probably St. Louis Cemetery Number One, where the infamous Quadroon voodoo queen, Marie Leveau, is buried. We should take a ride around the Garden District, which has beautiful antebellum homes and celebrity residents like Anne Rice, Nicolas Cage, and Sandra Bullock. There are lots of restaurants there; maybe we could have lunch? And that's not even mentioning the art museum, the arts district, or the botanical garden. And, of course, the music that pours from hundreds of establishments in this city, and the unique and interesting neighborhoods, each offering something different in character. Sure you don't want to stay longer than this weekend?"

"Goodness, that is a lot. I think some will have to wait for a return trip. But I don't think I can do lunch. I was going to pick up takeout for our cruise on the Steamboat *Natchez* this afternoon."

"Ah, a return trip! Music to my ears. I have one other local attraction to offer this time, too: dinner at my house. I come from an interesting background, which has blessed me with fabulous old Louisiana recipes. Won't you come?"

"Well, that sounds like an offer too good to pass up," Charlene responded with a smile. "One thing you should know about me is that I have totally overdeveloped taste buds. I eat, therefore I am, and I'm an omnivore who is game to try almost anything at least once. But I'm afraid I won't be able to this time. I'm pretty sure I'll be resting tonight. Not used to this travel."

"Oh, too bad," Lee said, clearly disappointed. "Well, shall we proceed, madame?" She came around the table to pull Charlene's chair out and then took her arm to guide her gently to the crowd on the street. "To the left you are right. Onward to St. Louis."

Dodging the main stages and crowds, they took in the sights of the Quarter. Charlene was impressed with the beautiful stained glass of the cathedral and the tales and history of the cemeteries. The beautiful above-ground graves easily conveyed vivid images of the past—battles, floods, and plagues, and the voodoo so well described in the guides' stories. They drove through the Garden District, admiring the stately old homes and well-tended yards and gardens. Stopping at a local deli, they bought a variety of sandwiches and chips for everyone's lunch on the steamboat cruise.

Finally, they strolled the Mississippi waterfront walk to the accompaniment of the Festival's stage performances, until they came to the berth of the *Natchez*, an impressive paddle wheeler. Lee bought Charlene's ticket, over her protests, and escorted her to the gangway to await her friends. Charlene assured her that she'd be fine and Lee should go on about her day, but she was undeterred. She gently assured her she had nothing better to do and wanted to wait with her. As they waited, they enjoyed the lighthearted piping of the calliope concert on the ship's top deck, laughing at the steam escaping from each pipe as its note was struck. Above, the fleur-de-lis New Orleans flag gaily flew alongside the Louisiana state flag.

Shortly, three of the others arrived, and then Jill raced up to board at the last minute. "Sorry, I was at Harrah's and lost track of the time," she breathlessly reported.

"Well, guess I'd better get aboard," Charlene said, and reached for the gangway rail. Her step up, however, was halted by Lee's hand tugging on her arm.

When she turned, curious, Lee pulled her into her arms and kissed her firmly on the lips, then released her with a wide smile. "Have a good time," she said, as hoots sounded from the four friends watching above.

Once aboard, Charlene leaned over the railing and waved to Lee, who smiled and waved back. The sounds of the calliope reinforced her time-warp feeling as the boat's horn sounded its three deep, sonorous tones and the craft slowly left the dock. She could not help but imagine how many others had seen exactly the same views on such boats, plying their way up and down the river. She had no trouble at all imagining hoop skirts, bonnets, and gloved hands on the ladies, as well as stiffly starched shirts with cravats, top hats, and spats on the gentlemen.

"My, my, my!" said Robby teasingly. "Looks like your morning tour went well, did it?" Charlene just smiled. While Robby rounded up five chairs along the ship's left rail to see the best view with the tour's narration, Jill and Charlene went to the bar to fetch some drinks.

"At Harrah's again?"

"Oh, yeah," Jill said airily. "The heat is getting to me and it's wonderfully air conditioned. And I enjoy it." Charlene looked thoughtful but said no more until they delivered the drinks.

"Here, girlfriends, have your delicious, grow-hair-on-your-chest beverage," Jill said, giving everyone a tall frosty glass, upon which the friends feasted and drank toasts to the mighty Mississippi River. After the tour guide was finished announcing the first part of the trip, Robby explored the three levels of the engine room and the four others went downstairs to hear the jazz band in the bar. By the time they were steaming back into port, the lights of New Orleans were coming on and the friends stood at the railing, taking it all in.

After they disembarked, they enjoyed more music as they walked back down the riverfront toward Canal Street. Charlene slowed down and declared, "I'm ready to quit and don't want to take the trolley. Anyone want to share a ride?"

"We're with you," said Robby. "I found out that the Uber app is blocked for the Quarter, though. Let's go over to the other side of Canal Street, where it does work, and get a car." Jill and Taylor agreed, and the five did just that. The car left them near home at Katie's Restaurant for dinner, where they split appetizers of fried green tomatoes and a crawfish beignet, along with pounds of peppery boiled Gulf shrimp, coleslaw, and giant onion rings.

After the short walk home, they collapsed on the comfortable porch with glasses of chilled wine. Robby and Dory claimed the swing, Charlene and Jill grabbed the recliners, and Taylor, unruffled, perched on an Eames chair.

"Oh, Taylor, at this particular moment I envy you your youth," Dory said. "And your slim figure, too, but mostly your youth. You could go out again, couldn't you?"

Taylor laughed. "Well, I could be persuaded, but I'm not in any fever to do that. I'd be just as happy to stay here and watch a movie."

"Youth isn't everything, although the media would have you believe it is," said Charlene. "But think of the advantages of age. I rely on a few of them, like 'being young is beautiful, but being old is comfortable, and your supply of brain cells is finally down to manageable size.'" As the others laughed, she continued. "Or, 'things you buy now won't wear out and your investment in health insurance is finally beginning to pay off.' Besides, as Bernard Baruch said, 'Old age is fifteen years older than I am.'"

When the laughter died down, Robby ruefully confessed, "Yeah, but it's a little embarrassing that the only way I know what day it is, is by the pill case section I open in the morning. And I'm with Woody Allen's philosophy: 'It's not that I'm afraid to die. I just don't want to be there when it happens.'"

"Oh, Dory, are you still obsessing over your weight?" asked Jill. "You know the important thing is to be fit, not thin."

"Oh, I know. But I'm not that fit, either. I'm kind of lazy about exercise, although I do exercise. Like, I am right now. I'm doing Kegels as we speak." Dory grinned self-consciously while the others laughed. "Well, we do have to do those these days, you know? Tighten up, in case we sneeze or laugh too hard. But, really, you know how I love to cook and bake, not to mention eat—"

"And don't I love it!" Robby crowed.

"Yes, but you still have the metabolism of a twenty-year-old, unlike me," Dory said.

Over time, the conversation became repeatedly peppered with yawns, and soon they drifted off to bed.

"Darling, you know that I think you're the sexiest woman in the world," said Robby. "I love your curves. And you're usually the prettiest woman in the room, too."

"Oh, thank you, sweetheart, and I count on your thinking so," Dory said, smiling. "You are absolutely the best thing for my ego. I just adore you."

"I love you more. Now, come on, let's go to bed. Besides, I think all the walking we did today helped to offset the way we're eating whatever we damn well please on this trip."

"From your lips to God's ears, honey."

And, snuggling, Robby drifted off to sleep while Dory checked her texts. Reading one, she caught her breath. "Now, what in hell am I going to do about this?" she muttered.

"Huh?" a sleepy Robby asked.

"Oh, nothing, babe, go back to sleep." She soothed her lover, but Dory long remained staring into the dark, brow furrowed.

Chapter Five

After another morning repast at Mimi B's, the group soaked up still more music from the cornucopia offered: Big Sam's Funky Nation, Buckwheat Zydeco, and Smokin' Bones. While the rest strolled some more, Charlene returned to the convent to hear the Symphony Chorus of New Orleans.

Afterward, she placed a group call to her wandering friends. "This concert helped, but I'm still feeling a little overloaded and I'm getting over the crowds. I'm going back to rest and then maybe take a nice quiet walk through the Garden District. Probably a short walk. This is the most strenuous vacation I've had in years."

"I'm up for a nap, too," declared Robby and, to Charlene's surprise, Taylor said she'd come along as well.

"Well, I'm going to relax in comfort at Harrah's again," Jill said.

"How's that going, Jill?" asked Dory.

"Oh, you know, sometimes up, sometimes down," Jill breezily replied. "It's a fun hobby."

Long as that's all it is. "Well, I'm on Chartres Street," Charlene said. "Why don't y'all meet me at Chartres and Toulouse? There's a restaurant named the Camellia Grill I read about on Trip Advisor that seems to be famous for omelets and sandwiches, and isn't expensive."

"Sounds good to me," Robby said.

Looking at the menu in the restaurant, Dory groaned. "Oh, I could get into a bacon cheeseburger, but I think I'd better be more sensible and have a salad. Although I could probably max out the calories on that too, with my add-ons. My 'see-food' diet—I see food, I eat it."

"Oh, God, there you go again, Dory," scolded Jill. "You're on vacation. Live it up and think about that when you get home, I say."

"Well, the caution is well taken," Taylor said. "It's so easy to gain and so hard to lose."

"Ha! Says the woman who still has a metabolism." Dory grinned. "But you're right. The way I look at it is like something I read: the older you get, the harder it is to lose weight, because by then your body and your fat are really good friends."

Everyone laughed, but Robby sympathized. "I know I'm still doing okay, but I understand. In fact, I wish I was as fat as the first time I thought I was fat. Especially in our thin-oriented culture, I'll bet young people still worry about their looks, even when they're at their most glorious."

"Oh, you have nothing to talk about, Robby," said Dory. "Now me, according to the BMI chart, I'm too short. As some wise person said, 'I have a condition that keeps me from having a diet that really works: I get hungry.' And at this point, cremation is my last hope for a smokin' hot body."

After all the laughter, Jill exclaimed, "Oh, enough. We're all doing just fine for our age, ladies. I see a lot of women even younger than us walking with canes. Let's just count our blessings, shall we?"

"Hear, hear," said Robby, and they all raised their

iced tea to toast.

Standing up to leave after lunch, Dory said, "I'm with you on the nap. After that, I want to visit the Besthoff Sculpture Garden in City Park. Then I'll meet y'all back at the house." Robby said she'd go with her after a rest, and the group separated, Jill to Harrah's.

A congenial Lyft driver ferried the four back to the house, where they collapsed with another iced tea around the kitchen table.

"Lordy, I'm going to shower before my nap, for sure," Charlene said. "The sun was so hot that I blessed every breeze and the convent chapel's A/C. And this is only April! I don't think I could live in New Orleans."

"Me, too," agreed Taylor. "What I'd like, ideally, would be to have enough money to have a little pied de terre in my favorite cities so I could be there at the best times. Or just to travel at will and rent, never worrying about maintenance and upkeep. Yeah, that might be better. I hope to do that thanks to this movie, in fact."

"Well, you get used to it, you know, when you live here. But you haven't said much about your movie, Taylor. What's it all about, anyway?" asked Dory.

"Oh, glad you asked!" Taylor beamed. "It's my passion. Well, you know, that's how I met Jill, at a cocktail fundraiser for it. It's based on the bestselling book about women of a certain age redefining their lives to live them to the fullest. It was optioned several years ago and I gathered some investors to buy the option. Now we just have to produce it. It's really exciting—we've circulated it in Hollywood and had interest expressed by several luminaries I could name. I won't drop names, but I can say they starred in recent movies."

She turned her attention to Robby, saying, "In

fact, the script is still in development, Robby, but there's some thought of having a police detective as an important role. Maybe you could even consult on that. Would you be interested?" Robby shrugged noncommittally and, after a second's pause, Taylor turned her eyes back to the others.

"There's still a ways to go, of course, we're only beginning. But especially with that kind of star power, I think this'll be a real money maker, not to mention helping to dispel myths about older women, including lesbians. I have a great cadre of investors in Hollywood and some now in Atlanta, but investments are still open. If you're interested I'd be glad to share all the relevant information with you. Early investors have larger percentage shares."

"Boy, that could be a *great* movie," Dory said. "There's certainly a huge population it would speak to. I'll think about it."

"Interesting." Charlene looked slightly skeptical, as did Robby.

"Well, no pressure," Taylor said smoothly. "I'm into the shower and that delicious bed. See you later."

Robby watched her leave and then looked at Charlene. "Something bothering you?" she asked.

"About Taylor? Well, I don't know. I just feel pretty protective of Jill, you know? She can be so impulsive, both emotionally and financially. Just being cautious, I guess."

Robby nodded. "I know what you mean. I find it hard to believe they wouldn't have the storyline pretty much outlined already, for instance. What's with this consulting on a role business? And Jill can be a runaway train, but she is her own girl. We can watch, though. I'm with you. Still, I'm interested in knowing more about this movie idea. She does apparently have some people signed on, so maybe it's possible. We'll see."

"Yeah, we'll see," muttered Charlene, a plan forming in her mind as she walked to the shower. She was still thinking as she spread the creamy bodywash over herself and rinsed in the brisk, clean water. "I'm glad I still have contacts in the law. I think I'm going to need them. And maybe Robby can help."

Jill returned to the house, flush with victory. "I won five hundred dollars," she said, waving the bills around. "Dinner's on me!"

"Nice!" Dory cheered. "But from what I hear, you might want to invest that in Taylor's movie instead, huh?"

Jill froze. "What?"

"Yeah, I asked her and she told us about it," Dory replied. "Why didn't you tell us that she was hanging with such luminaries in LA, Jill? That must be interesting."

Jill forced a smile. "Well, actually," she said. "I didn't want her to bring it up. I haven't even decided about it myself, and I certainly didn't want to endorse anything I wasn't sure about. In fact, I asked Taylor not to raise it at all."

"Oh, God, I did it again. I'm sorry," said Dory. "I did ask her, though. She didn't bring it up."

"Still, I would've rather she'd been more, I don't know, reserved about it, I guess. Well, whatever. I'm going to shower and rest."

But she was annoyed. *No, past annoyed*, she

fumed as the water sluiced over her. *Dammit, I told her not to discuss it. That was just tacky and I don't want to involve my friends, at least, not yet.* By the time she got back into the room, she was primed for battle.

Taylor cocked an eye at her as she swept into the room. "Hello, lover. Feel better? How was Harrah's?" She paused as she read the anger on Jill's face. "Uh, is something wrong?"

"I told you not to bring up investing in the movie this trip, Taylor! Why did you ignore that? Did you actually solicit them?"

Taylor slowly rose to sit, plumping the pillow behind her. "Now hold on, Jill. They asked and I answered. What was I supposed to do? Just zip my lips and not respond? That's crazy. And I didn't 'solicit' them, but I did mention that investments were still open, of course. Why not?"

"Because implicit in all of that is my approval," Jill spit out. "And they're my friends, of course that would bias them in making a decision. That's exactly why I told you not to bring it up."

"And I didn't," Taylor said. "I just answered a direct question." She rose from the bed, her robe opening to her naked body, and crossed to Jill. "Let's not quarrel about it, honey, okay? It just happened in the course of conversation. I won't follow up on it at all, okay?"

Jill huffed, but relaxed slightly as Taylor pressed against her, nuzzling her neck. "Well, okay," she said. "As long as we're clear on that, right?"

"Crystal clear, love." Taylor cooed, as she slipped Jill's robe off her shoulders. "Now, can we get on to more pleasant things?" Her hands roved down Jill's arms, then up her back. "Come to bed, sweetheart," she whispered, her teeth teasing Jill's earlobe.

Jill sighed, relaxing further, and then giggled as Taylor's tongue went in her ear. "Oh, you! What am I going to do with you?" But she let herself be taken by the hand to lie on the four-poster bed, where Taylor began to caress her breasts.

"Perhaps we can begin with a little massage?" She teased Jill slowly, one hand moving down Jill's body and brushing her cleft.

"Oh!" Jill's hips rose involuntarily. "Oh, you are a vixen, you know, Taylor?" She lay back, a smile curving her lips. Taylor's dark hair tickled her stomach as her lips explored Jill's terrain, until her face disappeared between her legs.

Jill stifled a scream at the first moist contact and tried to simply surrender to the sweet sensations. But there was an irritating murmur at the back of her mind, a nagging doubt about Taylor's motives. With an effort, she stifled the thought and let her consciousness just float away.

Charlene was just beginning to drift off to sleep when she heard a sound drifting down the hall. *Oh, God, they're at it again. Taylor certainly seems to have down the art of transporting Jill to the heights. I wonder how pragmatic she can still be in keeping her financial affairs divorced from that influence? There's just something about Taylor that I don't trust, and I don't think it's just a bias that someone young and beautiful couldn't be attracted to a much older woman. Jill is still a beauty. But I don't think her looks are what Taylor's after.*

As she drifted off to sleep, she was listing and prioritizing her investigative friends. "Soon as I'm home…" she murmured, then all was dark.

Robby woke refreshed an hour later and stretched luxuriously in the bed. She relaxed back into it, letting the soft hum of the ceiling fan lull her as she enjoyed the feel of the crisp sheets and the perfect not-hard-but-not-too-soft pillow. Dory wasn't in bed and, she soon realized, not in the bathroom, either. She sat up, looking out into the courtyard, to see Dory once again on the phone. She hung up and paced in an agitated fashion.

Okay, Robby thought, lips pressing firmly. *Enough is enough. It's come to Daddy time, ready or not. But not right now.* She opened the French doors and leaned out into the warm air. "Hey, sweetheart," she said, smiling. "Care to come into the cool before we go out and get hot again?"

Dory jumped at her voice but turned with a smile. "Yes, although that is a little counter-intuitive, isn't it? Well, let's get ready and get going to see some beautiful things."

"Besides you, that is," Robby said, kissing her as she entered. "I'll be ready in a flash. Why don't you call Lyft or Uber since you're already dressed?"

While Dory did so, Robby dressed, thinking, *What we need right now is a little privacy. The park should work out well for that, I hope. Something is going on with her, and I'm about to find out what the hell it is. Can't be good, since she's hiding it from me. Well, whatever it is, we can work it out, I'm sure.* She frowned, pulling the T-shirt over her head and slipping into her sandals.

Dory noticed. "Everything okay, honey?"

"Just fine, baby, just thinking. Let's go."

As usual, the Lyft driver was engaging and full of information about their destination. "Gallerie magazine named this one of the ten most beautiful sculpture gardens in the world, did you know? And to think it's free! What a gift to the city of New Orleans. Well, here we are, ladies. You have a wonderful time and call me when you're done. If I'm not on another call, I'll be glad to take you back."

The two thanked her and walked into the garden. They wandered its acres, marveling at the dozens of sculptures that ranged from traditional to avant-garde, as well as the drifts of native Louisiana irises in full bloom.

"Oh, this is heavenly." Dory sighed.

"I agree. Why don't we get some coffee and beignets at the café and sit by the river and picnic?"

Dory agreed, and so they did.

Passing the Cascade Garden Pool, they headed toward the lagoon and settled comfortably on a bench. Remarkably, there was no one around, and they munched and sipped in silence, lost in their own thoughts as they enjoyed the late afternoon's cooling breeze. When they had finished, Dory turned and said brightly, "Well, shall we go, love?" She began to rise, but Robby gently pulled her back down on the bench.

"Dory, look at me," she said seriously.

Dory stiffened, then laughed. "What, honey? Don't tell me you're going to propose?"

Robby smiled faintly. "Maybe someday, sweetheart. Maybe someday soon, actually. But right now I just want to talk to each other honestly. Please look at me, Dory."

Dory turned slowly and looked her in the eyes, her own reflecting distress. But she tried to lighten the mood again. "Oh, baby, no proposal? Aw, gee. Well, what then? You seem so serious."

"I am, Dory. I know something's going on with you. This is your butch Daddy speaking now. Is there something you want to tell me?" Her dark eyes looked piercingly into her lover's, who squirmed and looked away.

"Oh, gosh, honey, I've just been a little distracted lately. It's nothing, really."

"No, Dory. Look me in the eye and tell me that," Robby said, both hands on her arms to hold her gaze. "These calls from the reporter should be inconsequential, but they clearly are not. What's going on?"

Dory's eyes welled with tears as she looked at her lover, shaken. "Oh God, oh God, I can't, Robby. Please don't make me tell you. I couldn't stand it if you hated me. I couldn't, I just couldn't," she said, beginning to cry freely.

Robby stared at her, startled. *What could be so bad?* She was reacting far beyond anything Robby had anticipated. She sighed, taking her distraught lover in her arms and making soothing sounds. "Okay, baby. It must really be something to upset you so. But how could I hate you? You know I worship you. I love you, come what may, sweetheart. We'll work it out, whatever it is. Just spit it out, honey. Just say it. Now. What is it?"

But Dory was beyond speech. Robby held her sobbing lover and continued. "Tell me. Come on, now, tell me. You've been carrying something around all by yourself and you shouldn't. That's what I'm here for, baby. You know that. Just say it."

"I can't. I can't."

"You can, and you will, right now. Come on, baby. Tell me. You owe me that and you know it."

"I know I do," Dory said, trying to calm herself as she wiped her face. "Oh, Robby, I did something so wrong and it's going to ruin everything. I'm so sorry, so sorry. Please forgive me." And she broke down again.

Robby took her face in her hands. "Say it," she commanded firmly.

"I, I—it's my book. Oh, Robby, I made a terrible mistake."

"What, in God's name? What did you do?" Robby demanded, frustrated.

"I submitted it to several publishers and no one would accept it."

"Yes, I remember."

"Then after a half-dozen or so rejections, the last one told me…" Dory cleared her throat. "He, he said, 'You know, if this was a memoir instead of fiction, I'd take it in a minute.' So, I, I—"

"You rewrote it as a true memoir, as we discussed. Baby, I know you were reluctant to let go of some of the fictional embellishments, but that doesn't seem so tragic, especially given the sales of the true story. Unless you're worried about your personal life being too exposed? But we talked through that choice when you did the revision and decided you were strong enough and protected enough by all those who love you, that it was worth the risk. And you know Daddy will never let anything bad happen to you. I mean, really, I don't see the downside, as long as you were honest about your experiences." Robby paused, searching Dory's stricken face. Then realization dawned. "Oh, my God."

Dory could not speak. She looked at her lover in despair, red-eyed and tears pouring down her face.

"Is *any* of it true?" Robby asked, in shock.

"Yes, of course, most of it is. But the big events, the highlights, like being at Stonewall or in the Up Stairs Lounge fire here in New Orleans, weren't."

"And that's what the reporter uncovered?"

"Yes," Dory whispered, hiccupping. "She talked to people who had been there, especially the survivors here in New Orleans. I'd been to the club often and people remembered me, but no one could confirm that I was there that night and just narrowly escaped the way I said. In fact, some said they had no recollection of seeing me there at all that night."

They sat in silence as the enormity of the fraud seeped into Robby's brain. Exposing that would not only ruin the bestseller's sales, but it would destroy Dory's credibility and career forever. She might as well work as a cashier somewhere. But worse than that was Robby's even slower realization of the lie she had unknowingly been living with. Dory's credibility as a person, let alone as a writer, was seriously up in the air. If she would keep this from her lover—the closest person in the world to her, the person she allegedly shared everything with transparently—who was she, really?

"So, you've been lying to me for—let's see, how many years now?"

Dory stared down at her hands, twisting in her lap. "Not many years. Just one or two. I didn't mean to..."

Robby snorted. "Didn't mean to? You mean after

I read the memoir and asked if you really had been at all those places and you said yes, you didn't mean to lie, but you did anyway? And then you said they were intense memories that you could write about because that kept them at a safe emotional distance, but you didn't want to relive them out loud with me. I always tried to be respectful of that and not push you to talk about things that haunted you, but clearly it wasn't the trauma that held you back. It was that you *weren't even fucking there*."

Dory made a strangled sound and didn't answer.

In shock, Robby sat up, slowly disengaging herself from Dory, and looked straight ahead.

Dory searched her face desperately. "Oh, God, Robby, I'm so sorry, honey. Really I am. It's been like a millstone around my neck for the past year, keeping it from you and everyone else, but mostly you. The stories are absolutely true, they just didn't happen to me personally. Oh, Robby, please forgive me. It was a really stupid thing to do and it's so unlike me. I just didn't think it through. Oh, God, baby, please. I could stand anything, the public humiliation, anything, but I just couldn't stand losing you."

Robby finally turned to look at her and Dory burst into fresh sobs at the distant look in her eyes.

"Dory, I…I need time to process this. It's beyond being a really big deal, you know?" She raked her hand through her hair unsteadily and looked away again. "Who are you, really? The person I thought I knew wouldn't do that. She was honorable…"

Dory raised her head back in agony, and then bowed it, listening quietly, dispiritedly, like a person receiving her sentence from the judge.

"…and ethical. And above all else, she was totally

honest with me. She was the one person I could believe in this life."

She stood shakily. "I said we could work anything out, Dory, but this? I really don't know. I just don't know."

Dory shook her lowered head and moaned, folded her arms over her stomach and doubled over in obvious emotional pain. "I'm sorry. I'm sorry. What can I say to fix it? I swear, it's the only thing I've ever kept from you, Robby. I adore you. Please don't leave me. I just couldn't stand it. You're everything to me. I will never, ever, ever keep anything from you again, I swear it! Please, please, Daddy. Please don't leave me."

Robby shook her head. She was well aware Dory knew that calling on Daddy touched her in her softest spot, the part of herself that was the unequivocal caretaker, the devoted partner, the one willing to walk through fire for her lover. She was pulling out all her cards in her desperate attempt to keep them together.

But this. Robby felt as if she had been knifed in the gut, feeling the pain as much as Dory. This was going to be a hard one to get past, if they ever could.

"Come on," Robby said woodenly. "We'd better get back. Please compose yourself as best you can, as will I. I don't feel like explaining what happened to our friends right now. We'll just have to wing it. Or maybe go home early tomorrow. Oh, hell, we're leaving at one o'clock anyway. Surely we can hold it together that long."

Robby turned away and pulled out her phone. "I'll call for a car. Let's go to the street."

She walked off, leaving Dory to slowly follow.

Chapter Six

So, today's the day, huh?" Lee said the next morning, putting her menu down.

"Yes, this is it," Charlene responded. "April sixteenth, back to reality. Our flight leaves at one. I sure do want to thank you for your company and sharing your knowledge of New Orleans with me. If I can ever return the favor…although, I don't think Atlanta has quite the cultural riches to share. Sherman pretty much took care of that."

"Well, I'd like to take you up on that, actually. I've been curious about Atlanta and…" Lee gulped and reddened slightly. "Frankly, I'd like to see you again. How do you feel about that?"

They paused to give their orders and watch their coffee being poured.

Charlene traced the cup's opening with her finger, looking down thoughtfully. "Yes. Yes, that sounds good. If we were in Atlanta, it would be a no-brainer, but the hundreds of miles between us do give me pause, I must admit. When we met I thought, 'Oh, a fun fling. What's the harm?' But coming to know you a little bit, I am definitely interested in knowing more. But how would we manage that? Isn't it a little unrealistic?"

Lee smiled delightedly. "Well, it would be, if I wasn't swimming in flying privileges. Compliments of my twenty years as an airline customer service rep.

And besides, what's a few hundred miles to kindred hearts and minds connecting?"

"Oh. That's right, I forgot about that." Charlene smiled in return. "Well, in that case, why not? Use 'em or lose 'em, they say. You can't leave them to your heirs, I presume."

"Yup, that's right. Well, good. When should I come, not to be too pushy?"

"Well, Jill usually has a bash around Memorial Day at her house on Lake Burton. That's only a few weeks away. Why don't you come then?"

Lee grinned. "Deal. And in the meantime, there's always phone, text, and email. I'm going to look forward to getting to know you better and better, Charlene. And I warn you, I grow on people."

Charlene laughed, leaning back with her cup in hand. "I can believe that," she said, smiling warmly. "And we already share a lot of interests, so it'll be fun to explore them together. I can't wait to show you our botanical garden. It's small, but a real jewel. My favorite part is a huge moss-and-rock sculpture of the Earth Goddess's face, with her similarly large but graceful hand guiding water to fall in a reflecting pond. It's amazing. And I'm pretty sure there's a Chihuly exhibit planned for around that time there. His glass sculptures are wonderful. Don't worry, we'll find plenty to do."

Lee leaned forward and took her free hand, looking into her eyes. "No need to be frenetic, either. We also can just hang out and enjoy each other's company, go to a movie and have dinner, take a walk. Whatever it is, I'm sure I'll enjoy it. Thank you for, well, being open to my coming. I wasn't sure you would be and I'm sure glad you are."

Charlene colored. "Well, who knows what will come of it? But I firmly believe in enjoying life to the fullest, especially at our age. So," she said, extending her cup to toast Lee's. "Here's to fun times shared."

"To that," agreed Lee. *And to much more than that, I hope.*

Robby woke up from a restless night to the welcome scent of coffee and groggily reached for Dory, but found the bed empty. Suddenly remembering the night before, she put her arm over her eyes and softly groaned. How could things have gone from so right to so wrong so quickly? She felt as if the earth had dropped out from under her feet, but still she battled her disbelief. The woman she so loved had deceived her day in and day out, causing her now to question everything about their relationship.

She heard the soft click of the door handle and stiffened as Dory entered the room, carrying a tray. "I thought you might like some coffee, and we still have muffins and fruit." Her tentative smile vanished as Robby sat up, her stony expression unchanged.

"Thanks, but I don't think I can eat," she said. "And I don't really want to talk right now. I think I'll go for a walk. I need time to myself to process this mess, Dory, and to be honest I don't know where it'll end up."

Dory dropped her head in assent. "I'm not sure what to say, either," she said softly. "Except to reiterate how very sorry I am. I…I don't know, I feel horrible and yet relieved that at last you know. It's been a constant grief to me to have kept this from you. Maybe if I had shared it with you much earlier, we could have figured out what to do together."

"What to do?" Robby snorted. "Are you kidding? You lied, and you put the lie in print, for God's sake. And then worse, you lied to me. Face it, babe, your credibility is fucked." She clamped her lips shut to keep from saying anything more. She had never felt so conflicted in her life, and being cruel to the woman she adored was never a scenario she had imagined.

Robby could feel the grief emanating from Dory as she silently threw on her clothes. *Can't think about that now, I need to clear my head before we talk about anything else.* She grabbed her phone and slammed the door behind her.

Jill stretched in the bed, then rose to pull aside the damask curtains. The morning sun flooded the room and she closed her eyes, enjoying its warmth on her face. The door opened behind her and she turned to see Taylor placing a tray on the small table.

"Here you go, sleeping beauty," Taylor said, smiling. "Coffee, fruit, and muffin. I met Dory making up a tray, too, in the kitchen, and I'm wondering if something's wrong with her and Robby. She was just not her perky self. Looked like she hadn't slept a wink."

"Those two?" Jill scoffed. "Nah. They're as perennial as the mountains. I've never seen a couple more in love than they are."

"Well, I don't know," Taylor said, coming over to wrap her arms around Jill's waist. "Maybe not. Hopefully not. Will you come and dine, lover? But first, a kiss to start off the day right."

She leaned into Jill's warmth and kissed her

softly on the lips, short, affectionate pecks that led to a long, satisfying kiss. Then, taking her hand, she led her to the table and pushed her gently into the chair. "You eat, sweetie, and take your time waking up. I'm going to shower and then pack."

Jill smiled at her and sighed at the first sip of the brew. She leaned back and munched the muffin as Taylor went out, and shortly heard the water in the shower. Her gaze wandered around the room, alighting on Taylor cell phone. Taking another sip and bite, she eyed it steadily, then crossed the room and picked it up. She remembered Taylor's passcode from a conversation when they'd laughed about the weird combinations people picked to remember their codes. Taylor's was "casebet," gambling slang for all-in. She hesitated, and then entered it. The cell lit up to life and she checked Taylor's recent phone calls.

There were almost daily calls to Los Angeles—one number in particular—and to Atlanta, plus several to an area code she didn't recognize. She wrote them down and then moved on to the texts, where she found an interesting array of conversations about various investment deals she seemed involved in. There were reassuring texts to people she assumed were investors, and one that made her suck in her breath. It was from someone named Cisco who seemed to be coordinating her LA affairs, who lightly asked, *How's it going with the subject?* Taylor had responded that things were progressing according to plan.

What is that about? What plan? Am I the subject? Questions raced through her mind as she stared at the screen, until she suddenly realized she hadn't heard the shower for several minutes. She hastily put the phone back and resumed her seat just as Taylor entered, brushing her hair.

"Feel better?" Jill asked smoothly, sipping her coffee.

"Much. I highly recommend it." She reached for her buzzing phone and paused, glancing once at Jill before she picked it up and read the screen. Then, wordlessly, she set it back down.

Oh, my God, did I not return it to the right place? Jill looked back at her quizzically. "Text?"

"Trash," Taylor said, shaking her head.

"My turn." Jill grabbed her towel and headed out. "Back in a flash."

Wow, that might've been a bust. Tell ya, I'm not sure I'm cut out for cloak-and-dagger stuff. It's nerve-wracking.

Dory had sat frozen on the side chair watching Robby leave her. Overcome with grief and fear of what was to come, she simply crawled back into the bed and shut her eyes. Unconsciousness was infinitely preferable to reality but, try as she might, she could not sleep. Picking up her phone, she called the airline and changed her reservation to an earlier flight, dressed and packed rapidly, and dialed a car service for a pickup. She could not bear to face Robby or anyone else again. Taking a last look around the romantic room in which she had been so happy only twenty-four hours earlier, she walked around the house to the front to wait for her ride, her heart a physical ache in her chest.

Robby returned to the room, eyes widening when

she realized Dory was gone. She checked her phone and found the text: *Gone home early. I'll stay a few days with a friend until you think you can talk. I'll always love you. Please forgive me.*

She raked her hands through her hair, mind still roaring in confusion. The walk had helped her calm her nerves a little bit, but not her mental confusion. She felt Dory's absence acutely and imagined that it would probably get worse before it got better. She'd always felt like they were almost psychically joined. Beyond just being used to having each other physically present, they could read each other's feelings, guess each other's thoughts, and their opinions generally were in sync.

And how was she going to explain Dory's absence to the others? Oh, shit, her leaving left Robby with even more crap to deal with. *Damn it! Well, one step at a time*, she thought grimly, and pulled out her bag to pack.

She met the others in the living room. "Dory still packing?" asked Charlene.

"No, she's gone on ahead earlier this morning."

"What on earth for?" Jill asked. She glanced at Taylor, who cocked her eyebrow.

"Some kind of emergency, but nothing life-threatening," Robby said. "I'm sure it'll all become clearer soon. I'll call for a ride to the airport."

The others looked at her quietly as she called, and she knew they were noting her tension and the fatigue etched on her face. She was relieved that no one said another word about Dory. The conversation on the way to the airport was quiet except for the friends laughingly pumping Charlene for more information about Lee. Still, it was an uneasy ride.

Chapter Seven

Lord, it's good to be home. Kicking off her shoes, Charlene tossed her bag on the bed and went down to the kitchen for a glass of wine. *I love to travel, but it sure takes more out of me now than it did when I was younger.*

And what on earth is going on with Robby and Dory? Obviously, Robby would have had a logical explanation if it really was nothing earth-shattering. And even if it was urgent, she would have shared that. Something isn't right with them. Could they have had a fight? Lord, I never thought those two would have a serious dust-up, which this certainly does seem to be. I wonder if I should say anything, if I could help? We all share everything, pretty much, but this seems way out of the normal topics for discussion. Oh, I just hate to see them in trouble.

She sighed, sipping her wine contemplatively as she walked back to the bedroom, enjoying the familiar comfort of her surroundings: the painting she'd gotten at the Piedmont Arts Festival, which extended her art collecting beyond the Native American pots she'd gathered in her travels; the just-right restful gray of the walls; the sleek fabric shades on the windows overlooking the garden she loved. She hoped Lee would like it.

Lee. Should she offer Lee the guest room when she visited? Of course, what was she thinking? It had been a while since she had been attracted to anyone on other than a purely physical level. Lee was…interesting, and it unnerved her a little to find that it...well, unnerved her.

Oh, get over yourself, girl, she scolded herself. *What will be, will be. Just have fun. You surely know how to do that!*

Still…

She settled into the comfortable chair by the window, taking in the exuberant emerging blooms of the azaleas and daffodils, and the perfect, delicate green of the old trees' new leaves. She smiled to see the helicopter seeds flying off the maple, remembering how as a girl she would use their "glue" to stick them on her nose and pretend to be a unicorn. When had such simple pleasures been lost? Sipping her wine, she eyed the glass and murmured, "I guess about when you became the simple pleasure, my friend."

She settled back and reflected on her life. She was a survivor, no doubt about it, and she was proud of that. That trait had carried her through some challenging times, and her methods had sometimes been unorthodox, but the past was the past. Wasn't it? She huffed a little breath. Of course it was. Long past. *But the past does have a way of insinuating itself into the present,* an annoying little voice whispered.

Why have I never had a lasting relationship? she thought, not for the first time. *My friends can do it, at least in serial monogamy if not lifelong commitments. What's wrong with me? It wasn't an issue when I was working, but now, with time on my hands, I feel an absence. It would be nice to have someone to travel with, like Jill does, except…*She grimaced. *I think I'd be a little more selective in companions. I just have an* *uneasy feeling that something's not right with Taylor. She has a secret, I'm sure of it.*

"Huh, but don't we all? Oh, I don't know," she said aloud and sighed. "I'm tired. A nap sounds like what I need right now."

Entering the custom walk-in closet, she quickly separated clean clothes from laundry, tucked her travel cosmetics bag in a drawer, and slid her suitcase on the top shelf. Then she ducked into the shower, moaning in pleasure as the hot water sluiced over her body, flooding the drain with the dust of travel. Rubbing down with a thick towel, she slipped into a comfortable cotton T-shirt and padded over the thick carpet back to her bed. She put her clock on to surf sounds and, with a sigh of relief, crawled between the Egyptian cotton sheets and closed her eyes.

Just as she dropped off, the last conscious image she had in her mind was Lee's smiling eyes.

Dropping her suitcase in the foyer, Robby closed the door and glumly looked around her. The house that had been her home and refuge for the last twenty years seemed preternaturally quiet and empty. She felt Dory's absence like a sharp wound in her heart.

"Oh, it's better that we have some time apart," she muttered to herself. "It would be horrible to be bumping into each other here, trying to avoid the elephant in the room." But her heart could not agree. She missed her, the yin to her own yang. But her cop heart was outraged at Dory's deception, and perhaps more to the point, utterly insulted. She felt like a fool. She was a cop, with good cop instincts, for God's sake.

How could she have been so deceived?

"Goddammit! How could she *do* that?" she fumed as she stomped up the stairs to the bedroom. "We had a deal between us. No secrets, complete honesty. What else don't I know?"

When she realized she'd been standing in the middle of the room still holding her bag, she dropped it with a thump, swearing. Then, throwing it on the bed, she viciously attacked the contents. T-shirts and jeans flew on the floor or were left folded on the bed. She ruffled her short hair in aggravation. "Oh, shit, just put it all in the wash. Who gives a fuck?" She tossed it all in the hamper and the empty bag in the closet, and headed down to the kitchen.

She hung at the open refrigerator door, bleakly taking in the empty shelves. Dory had planned to stop at the grocery store on the way back from the airport to restock at least for the evening, but that was the last thing on Robby's mind. Well, there was beer, at least. Sighing, she pulled out a cold bottle and popped the top, restlessly pacing around the kitchen and peering out into the yard.

She didn't know what to do with herself. Normally, she would have settled in front of her computer to catch up on email and Facebook posts while Dory puttered around the kitchen. But her world had been disrupted and nothing felt like the next logical thing to do. She looked at the bottle in her hand and poured it down the drain. The gym, that's what she needed. A good workout to help untie the knots in her stomach and brain. A little post-exercise endorphin rush to balance the flood of whatever the opposite of endorphins was. She felt fucked up to the max, an unfamiliar and unpleasant state for her. She was used to being certain, balanced, fearless, and now none of that was true.

Shit.

Dashing back upstairs, she changed into her workout clothes. Slamming the door behind her, she ran out to the car like the devil himself was on her heels.

She greeted the receptionist at the gym absently, stashed her bag in the locker, and dove into an Olympian workout unlike any she had done before. Finally, spent and sweaty, she walked back into the locker room and grabbed her towel. She felt calmer, less panicky, but a heavy feeling had settled around her heart.

Once home, she stripped and entered the shower, turning the water up. Standing under its pounding power, she let go and allowed her tears to come as images of her years with Dory flooded her memory. She leaned against the wall and sobbed quietly, mourning the loss of trust and faith, and maybe love. Her shoulders shook as she imagined never holding Dory in her arms again, never waking up to her sleepy smile, never shaking her head fondly at her occasional ditzyness.

But she felt betrayed and it was a hard pill to swallow, harder than the disappointments and tragedies she had dealt with as a detective, harder than the emotional toll her family's rejection had been when she came out. She felt completely gutted emotionally, adrift and hopeless. She let herself simply weep for as long as she needed to, until the cop emerged again to take control.

Enough, she thought grimly, straightening up. *Welcome to hell, but you've been here before and gotten out. You'll do it again.* Emotion swept over her, but she fought the temptation to succumb again. Turning the temperature to cool, she lifted her face and let the water sweep over her, pressing her hair back and standing straight up. Turning off the faucet, she rubbed herself hard with the towel and wrapped it around her to walk back to the bedroom.

"I can do this," she said to herself. "I can do this. Maybe it's not over. Maybe Dory and I can find a way through this." The thought of her lover brought a mammoth lump to her throat, but she swallowed it. "Time. We just need time, one way or the other. And I'm retired." She chuckled humorlessly. "And Dory's freelance and controlling her own schedule. So time is one thing we have plenty of, but then again, maybe very little of. Who knows?

"One step at a time, Robby girl. One step at a time. It's just about time for Killer to get home, anyway."

She finished toweling off and quickly dressed in jeans and a black T-shirt. Hearing the bus coming up the street, she ran down to the front door and flung it open, crossing the lawn just as the bus door opened.

"Killer! Hey, dude. Welcome home!" A golden flash leaped out of the Doggy School Bus and raced to her, almost knocking her down with his enthusiastic greeting. She reached down and hugged her best buddy, then stood and waved to the bus driver, laughing.

"Thanks, Tamara! Was he good?"

"Oh, are you kidding?" Tamara called back, grinning. "We hate to see Mr. Handsome go. Take another trip soon so he can come play with us some more. See you next time!" With a wave, she closed the door and proceeded to deliver the rest of her charges, all of whom were grinning at Killer out of the windows.

"Man, with all those wagging tails, she probably barely needs A/C in the summer, right, Killer?" She knelt on the grass and wrapped her arms around his wiggling golden body, burying her face in his soft coat. "Oh, Killer, it sure is good to see you again, sweetheart." She laughed as he successfully knocked her down, twisting her face to escape his wet kisses as she stared at the blue sky. Struggling back up, she got to her feet as he danced around her, barking vigorously.

"Come on, Killer, help me fill this house back up with love," she said, clapping her hands. "Race you!" She ran after the bounding dog up onto the porch, looked out at the street with a sigh, and closed the front door.

"Come in, girlfriend," Serena said, eyeing Dory sympathetically. "You look like you need a hug."

"Oh, yeah," Dory said, losing herself in her friend's warm embrace. Rolling her bag into the kitchen, she hopped onto the counter barstool and looked down glumly, arms folded. "I've really done it this time, Serena."

"What on earth happened?" Serena asked. "The last I knew, you all were doing great, as usual. Did something happen in New Orleans?"

"Yeah, you might say that, although it really happened about a year or two ago, or at least since my book. I've been living a lie for all that time, and it may have cost me the most important relationship in my life. And I'm even afraid to tell you. I don't want to lose you, too, my best friend."

"Good grief, girl, give me specifics, please," Serena said, alarmed. "But you're never going to lose me, you should know that by now. Come what may, you're stuck with me since you saved my ass from indefinite detention in seventh grade and gained my undying loyalty. Now, give. What's up?" Taking a couple of glasses from the cabinet, she opened the refrigerator to fix them both cold glasses of juice.

Reassured that at least she wasn't looking at her, Dory launched into her explanation. "Well, the long and short of it is that my bestseller's success is built on a lie. It's not a memoir. Well, not entirely. It's got a healthy dose of fiction in it. That's how I wrote it to begin with, as a novel, and it was rejected everywhere. But when the last editor told me that he'd publish it in a minute as a memoir, I just ran with it. I rewrote it and presto, success.

"But that made me semi-famous in the gay community, and a reporter who interviewed me for *Out Proud* magazine did some digging. She suspects the truth, and now I don't know what's going to happen. I'm pretty sure it'll get out, though, and I'll be disgraced. My life as an author is probably over and worse, Robby is completely disillusioned with me. She feels like she doesn't know me, and maybe she doesn't. Maybe I don't even know me."

Dory stopped abruptly as her voice began to shake.

Serena looked thoughtfully at her friend as she returned with the juice. Sitting next to Dory, she leaned over and hugged her again. "Oh, boy, yeah. I see what you mean. This is a big deal, isn't it? But you'll make it through, sweetheart. It's not a killin' offense. Tell me about the reporter. Where does it stand with her?"

"Well, she's still uncertain, so she hasn't done anything yet." Dory wiped her eyes and plowed on. "She's been calling me to ask about the discrepancies she's found. At first I tried to explain them away, but lately I've been avoiding her. That can't go on forever. I guess I'll have to come clean. She doesn't seem like the blackmailing type, so I expect she'll just be delighted to have stumbled onto a pretty big story. She's young and ambitious. Who wouldn't seize on that? Oh, God." She moaned. "I'm ruined. And Robby. Oh, God." The threatening tears finally broke loose and streamed down her face.

"What in God's name am I going to do, Serena?"

"Okay, we'll have to think about this and strategize. First thing always is to do damage control. Maybe you should start with the most important component, Robby. Can you talk to her?"

"I don't think she even wants to see me, let alone talk." Dory sobbed. "I figure I just have to give her time, but I don't know how long to wait. And it's so ironic. This is probably the biggest crisis I'll ever have in my life and now is exactly the time I need her love and advice and feedback the most. I could just shoot myself. At least I'd be out of my misery."

"All right, let's not let this dissolve into a pity party," Serena said gently. "You're going to need all your wits about you, sweetie. How much sleep have you had?" she said, peering at Dory's face.

"Sleep. Oh, I don't think so." Dory snorted. "My brain is on overdrive. Despair and desperation have a way of doing that to you. I haven't slept well for weeks, and not at all in the last twenty-four hours."

"Then that's the first thing to do," Serena said firmly. "I have some Valerian that you need to take right now. It's a herb that really works. But it takes about an hour to relax you enough to sleep, so you should do that right away. In fact, take two," she said, taking the top off a pill jar. "Good thing that was juice and not coffee I served."

"Eeew." Dory wrinkled her nose, sniffing the bottle. "It stinks."

"You should be glad I didn't have the liquid form." Serena laughed. "Yeah, it doesn't smell pretty, but it's effective. Why don't you go on up to the guest bedroom and get settled in, then take a walk around the neighborhood?" She stood behind her friend and began kneading her shoulders, drawing moans from Dory. "Wow, you are tight as a bow. The exercise might help unravel some of those knots, clear your mind of some of the panic, and help you to relax enough for the Valerian to work. Things will still be there when you wake up, but you'll probably be better able to think and plan.

"And I'll be here for you, girlfriend. Don't you worry about that. We'll figure out a plan of attack together. You are a good person, you just made a mistake. And you didn't even dream it all up yourself, you essentially were advised to do it by an expert. Everybody has their weakness and you fell into this one, but you'll survive."

"Yeah, maybe as a hermit living out in the woods somewhere because no one will want to know me." Dory scoffed at her lame joke. "But you're right. I'm just completely overwhelmed now. I need to regroup to face the music. And now that you mention it, I do feel tired down to my bones. If I could just turn off my brain..."

Serena smiled. "Okay, start with the unpacking and walk. Literally, one step at a time."

"Right," Dory said, slipping off the stool. "And Serena?"

"Yes?"

"Thank you. I don't know what I'd do without you."

"That's what friends are for, sweetie. Now go on."

Dory awoke to the early evening sun streaming in the window and the distant sound of lawn mowers. *Hmm, summer's coming, for sure*, she thought drowsily as she stretched. She turned to snuggle with her lover but, heart sinking, woke fully at finding the empty space beside her. Looking at the clock, she was shocked to see she'd slept for three solid hours and the light of day was waning. The memory of recent events crashed down upon her and, with a moan, she rolled back over, wanting to lose herself in sleep. "Nope, won't work." She sighed.

Throwing back the sheet, she sat up and rested her feet on the cool wood floor, bracing her arms and dropping her head. "Okay, Dory, time to face the music. You've got a lot to do, but where to start? Ohh, coffee. Or something. I need something."

She splashed water on her face and peered into the mirror. "Yikes, not looking too good, girlfriend." She moaned. "Oh, well, that's the least of my worries, including that I'm talking to myself."

Putting her clothes back on, she padded down the hall to the stairs, to Serena's cheery "Hey, there!" from the kitchen. She managed a small smile in response and settled back down onto the barstool.

"How'd you sleep?" asked Serena, clearly noting her sad expression. "I'm so glad you had a good long nap."

"Actually, pretty good. That Valerian really works. I feel better. And to think it's just a herb. Thanks. "

"Anytime. In fact, you might repeat that tonight until you catch up a bit. You look like you're still dragging a little, if you don't mind my saying so."

"I know," Dory said, grimacing. "I noticed in the mirror. Boy, stress can really age a person in a hurry, it seems. I mean, even more than I am."

"Not to worry, baby, you'll be back to your enthusiastic, gorgeous self before you know it. Today, your task is just to rest up and restock your resources. Would you like some tea? Or maybe a glass of wine? It's a depressant, which you certainly don't need, but it might help you catch up more on your sleep. Then, once you're rested, what's your plan, if you have one yet?"

"Wine, yes, just what the doctor ordered, please."

"Sauvignon blanc okay?"

"Yes, perfect. To answer your question, I was thinking as I dropped off that the first thing I want to do is write Robby a note," Dory replied, accepting the glass and settling back onto the barstool. "I don't have quite enough courage to just go over, in case she just turns me away, but I really need to try to explain and apologize. At least, I hope that'll crack the door open between us just a little bit. I can build on that. So, that's the most important thing.

"Then, I need to talk to my lawyer about my contract and any liability. Then my agent and publicist to break the bad news, and then based on what they say, just maybe I'll be prepared to talk to my publisher. Or maybe I'd better do that in person. Yeah, I'd better just fly up there and throw myself on his mercy." Gloomily, she sipped her wine, staring out the French doors to the deck and the darkening yard behind.

Serena came around the counter and began massaging Dory's shoulders again. "Oh, lord, child, you're still stiff as a board. Do some stretches and I heartily recommend that you keep taking walks. And are you hungry? You need to keep up your strength."

"Yes, mother." Dory groaned, hanging her head loosely before her and reveling in the relief to her aching muscles. "You're the best. Oh, thank you. Maybe something light to eat. I don't think my stomach will tolerate much."

Serena pulled out a pot of homemade soup from the refrigerator. In a matter of minutes, she had a steaming bowl in front of Dory, alongside a healthy chunk of baguette and butter. "Eat," she commanded. "I'll refill your glass.

"So, I'll give you a key to the house and you can come and go at will," she continued. "I'll be at the gallery in the morning, but the rest of the day I'll be in the studio out back, because I'm working on a new series. If you need anything, just cross the lawn and come on in, okay? The PIN to unlock the office computer is in the top right drawer of my desk, so feel free. I won't be using it at all for the next few days, most likely. If I want to check my email, I'll do it from the studio.

"And oh, lord, don't be getting all mushy on me," she exclaimed as Dory looked at her in gratitude. "You'd do the same for me. Just take good care of yourself, okay? Distress and grief affect the body physically as well as emotionally, you know. Do those stretches and remember to eat, and for goodness sake, keep hydrated! You hear me, girl?"

"Yes, mama," Dory said, laughing. "Yes, ma'am!

Whatever you say, ma'am! You should've been a drill sergeant in the Army."

"Yes, well, sometimes a body just needs to be taken in hand by someone who loves her. So, I'm off to bed. It's been a big day. And even bigger for you, so I recommend you hit the sack, too. There are novels and short story anthologies that you can pick from if you don't feel sleepy right away. I put the Valerian in your room if you need it again. And tomorrow, you have as good a day as you can manage, honey. Call out if you need anything."

"Thanks, Serena. Love you," Dory said to her departing back, and finished her meal with a smile. *Friends*, she thought. *People may come and go, but your friends are always there*. That, of course, made her think of Robby, and she gulped. One quick call and then to the most important letter she might ever write.

Sipping her coffee, she picked up her phone and dialed. "Hello, Charles, I hope I'm not calling too late," she said to her lawyer. "I'm back and I think I might need my legal beagle. Do you have time tomorrow?"

"Dory," her attorney and friend exclaimed. "You're back. How was New Orleans?"

"Well, wonderful and awful. I'll tell you all about it. Got some time?"

"Uh-oh," Charles said. "For you, always, my love. Let's see...yes, I actually have some time in the afternoon. Want to come at noon and we can have lunch, too?"

"I don't know about lunch because I have another appointment to make, but that might have to wait until later. But I'll see you at noon tomorrow. Thanks." Dory hung up and walked out the back door onto the deck. She finished her wine leaning against the rail, breathing in the fragrant air and thinking. Then, squaring her shoulders, she headed for Serena's office and sat down at the computer. Time to write to Robby.

She sat quietly before the monitor, staring at the blinking cursor as she gathered her thoughts. She had thought that she would write a long epistle, explaining and begging, but she had changed her mind. What was in her heart was very simple, really. *My darling Robby,* she began.

I know we are in a terrible situation and it's all my fault. I would do anything to turn back the clock and reverse the very bad decision I made. But since that's not possible, I just want to say these very basic, most important things to you, and I hope you'll hear them with an open heart.

I love you. I will never, ever, stop loving you.

I am sorry beyond words that I've screwed up so badly. I will do anything to make it up to you. I know I don't deserve it, but please forgive me.

And I know I don't deserve this either, but I need your input now more than ever, and I am begging you to please, please talk to me. You've always been the thinker and problem solver in our little family; I've always depended on your wisdom and I so need it now. I know I need to make penance to everyone, especially to you, but also to the whole damn world, and I don't know where to even begin.

Please see me, Daddy. I'm staying at Serena's, But you say when and where, and I'll be there; in public, in private, I don't care. Please.

My love forever,
Dory

She read it over and over until she knew there was nothing more to say. She printed it, signed it, and put the letter and her heart in an envelope to await her judgment. Trudging up the stairs to the bedroom, she decided to take it home first thing in the morning. She didn't know whether to pray that Robby would be there or gone. Either way, she knew that she was fighting for her life, which she just hoped wouldn't be spent alone in regret.

Top down to enjoy the fragrant spring air, Jill moved her silver Mercedes up the circular drive and then behind her home to the garages. Entering, she coasted to a halt and turned the purring engine off. "Bye, Baby," she said, giving the sleek car an affectionate pat. Riding in it always made her feel good, and she always named her cars. Her friends teased her about it, but she didn't care. Her cars were dependable and luxurious; what was not to like?

A slight frown furrowed her forehead as that thought led to another. Taylor. Huh. Was there really trouble in paradise with Taylor? She sensed her friends' reservations about her, although no one had said anything about it, and the peek at Taylor's cell phone had raised some troubling questions.

What did she really know about Taylor? On the surface she looked fine—and under the sheets she was undeniably great—but her friends' unspoken misgivings had alerted her own antennae. She'd have to think about that. Perhaps some due diligence was called for. Robby could probably help her with that if needed, but she had her own private investigator contacts to draw on as well. That was one of the resources rich people needed, Daddy had told her, and she'd availed herself of that before. Particularly since the subject of cash investment had arisen, that might be a timely intervention. And especially since Taylor was drawing her friends into it, too, something that still annoyed her. She might risk her own capital, but she'd darn sure protect her friends'.

She entered the house, simultaneously loving the perfect climate control and wishing the windows were wide open to circulate the fragrant air. "Well, with the air comes Atlanta's yellow rain of pollen," she admitted to herself. It was true—in the spring, every Atlanta car not in a garage was yellow, coated with a thick dusting of pollen. And that was all her asthma would need, not to mention how disgruntled her house cleaner would be. So, climate control it was.

Placing her bag on the luggage rack in her walk-in closet, she began to unpack, returning her thoughts to Taylor. It was odd, she thought, how her expectations of relationships had changed with age. In her youth, everyone had the potential to be "the one," and her selectivity was broad. After all, they all thought they were immortal, with an unlimited amount of time to live and love and experiment. But now, she felt the faint chill of age at her back, and her requirements of romantic relationships had changed. There probably was no "one" out there. Everyone in her generation had decades of experiences, good and bad, that had molded them into the person they were. Everyone was pretty set in their ways. Those who had remained with their partner for decades were comfortably ensconced. A few even still having sex, she thought wryly. The rest seemed happy to just be content.

But contentment was never for her. She wanted the thrill of the highs and tolerated the accompanying lows, and she'd never met anyone who could enjoy the ride with her. She had felt in the past like there was something wrong with her but, over time, had simply accepted that this was who she was. Devil-may-care Jill, lucky girl, able to indulge her whims. Always with a companion, but never a bride. It used to bother her, but now she was content that this was her life.

That was okay. But with wealth came the hazardous potential of people with ulterior motives disguising them with attractive faces and flattery. Normally, she socialized with successful people because that risk was greatly reduced with them. Taylor, although she presented the image of success, was an unknown entity, but her radically different career and the peek into the Hollywood sphere had attracted Jill like a moth to a flame. Not to mention her looks.

"Yup," she reminded herself. "She's a looker and she's interesting, but that doesn't make me stupid. I'll make some calls."

Chapter Eight

Charlene pulled her Audi into the short-term parking space in front of the coffee shop and jumped out to get her morning fix.

"Good morning, Julius." She smiled at the neatly ponytailed barista behind the counter.

"Good morning, Judge." He smiled back. "The usual?"

"Yes, please," she replied, hand immersed in her bag searching for her wallet as she absently glanced around.

An entering woman caught her eye as Charlene happened to look toward the door. To her surprise, she looked directly at her, seemingly in a deliberate manner, then looked away quickly when their eyes met. There was something familiar about her, as if she had seen her before, but Charlene was sure she didn't know her. She looked careworn, tired, a little rough around the edges. *Well, who wouldn't be, early in the morning with this crowd*, thought Charlene, and dismissed the thought. Still, she felt a little uneasy until the time came to pay. Taking the coffee to the prep counter to add chocolate powder to her latté, she glanced around again, but the woman had vanished. *Silly. It's nobody.* She dismissed her from her mind.

She stopped at her small campaign office and checked in with her staff, set up media interviews, and updated her schedule of campaign event stops. She picked up a quick sandwich for lunch and then headed farther into town for the candidate forum.

Arriving at the middle school a short time later, she walked down the auditorium aisle to the panel's table on the stage, accompanied by the stares and clicks of media cameras. The forum had been organized by the local party chapter, and the butterflies in her stomach reminded her that she had been out of the public eye for a while. Taking a deep breath, she shook hands with the moderators, smiled at the other candidates, and took her seat.

As she settled in, a woman seated at the end of an aisle caught her eye. She seemed to be staring at her, and she gave Charlene a small humorless smile that chilled her. Distracted, Charlene's brow furrowed as she searched her memory for a connection. *Of course—she was at the coffee shop this morning. How could this be a coincidence? But who is she?*

After chatting with the other candidates for a few minutes, she excused herself to visit the restroom before the panel began. And when she came out, there the woman was, washing her hands at the sink.

Charlene moved to the sink next to her and the woman glanced over.

"Pretty warm out there, isn't it?"

"Yes, I guess so," answered Charlene, the hair on the back of her neck prickling.

The woman was dressed in old baggy jeans and a well-worn T-shirt, her thin hair tied back in a loose ponytail. Her face was lined and she appeared older than she likely was, as if she was aged from a hard life. She smiled or, rather, grimaced, and said, "You don't remember me, do you?"

"No, should I?" Charlene answered, on full alert,

her mind racing, still mystified, uneasy.

"Does the Pink Pony jog your memory? The name Connie?"

Charlene froze, her hands paralyzed under the water stream.

"Oh, yeah, I see you do." Connie laughed mirthlessly. "Old friends, right? How've you been? You look good. In fact, I've been keeping up with you, Your Honor. Hear you're running for State House. Hmm, bet that'll involve a lot of publicity, won't it? Bet your competition will be looking into your background, won't they?"

Charlene took a deep breath, turned off the water, and dried her hands with paper towels. Slowly, she turned and faced Connie squarely.

"Of course I remember you, Connie. We weren't friends, exactly, but good acquaintances. You seem to have something on your mind. What do you want?"

"I do, I do indeed," Connie said, drying her hands. Her eyes shifted uneasily, avoiding Charlene's. "I seem to remember doing you a lot of favors in the old days when I bartended and you waited tables. Connie wasn't someone to look *down* on then, was she? No, no, Connie was a positive Godsend sometimes, when she knew which frats were planning kegs and might like to have a party girl there to…liven things up, right?"

"I don't recall looking down on you at all," Charlene said coldly. "And you got a cut of those jobs."

"Oh, yeah, peanuts, even then. But I need more now. I've got a kid in college, and I'm kind of short on her tuition." Connie's demeanor seemed to shrink a little bit as she paused, but then she drew herself up and thrust out her chin. "You wouldn't mind helping an old friend now, would you?"

Charlene took a deep breath. "How much?"

"Well, tuition's right expensive these days, you know? It seems to go up every year. I'd have to figure it all out, but how about a thousand to start?"

"One thousand dollars. For tuition, is that right?" Charlene concentrated to keep her voice from shaking. "I'd have to think about it. Where can I reach you?"

Connie snorted. "Oh, I'll reach you, don't worry. And I'm going to need an advance on that tuition right quick. The trip out here just tapped me out, I can tell you." She turned to go and then paused. She seemed to deflate and her gestures were birdlike, nervous. She turned back, stood for a moment, silent, and then said, "I know this is awful for you. I'm uncomfortable, too. And I have to admit, yes, I do remember you well from those days. But things change, you know? I have a situation. I'm kind of sorry to pull you into it, but I have no choice."

Charlene just looked at her, and Connie, eyes down, walked out. Charlene leaned against the wall, white-faced and breathing hard. "Okay, okay, get a grip. It'll be okay," she whispered to herself. "Think. You just need to think about it. There's a solution, somewhere. Breathe."

She splashed cold water on a paper towel and placed it on her neck, standing there for a few minutes until her breathing quieted. She looked up and studied herself in the mirror.

"Well, Charlene girl, seems the past has come back to visit you, eh? Now, how are we going to handle this one? Well, time will tell. For the moment, onward." Squaring her shoulders, she tossed the towel in the bin and marched back into the auditorium. She quickly scanned the audience, but saw no sign of Connie.

Later, the panel over, she drove home slowly, racing thoughts competing for her attention. The panel had gone well, she thought. Her novel approach to juvenile crime while on the bench, involving mandatory work-study rather than incarceration, had been demonstrably successful and won her a lot of respect and community support. So did her ideas about building economic infrastructure in the poorer areas of the city, which were grounded in both reality and urban planning science. The key would be to get her messages through to the public and inspire them to vote for her. To do that, she had a full schedule of public appearances planned from now until election day.

She sighed. Sometimes she felt that her life was moving too fast for her to feel balanced, but hopefully that was temporary.

Suddenly the specter of Connie jumped back to the front of her mind. *Oh my God.* Connie could derail everything, completely destroying the respectable reputation she had built over decades. Her friends knew that she'd worked her way through college, but she'd only told them about her normal jobs. She never confided her party girl gigs. Dear God, once she'd even jumped out of a cake. But mostly she danced, sinuously inviting and smiling at the males ogling and whistling at her youthful self. But it wouldn't matter that that was the extent of her wildness, probably, if the word got out.

Ironic, she thought to herself. *It was exactly having to do that kind of work that made me at least partly understand the young offenders who came before me. When you're faced with critical decisions well before you are equipped to strategize and address them, you fall back to the obvious fixes. For them, it was crime. I was lucky to have another, although unconventional, way to survive.*

But what to do about Connie?

Well, first thing, she had to find out all she could about her. Did she really have a daughter in college, or was that just a convenient scam for her blackmail?

Charlene sat back in her seat at the red light, fingers drumming on the steering wheel. She mentally reviewed all the prosecutors and lawyers she had met in her career, casting about for someone who might be able to help her with this problem. Moving ahead with the green light, she shook her head. It wasn't really legal aid she needed; it was pragmatic investigative work.

"Of course!" She almost hit her brakes with the suddenness of the thought. The help she needed was right in her own backyard. *Robby.* God bless the woman. She'd been one of Atlanta's finest detectives, wearing her trademark fedora with pride for years. Robby could help, she was sure of it, and her thumb reached for the Bluetooth button. "Dial Robby," she instructed, and drummed her fingers again on the wheel as the rings sounded.

"Hello?"

"Robby? It's Charlene. Do you have a minute?"

"Oh, sure, for you, anytime."

With a quick intake of breath, Charlene suddenly realized that this was not a normal time for Robby. Something was going on with Dory and she could hear the tinge of sadness in her friend's voice.

"Oh, God, Robby, I just remembered this might not be the best time for you. I'm sorry. I have a problem I thought you might be able to help me with, but maybe you might want to be talking to *me* at this particular time. Or maybe not. None of us want to intrude on you all, but we all worry that something's not right with you—but none of us want to butt in. Oh, I'm making a hash of it. Long and short of it, how are you doing, darlin'?"

By this time, Robby was chuckling. "Charlene, you were the pluperfect judge, but when you get tied up in your thoughts, you are so sweet and funny. Thank you for your concern. Yes, of course, your Spidey senses were correct that something's awry with me and Dory, but we're working on it. We probably just need a breather to regroup before we address it. Not to worry. What can I do for you, girlfriend?"

"Probably" need a breather? Interesting.

"Well, you know we're all here for you both if needed," she said. "As for me, it's complicated. Can we meet?"

"Oh, sure. In fact, now would be okay," Robby said. "I'm just rattling around this house, a little at a loss as to what to do with myself, so your company would be most welcome. I'll put on the coffee."

"Deal." Charlene grinned with relief. "I'm only fifteen minutes away. Shall I stop for some Krispy Kremes and we'll both be decadent?"

"You got it, although after our deliciously indulgent trip I probably should say no. But, go for it. Coffee's going on now."

Charlene hung up, breathing more easily than she had for the past three hours. With Robby's help, she would figure a way around this. She badly wanted to win the election, not just because it was a challenge, but because she felt driven to do some good for her community, more than she could do from the bench. In fact, that experience had just whetted her appetite.

"Who knows how much time I have left?" she mused to herself. "I'm healthy as a horse, but no one knows. I want to make some mark, make my world a little better, and one way to do that is to win this election.

"Robby, here I come. Let the brainstorming begin, well fueled by doughnuts and coffee!"

Chapter Nine

After Charlene left, Robby paced the floor as she waited for Jessie to pick up. *Does everyone have secrets? What, is Mercury in retrograde or something? First Dory, now Charlene, and I'm wondering about Taylor's motives with Jill. Good God.*

"Oh, hello, is Jessie there? This is her friend Robby. Thanks, yes, I'll hold."

She settled on the breakfast barstool, absent-mindedly shuffling through the mail she'd brought in earlier. A return address caught her eye—Dory's publisher. *Probably with details about her contract for the next book.* A stab of pain hit her at the thought of her lover, but she resolutely put that out of her mind when she heard Jessie's voice.

"Wow, partner, what a surprise to hear from you so soon. And a pleasure, I might add. What can I do for you?" Jessie asked.

"It was good to see you and catch up in New Orleans, and I'm glad we've renewed contact. But this call isn't just social. I have need of your particular expertise. Interested?"

"You bet. And I'm intrigued. What could be beyond your own legendary sleuthing ability that you would need me, I have to ask?"

"Well, I haven't maintained my old contacts and I certainly haven't made any new ones, and you've stayed in the game. Plus, you're probably more electronically up to date than I am. And, as we've seen in the past, two heads are often better than one," Robby said.

"You're right there, pal. I still remember how you pulled the rabbit out of the hat on the Ormewood case. I'd missed the essential clue completely. So, what's up?"

"I don't know if you remember my friend Charlene?"

"The judge? Absolutely. Don't tell me she's in trouble."

"Well, she's had an unpleasant reminder of past indiscretions. Nothing illegal, but she's running for a House seat and the timing is particularly bad." Robby went on to outline the story for Jessie. "Name is Conway, Connie or Constance; last known residence is Los Angeles. She's here in Atlanta, but wouldn't say where. She's going to get back in touch with Charlene."

"Okay, that's where we start. Charlene needs to insist on meeting her in person, and we can pick up the trail then. I imagine she's rented a car to get around—you can't function in Atlanta without one—so she'll have her ID on her and we can go from there."

"I agree. And I won't ask how you're going to access that information, Jessie."

"Nor should you, my friend. I've found the private sector is a lot more forgiving and supportive of investigative activities than the public one. Thank goodness. Well, you remember. We never talked about it for obvious reasons, but we had our own dubious sources of information even when we were on the force. Bless their hearts."

Robby laughed. "Yes, indeed. Okay, Jess, I'll wait to hear from you and then I'll develop my own path to follow in conjunction with yours. Thanks. Oh, and I forgot to mention, this is of course a paying gig, you know, so have at it."

"Good to know and you're quite welcome. Talk to you soon."

Robby resumed her pacing, brain on overdrive. Charlene's problem offered a whole new area to fret about, and she was anxious to get started investigating it. Jessie probably would have some information pretty soon; they just had to wait on Connie to get back in touch.

Restless, she collected her pistol, ammunition, earplugs, safety glasses, and gloves, and headed for the firing range. The drive there left her trapped with her thoughts, though, so she finally succumbed and started analyzing the Dory problem instead of ceaseless circular thinking.

Why did she do it?

What does that say about her as a person? Is she still the same person? Of course she is. Did I think she was perfect? No. Well, she was perfect for me. Dammit, she still is perfect for me. What did I expect, that nothing would ever arise to disturb our relationship?

She grimaced. *Well, no, but I guess I always thought that if it ever did happen, it would be another woman. I just knew that would never be me to stray. I pick my soul mate and that's that. No one else exists. But Dory, bless her, she's so freaking social. I guess I always reserved a protected spot in my heart in case she met someone and just got bowled over. But she never has.*

I always thought we were so solid. Well, we are solid. What the hell is the real problem here?

"Hey, pick a lane, air brain!" Robby honked at

the car invading her lane, then raked her free hand through her hair. She could hardly wait to get to the range and start blowing the target to smithereens, to relieve the pressure building inside. She felt anxious, almost desperate, at her wit's end. Being the one to part from Dory had never entered her mind as a possibility. Was that what she really wanted?

No. God, no. I'm just so freaking confused, is all. It's all so unexpected. If there's not a target lane open, maybe I'll go for another run. Got to clear my head.

Arriving at the range, she registered at the desk and entered the gallery. Finding a lane open, she pointed her weapon to the floor and loaded it, checking the chambers carefully when she was done. She put on her earplugs, earmuffs, and safety glasses, and stepped up to the line, placing the Sig Sauer on the shelf before her while she hung the target in place. She moved it to the far back wall, raised her gun, and let instinct and skill take over. The bullets tore into the paper, some to the heart, some to the head. As she shot, a sense of calm settled over her. Having a sense of control always did that for her when the rest of her world seemed chaotic.

When there was little left of the target to mangle, she rolled it back and headed to the desk.

"Good shooting today," commented the manager, eyeing her target. "Looks like you needed it."

"Yeah, I guess you could say that," she said, laughing. "Nothing like blowing something up to release the tension."

He grinned back. "Yeah, I've heard that before. Have a better day."

Feeling calmer, Robby walked out to her truck and checked her phone as the engine warmed. A message from Jessie surprised her and she called her immediately.

"Hey, girl, we got lucky," Jessie said without preamble.

"What's up?"

"Charlene heard from Connie and set up a meet in five days. That's the soonest she could manage with her campaign, and it gives us more time to investigate Connie's story. I've got a guy who can pick up her tail, or do you want to do it yourself?"

"Oh, definitely me," Robby said promptly. "Wouldn't miss it. Where's it going to be?"

"At the Big Steer Steakhouse on Howell Mill Road, so I'm guessing she's staying at some cheesy hotel near there. Five o'clock. Want some company? I've got a new client meeting but I can probably make it to meet you there. Or we could meet up back there afterward, eat and debrief."

"Yeah, let's meet afterward. After I stake out the steakhouse. Get it? Stake? Steak?"

"Oh, geez, I see your jokes haven't gotten any better, partner."

"I don't want to bump into your schedule if we don't have to. I'll call you, but I'm guessing to meet at about seven?"

"Sounds good. Hey, how does it feel to be back in the saddle?"

"Good," Robby responded, smiling. "Good, actually. I went to the range today, too, and it really helped. You know, I might be missing my old calling more than I thought."

"Interesting," Jessie said. "You might regret saying that, friend. I can always use good talent."

"Hmm. Well, maybe. After this is over, maybe we can talk about it. Talk to you later. I have to go walk

Killer."

"Glad to hear sweet Killer is still around. Talk to you later."

Robby drove home slowly, turning over events in her mind. She felt a little bit more separate from the shock of Dory's news and better able to think about it.

Long-term relationships are tricky, she thought. *They look—and feel—so settled, so permanent. You get to thinking things will never change, except maybe to get better, but life ain't necessarily so, and the ripple—or worse, the explosion—is even more magnified.*

I need to just step back. For one thing, this is Dory's problem, not mine, except as I relate to her. So granted, that's been shaken considerably, but...

She paused her thought as a van with peace signs and a "Namaste" bumper sticker cut her off to take an abrupt right turn. "Well, so much for that philosophy," she muttered, accelerating again. "Namaste to you, too, idiot."

Yeah, how I feel about Dory. Well.

Entering the expressway ramp, she leaned forward to check the side mirror and hit the gas as she merged. Settling back, she put the truck on cruise control and turned on the New Age channel that helped her maintain her cool in traffic.

"Okay, Dory." She took a deep breath as images of her lover flooded her mind, and she found herself smiling. Dory at the beach, gritting her teeth and still diving joyously into the waves, coming up with a laughing shout. Dory merrily chatting at a party, then coming over to adorably lean on her, whispering "Uh-oh, Daddy, I'm a little tipsy." Dory in the garden, making things beautiful. *Damn, moving plants so often they ought to be on wheels.* Coming in dirty and happy, asking what she wanted for dinner. Dory in bed, snuggling close and then on waking, telling her dreams, always a good story. Dory in bed… She shook her head. *Oh, boy, better not go there, I have to concentrate.*

A feeling of conviction seeped into her heart, easing the clenching she'd felt in her solar plexus for the last few days. She knew Dory, she did. So her police officer ethos had been outraged. But she knew Dory's heart and character and soul. She was her soul mate. So she wasn't perfect, and she'd fucked up in a very big way.

"She hardly ever does, which might be why this hit me so hard," Robby muttered to herself. "I'm overreacting. Not for the first time, either. Poor Dory, she does put up with me."

She exited the expressway and made her way up the tree-lined streets to their home, smiling at Killer's face grinning at her from the window. "Don't knock stuff off the coffee table with your tail, Killer," she said, grinning back. Killer. Dory. Her family, her universe.

She would go see Dory. They would work this out, together, just as they had with everything for the last twenty years.

Opening the door, she found an envelope on the foyer table. It was from Dory.

Chapter Ten

Dory pulled into her attorney's parking lot and parked under the shade of a tree. "Okay, next step in my rehabilitation," she said to herself. "Let's hope the answers aren't too bad here."

After his receptionist announced her, Charles came out to greet her. "Hey, Dory," he said, giving her a hug. "Great to see you. Come on in." He closed the door behind them and guided her to the sofa in his office's seating area. "So, what brings you by today?" he asked. "Your call was so cryptic, it had me a little worried."

"Well, Charles, this has been one of the worst weeks of my life and promises to continue, so I hope you can advise me. Although," she added. "I have started to take steps to fix the mess I've made."

Charles gave a low whistle, eyebrows raised, as he settled back into the sofa. "Yikes. Okay, lay it on me."

"I'm beginning to feel like I should just record this and play it each time, given the number of people I need to involve." Dory took a deep breath and launched into her story.

Charles leaned forward and said nothing as he listened attentively, his expression growing more concerned by the minute. When she finished, he exhaled slowly and leaned back, steepling his fingers before him. He closed his eyes for a moment, thinking, and then moved to his desk, picking up a legal pad and pen.

"Okay. Let's start with who you've told about this so far."

"Just Robby. That didn't go well. We're separated, at least for now. I'm holding on to hope that we'll work this out."

"Oh, Dory, I'm so sorry. But yes, you're both strong and committed to each other; I'm sure you will. All right, next question: do you have your contract with you, perchance?"

"I thought you'd want to see it, so yes," she said, pulling it out of her bag.

"Excellent. I'll look at it. Do you know offhand if it has a clause specifically requiring you to tell the truth?"

Dory winced. "Ah, no, I don't know. Is that normal?"

"It depends. There have been some famous fraud cases in the last few years, so some publishers are getting conscientious about covering all possible eventualities. But mostly I think they are worried about plagiarism more than a case like this. You haven't appropriated anything, you've just taken literary license, is how we'll approach it. But, just in case, do you have media liability insurance?"

Dory paled. "I don't think so, but I don't know. I remember sitting down with my insurance agent at about the time I was shopping the book and merging all my coverage with one company, but I don't exactly remember what was in the portfolio other than the usual, home, car, etc. Do you think I could be in real financial trouble?"

"We'll have to see. I'd love to be reassuring, but

this is a relatively open area. At the very least, your publisher could demand your advance back. How much did you get?"

"Oh, for a first book, it wasn't much," Dory said. "Three hundred dollars."

"That's good. You can handle that. But if the publisher recalls all the books sold, they could come after you for those damages. Call your agent and ask about the literary insurance, and cross your fingers."

Dory looked at him bleakly and moaned. "I can't believe all the trouble I'm in from one impulsive mistake, Charles. And the more successful the book was, the more scared I became. I haven't even been enjoying my success with all the dread I've had, and when the reporter called me, I had a feeling disaster was coming. So, what do you advise, if there's anything you can advise? Or am I just totally fucked?"

"Well, things aren't completely dark. For one thing, don't forget that authors who've done this in the past—in fact, worse than this, ones who outright plagiarized—have bounced back in their careers.

"So don't despair, honey. You may just be looking at a financial hit, and you can recover professionally because you have real talent. You'll just have to work hard at it, which is a shame, because you'd just gotten to the point where you could maybe coast a little bit with your success. But you can do it."

Dory sighed. "Oh, thanks, Charles. I really needed to hear some good news. One thing I've never been afraid of is hard work, so I certainly won't stint in that regard. My biggest worry is Robby. She is so essential to my life, I can't imagine being without her. But the ball is in her court, that's for sure. I wrote to her and begged for a meeting. I hope that if we could just talk face-to-face, I could win her back, or at least get a temporary reprieve so that I can win her back."

"I know. And I know how much you love each other. You've been together for twenty years or so, right? You've got a solid basis to rebuild on. I have confidence in both of you. And you know, if there's anything I can do to help, just let me know.

"Now, what else are you planning? Who else are you going to talk to besides me?"

"Well, you're my first stop, of course. Not much I could do in jail."

"You're not going to jail, so give that idea up."

"Good to know. Okay, so I need to talk to Annabelle, my agent and publicist, to give her a heads-up."

"Good. She'll probably have some good ideas about spinning this, too."

"And then of course, when I have some idea of where I'm going with this, there's my publisher, Robert. I'll have to fly to New York to meet with him. I'm making plans for that now, but wanted to talk to you and Annabelle first. He and I have a good relationship, but I've strayed so far out of bounds with this, that I don't know how far his grace will go. I can only cast myself on his mercy I suppose."

"Okay, so let's go back to the starting point: the reporter. Do you have any kind of relationship with her? Can you influence her in any way to tread lightly, at least, or even better, give up the story? At least until you can take some steps in damage control?"

"No. I don't really know her. She seems nice enough, but this is a plum story any reporter would salivate after."

"Meet with her sooner rather than later. You

want to stay ahead of this. The absolute worst outcome would be to have her publish and blindside you. Make an appointment and, before you meet, talk to Annabelle and pick her brain. She might could help you. Maybe there is some way you could give the reporter an exclusive on some aspect of the story that would give her some notoriety and simultaneously help take the edge off the whole thing. I don't know. I'll think more on it, of course. My first task will be to study your publisher's contract, which I wish you'd given to me before, by the way."

Dory blushed. "I know, Charles. Guilty as charged. It was really stupid. But everything was so rushed and heady at the time. I couldn't believe I was actually going to be published! And come to think of it, though, even if you had and the truth clause was in there, I wonder if I would have come clean?"

"Well, water under the bridge, Dory. Let me do my thing and I'll get back to you as soon as possible. Now, can you get some lunch with me? You can tell me the upside of your vacation in New Orleans. Always meant to go there, but haven't made it yet."

"Well, maybe an iced tea," said Dory. "I haven't been able to get in touch with Annabelle yet."

The two went into their local favorite restaurant's bar and caught up on the more pleasant and mundane areas of their life. As they rose to leave, Dory said, "Thank you so much, Charles, for the reassurance as well as the reality check. And the support. It makes me feel a little less like an absolute heel."

"We all make mistakes, Dory," he said, giving her a hug and walking her to her car. "You take care of yourself and I'll talk to you real soon. Oh, where are you staying, anyway?"

"I'm staying with my friend, Serena, in Roswell," Dory said. "I'll text you the address in case you need it. I'm still hoping I won't be there long."

"Okay, good. I remember Serena. Good luck with the traffic, girl. And please do keep me in the loop with whatever else you find out or do, okay?"

"Sure thing," Dory said, starting the engine. "I'll talk to you later."

Weaving in and out of traffic, Dory cast about for anything she could do to make the situation better. "Fruitless," she muttered to herself. Pressing the Bluetooth connection on her steering wheel, she placed a call to Annabelle to set up her next crucial appointment.

"Dory, my favorite author. How are you? How was NOLA? Sorry I haven't gotten back to you. I just heard your message and was about to call."

"Oh, I'll bet you say that to all your clients," Dory replied. "I'm doing okay, thanks, Annabelle. How are you doing?"

"Good, good, thanks. Waiting to hear when your next opus will come out. How's it going?"

"Well, I need to talk to you, but not about the next book," Dory said. "When can we get together?"

"I'm about to leave the office on an appointment, but I have no plans tonight. How about this evening?"

"Sounds great. Let's meet at the Idle Hour and I'll buy you a good glass of Sauvignon Blanc."

"Well, perfect. Barring a crash slowing everyone down, which is all too likely knowing Atlanta, I'll be there at six."

"Deal. Drive carefully."

Later, Dory slipped into a parking space, cut the engine, and sat for a moment to gather her courage. *Ye Gods, what a day,* she thought wearily. *Okay, this is the last meet with my advocates before I have to meet with the Gorgon publisher. Oh, that's not fair; Robert is a sweetie, but he may transform before my eyes, and I wouldn't blame him at all.*

Sighing, she got out and walked toward the restaurant. A movement caught her eye and she spied Annabelle at a window table, waving and beaming. She waved back and strode to the door.

"How goes it, Dory? Good to see you."

Her plump agent was dressed in her trademark designer pantsuit, red this time, complemented by an emerald-green silk blouse. Her long peacock earrings swayed below her spiky gray and blue hair as she jumped up and hugged her client. "I already ordered for both of us, so just sit right down and relax."

"Hi, Annabelle, good to see you, too," Dory said, settling into the chair. "Isn't this weather gorgeous?" she said, stalling for time.

"Yes, but I'll bet New Orleans was even prettier. How was the trip?"

"Oh, good." Dory outlined their activities while another part of her brain wondered how to start telling her news. *Well, just dive right in.*

"Annabelle, I have some not so good news to tell you."

Annabelle's eyebrows arched. "Hey, you're not firing me, are you?"

"No, no. But you might want to fire me." Dory paused as the waiter delivered their wine and then took a big sip. "Okay, here's the deal," she said, and launched into her story.

Annabelle's blue eyes opened as wide as saucers behind her big glasses as she listened. She leaned on the table, inserting an occasional "holy shit" and "oh, crap" during her client's narrative. The only time she interrupted was to ask who the reporter was, hoping she knew her, and swearing softly when she didn't. When Dory was done, she remained staring at her, transfixed by what she'd heard.

"Wow. Just, wow," was all she could manage.

Dory could just imagine what was going through her mind, lost potential income probably coming in first. "I know," she muttered, looking down into her glass. "I've been something of a basket case since I made this unbelievable mistake, just waiting for the other shoe to drop. And now that it has, I don't know whether to be relieved or panicked. No, that's not true—I'm totally panicked. I hope the relief comes later.

"So, I don't know if you want to have anything to do with me, or this mess, now. But if I'm lucky enough that you stick with me, I'll be eternally in your debt. I don't know if there's any way this could be spun to be less than the cluster fuck it is, but if anyone can dream one up, you can. But it's all up to you. If you want to bail, I completely understand, and I wouldn't blame you at all. But oh, I'd really miss you." She looked at her, miserable, as Annabelle sat silent and still.

"I've heard of cases like this, of course," she said finally. She leaned back in her chair, eyeing her client speculatively. "But naturally, I never thought I'd be involved in one. Holy cow. Just, holy cow."

Annabelle paused, took a long sip of her wine, and looked out the window. "We've been friends and associates for a long time, haven't we?" she said. Dory held her breath. "Well, that has to count for something."

She looked back at Dory and smiled a little ruefully. "Damn, girl, you've set me up for a *lot* of really hard work. I could just kill you. Like, with my bare hands. But I won't, and I'm not going to bail on you. You're a friend as well as a good client, and a phenomenally good writer. I believe you'll come out of this still working, so I'm staying on for the ride."

Dory smiled, feeling relief starting to slowly seep into her consciousness. With the team of Charles and Annabelle behind her—*and God, please, hopefully Robby*—she just might make her way through this. Not unscathed, for sure, but at least surviving.

"Oh, thank you, Annabelle," she blurted out. "You can't know how much that means to me. I so appreciate it."

"Oh, dear lord, don't tear up on me. All right, let's get started right now, beginning with another glass of wine and an appetizer so we don't get crocked. Brain food, that's what we need. And, of course, comfort food."

She signaled for the waiter and ordered a spinach-artichoke dip with pita chips, then pinned Dory with an intense look.

"This won't be easy. It's going to be really hard, as a matter of fact," she said evenly. "But we can figure out the best way to approach it and then cross our fingers for a good outcome. Now tell me, who have you told and what have you done so far?"

When Dory outlined the situation with Robby, Annabelle's face softened in sympathy, and she nodded approvingly when she heard about the meeting with Charles. "Good. Good. Charles is good. If anyone can protect you legally, he can. And I hope to God you do have that insurance. That should be your first call tomorrow morning, to the insurance company.

"I know a little about writer's insurance. There's usually a five-thousand-dollar deductible, but it would cover everything else in settlement, judgment, and defense costs, up to the limit of liability, which could be anywhere from two hundred thousand to a million. But without it, if you wind up in court, you'd have to pay all the court, defense, and award costs. And you have to know, you could lose major time—a year, even—just working on the case. Forget writing.

"Okay, now let's get started brainstorming. How would you like to approach this? Is there any chance the reporter could be persuaded to bury it?"

"I don't think so," Dory said mournfully. "I wouldn't, if I were in her shoes. And besides, I can't live with this anymore. I'm almost grateful it's come out. Can you think of any way we could give her a story that would be true but do less damage?"

Annabelle looked out the window as she contemplated, rubbing her blue manicured nails thoughtfully on her chin.

"Let's see. Bottom line, you're going to have to do a huge *mea culpa* to the world. She could break the story, which should help win her over to your side. Shit, you should ask to go on Oprah—I'm only partly kidding. She had James Frey on her show to publicly castigate him for his fraud, which she unwittingly enabled by selecting his book for her book club. And he survived.

"We have a little time to minimize the negative public perception you'll get, but not much. The reporter will be ready to knock that story out in no time, but she might want to shop it to bigger media outlets. That might buy us some time, which would be lucky, because we have a lot to do."

"Anything," Dory said fervently. "Just let me know."

"First thing: list all your stakeholders. Obviously, the general public, but anyone else, specifically? Other than your publisher, of course.

"Then, do what you do best: write. Write an email with a sincere and honest apology. You can tell them the idea came from a publishing pro's comment, but acknowledge your personal responsibility in doing something wrong in a moment of weakness. Tell them how much it's been bothering you to feel like you were somehow cheating your wonderful readers. Send it to all your email subscribers and personalize it. We can do that in Gmail; I just need your subscriber spreadsheet. Tell them that you're sorry and how much you appreciate and value them. Your readers deserve better, and to make it up, you'll provide your next book to the email list for half price."

Dory's mouth formed a perfect "O" at this.

"Yes. And do the same for a post on your Facebook author's page. And here's where the silver lining to the dark cloud comes in: this could very well build your email list, because they'll have to get on it to get the half-price book. Do the same on Twitter and Pinterest and any other platforms you're on. And, very important, listen to your feedback and answer it. Communicate as if your professional life depends on it—which it does.

"In the end, this could be a good thing. You know, Brendan Behan said, 'There's no such thing as bad publicity except your own obituary,' and you ain't dead yet, honey! And you're not the first by a long shot, either. Frey should have been completely ruined after *A Million Little Pieces* was exposed as not biographical, but he bounced back with his best-selling *Bright Shiny Morning*. And even after Irving's *Autobiography of Howard Hughes* was exposed and he was even jailed, it became a film, and he's still writing eBooks. And don't forget, people love to forgive people who are genuinely contrite, especially if they'll get something for it."

"My God, Annabelle. You're a genius."

"Classic damage control, honey." Annabelle smiled, eyes twinkling. "Always thinking. Now, let's eat these yummies. Should we get dinner, too?"

Chapter Eleven

"Good grief, what the hell is my fund manager thinking?" Jill glowered at the monitor as she tracked her stocks' performance. "He should be making us all rich with the fortune he's making as the fund manager. Some money manager. I mean, really. I could pick better."

"Well, maybe not." She frowned as she pulled up her stock performance spreadsheet and flipped to the tab with the graphs. "But my God, Old Boston. That company's been around for a hundred and fifty years. Who knew it could go bankrupt? That was supposed to be my sure thing.

"Better do some trades to catch up. Okay, what looks good today? What's the next FedEx or Microsoft, at least for the next twenty-four hours?"

Her eyes roved restlessly over pages of analyses, charts, newsletters, and emails from the deluge of prognosticators who had somehow found her email address. They were annoying, but in a way she didn't really mind. They might actually have that one nugget that would indicate a gold mine.

Jill was addicted, which she freely admitted to herself if not to others. *What can I say?* she thought to herself whenever she paused long enough to think about it. *My brain's pleasure centers are jazzed by the thrill of it all.* She gave a mental shrug. *What the hell. I can afford it. I still have a nest, if a smaller nest egg on occasion. It's just expensive entertainment. Besides, it makes me really grumpy to not check in daily on the market.*

Still, a nagging little voice made her doubt her nonchalance about it. She vividly remembered the night on vacation in Monte Carlo when she dropped $50,000 before finally admitting the odds were not with her. Roulette, blackjack, poker—no matter what she tried, it all turned to shit. Then there was the time she invested $25,000 in a new casino, which turned out to be so badly mismanaged that it was the only one on the street to lose money and close down.

Well, win some, lose some, she thought, but her conservative side was still appalled. And she knew that her friends were becoming suspicious from the little comments they dropped in New Orleans. *Geez, if they only knew the full of it, they'd probably stage an intervention.* She returned to the screens. "Okay, this morning I'm only going to give this one hour," she vowed.

Two hours later, she was the intrepid new owner of 10,000 shares of a promising-looking penny stock, and a big chunk of MegaCell, a biotech start-up. It was involved in a suit, but it would gain $8 billion if it won it, a tidy profit. That was worth a gamble.

She stirred restlessly in her seat, looking at the screen. *All right, enough. This is a little too heavy. How about some poker?*

An hour later, she glanced at the clock in shock and jumped up. "How did it get so late?" she muttered. She had things to do.

Pulling out her phone, she scrolled through her contacts until she came to her favorite private investigator, Wallace. She loved Wallace; she was the best. A diminutive little old lady with an old-fashioned curly perm on her white hair, she had a mind as sharp as a tack and no one ever suspected that she was investigating them. But her fingers paused as she punched the keys. Even Wallace might not be the right bloodhound for Taylor. No, it might be better to sic a similar type on her—someone young, clever and friendly—to win her confidence and find out if anything was awry. But Wallace just might have someone like that in her stable. She dialed, and fifteen minutes later the mission was accomplished. She dressed and headed over to meet the investigator at Wallace's offices.

Wallace met Jill in the lobby and gave her a big hug.

"How've you been, baby girl?" she asked with a broad smile.

"Pretty good," answered Jill. "How about you, Wallace?"

"Just fine for an old codger." Wallace ushered her into her office. "So tell me, darlin', what brings you in today?"

"Curiosity and caution, Wallace. I have a new sweetheart and an uneasy feeling that perhaps all is not right with her."

Wallace nodded gravely. "Uh-oh. Yes, caution is well wedded with curiosity, generally speaking. Tell me about her. What makes you uneasy?"

"Well, she's younger and gorgeous…"

"Of course!" Wallace laughed.

"Yes, well. Life's little pleasures. But she's collecting backers for a movie she's promoting, an unusual investment to say the least. When she was just asking me, I was fine with putting it off, but she's moved on to my friends, so I want to know more about it, and her. I happened to look at her phone while we were in New Orleans..."

"Happened!" Wallace grinned.

"...and there were repeated calls from a number in LA. Now, she's from LA, so that doesn't necessarily mean anything, but she told me she has no family, so I'm wondering. She never mentioned a close friend she might talk to every day, either. And there was one number that looked so weird I had to look up the location, and it was the Cayman Islands. Why would she be calling them, I wonder?"

"How much do you know about her?"

"Well, actually, not that much. I met her at a fundraiser and she seemed pretty well connected, given that she was from out of town. I'm sure she was there looking for investors. But anyway, we got together and she's staying with me."

Wallace rolled her eyes.

"Yes, well, you know. We get along well and our interests match, so it's been pleasant. I took her to New Orleans with me and my posse."

"And how did your friends take to her?" Wallace asked.

"Hesitantly, although you know they'd never be rude. But she surprised me when she hit them up for the movie, too, and my Spidey senses kicked in."

"Probably a good thing," Wallace said. "Movies—an indie film, I presume?" Jill nodded. "Those can pay off in a huge way, of course, but not many do. But I suppose you can still use tax write-offs, but your friends might not."

"Exactly." Jill nodded. "So, I was thinking you might be able to help me. My ideal sleuth for this particular assignment would be young and attractive, maybe hitting Taylor up for friendship as well as doing the normal investigating. It would be great if she knew something about investments, too."

"Say no more, I have just the gal. Vivian Rhodes just joined us recently. She used to be in trusts and investments with a huge bank, so she's familiar with those matters. She got tired of the corporate life and has taken to our profession like a duck to water. I'll work with her to make sure you're well taken care of, not to worry."

"Oh, with you I'm never worried." Jill sighed. "Thank you. Is Vivian in now?"

"Yup. Come on and I'll introduce you."

They walked down the carpeted hall to a bright room with a wall of windows overlooking the office park pond. An attractive woman looked up and smiled as they entered.

"Vivian Rhodes, this is Jill Hunt, an old friend and one of our best clients. I'll work with you on her case, but now I'll leave her in your capable hands. Good to see you again, Jill," she said, giving her a final hug. "Don't be a stranger, and we'll be in touch."

"I know you will, Wallace, and thank you." Jill settled herself in the comfortable arm chair across from Vivian and the two women eyed each other with frank curiosity.

Jill saw a slim brunette woman in her early forties, impeccably dressed in a gold tailored suit. It was stunningly accented by the black silk blouse beneath and a tasteful gold chain necklace. Her long, graceful fingers sported subtle but elegant rings, and her watch was crafted with delicate gold links. Her perfectly manicured nails were a conservative short-medium length and finished with a subtle clear polish. *So far, perfect.*

"I am happy to meet you, Jill," Vivian began, drawing a legal pad to her. "How can I help you?"

"Well, I have a friend who I don't know very well, who is soliciting me for an investment. I'd like to know more about her and about it."

"Okay, and the nature of the investment?" Vivian asked, making a note.

"An indie movie."

Vivian's eyebrows rose just a touch, and Jill smiled. "I know, I know. Well, at least it's not a gold mine in the Andes."

Vivian laughed. "Well, indies can return a whopping profit if they make it. Look at *Slumdog Millionaire* and *The Blair Witch Project.* It's just infrequent. And the entertainment industry can be a great investment in good times and bad. People go to the movies when times are good and maybe even more when they're bad, when they need the relief of fantasy.

"But my guess is you've been on this path before about investment," she said, looking sharply at Jill. "You're wise to do your due diligence."

"Oh, you betcha," Jill agreed, noting how Vivian's dark eyes crinkled with amusement, and admiring the clean sweep of her dark hair under her chin. *What an attractive woman.*

"All right, let's get started," Vivian said. "Tell me what you know about her. I don't suppose you know her Social Security or driver's license numbers?"

"No, but I'm sure I can give you at least her license number by tomorrow. And I'll get you the phone numbers I noticed that have been bothering me. One is a number in LA she's been calling a lot, and the other is in the Caymans."

"Caymans, that's interesting. Yes, those would all be terrific starting points. So, I have a few areas you could explore with her, and I think you should. Since she's approaching your friends, it shouldn't arouse any suspicions that you want to know more about her business. In fact, you could couch it that you're interested yourself, so you'd like to know more. The producer's name, for sure. It would be interesting to know if she or he has submitted other films to any festivals, and/or won any awards. Did she or he complete the projects on time and under or in budget? Did they make a profit?

"Another is what company name Taylor is operating under, or what legal entity. Is she licensed as a broker? Same for the producer—what company name? Does she have a contract with him or her that you can see? I'd also like to know if there's an executive producer. Often, they're the ones that do all the work, not the producer.

"I'll also start a thorough search on her and the producer for civil cases. That's where disgruntled past colleagues show up. I'd like to check on past partners' experiences. We have access to non-public databases that go back well beyond the seven years that consumer reporting agencies check.

"And, oh, this is important. What is the contracted distribution plan for the film's proceeds? It shouldn't be a fifty-fifty distribution of all profits. That's a red flag that the producer is in it for the money and nothing but. It should be one hundred percent for first monies—they pay back the production costs—

and then it should be seventy-five percent of second monies—the profit—to the principal investors.

"Anyway, it's a lot to take in, I know. Don't worry, I'll document all these questions and send them to you so you'll have them for future reference. I'll mark the most important things to find out first. You don't want to swamp her with all of it at once anyway. That could alert her to be more careful if she is trying a scam. Better if she thinks you're relatively oblivious, or at least not that concerned, just curious."

Jill sighed. "Oh, it's so good to have a pro on your side. Thank you, this all relieves my mind considerably. Well, I'd better go, but I'll look forward to hearing from you. And perhaps we could meet for a glass of wine sometime?"

Vivian's eyebrows arched just a bit again, but she smiled. "Yes, why not? That would be pleasant. In fact, if you like I'll be glad to meet you to fill you in with my findings that way."

"Great. Well, thank you again. I'll look forward to hearing from you."

Jill walked out into the sunshine of the late spring afternoon, smiling to herself. Ah, life had such riches to offer, truly.

Jill's feeling of well-being vanished the following morning. She was alone because Taylor allegedly had some meeting, for what she had no idea. Restless, she settled in front of the computer and checked the markets. As the first screen scrolled up, she choked on her coffee. The readings were dismal, with steep losses in all sectors. She pulled up screen after screen, growing more unsettled by the moment. She did a quick mental calculation and paled at its conclusion. She quickly opened Money Manager for reassurance.

She wasn't reassured. Almost fifty percent of her portfolio's net worth had vanished overnight.

She turned on the financial news station and her heart dropped even more, if that was possible. The overnight downturn had wiped out over twenty percent of the market's value. "Oh, fuck," she whispered. "It's 1987 all over again." She had suffered big losses that year and had to curtail her bad spending habits considerably. But now she was more overextended than she had been then, thanks to her affinity for day trading and high-risk investments. "But 1987 didn't lead to a bear market anyway, so maybe I can recover again. But damn, this is mighty inconvenient, to say the least."

She had to admit she was shaken. She never paid much attention to her money because she'd always had plenty. Even though her father's estate was split between so many heirs, there was more than enough to go around. But maybe it was time for her to pay more attention, and just maybe to be a little less impulsive in her investing.

Taylor picked this time to return home, breezily reporting she'd had breakfast with a friend. Jill had to wonder who it was, but she didn't ask. Instead, she invited her for another cup of coffee and brought it to her in the bedroom, after quickly scanning the questions that Vivian had emailed her.

She settled in the Queen Anne chair, sipping her brew. "I don't suppose you heard the financial news today?"

"Oh, yes, I did," said Taylor. "I hope you weren't

too affected?"

Jill laughed mirthlessly. "Well, a little bit, for sure," she said. "So I'm paying more attention to the investments I'm thinking about, including the movie. I'd love to hear more about it. Who is the producer? Anyone I know?"

Taylor's eyebrows rose and she smiled. "I'm delighted you want to know more. But I don't know if you'd know him. Are you a fan of indie films?"

"Not really, unless they win Oscars."

"Well, he hasn't won one yet, but he's been nominated," Taylor said. "Two years ago, for a film about micro-investing in Third World countries. He focuses on real issues, generally speaking. I thought that this movie would be of interest to you and your friends, since it's about women aging gracefully in the twenty-first century."

Jill wrinkled her nose. "Really. Aging made you think of me? Oh, tell me more. But first, what's his name?"

"No, no! The emphasis is on the 'gracefully' part." Taylor laughed. "You and your group would be perfect models as heroines in the script. The director is Paolo Brocca. He's Italian, studied under Roberto Benigni, who won Oscars in the nineties for *Life Is Beautiful*. A wonderful man. And the screenwriter is Marco Rizzi, a fabulous writer. He's done a lot of TV shows and is branching off into films now."

"Hmm. And how did you meet these guys?"

"Oh, the typical LA way." Jill snorted. "At a cocktail party. But I was really intrigued with Paolo and when I heard about his planned project, I thought, 'Well, I'm a woman and better yet, a lesbian. This is the kind of work I'd like to support.' So I started making inquiries among my LA friends to find out if anyone else might be interested. They were, and then the word spread, which was how I got invited by a mutual friend to the party in Atlanta where I met you."

"Well, have they shared some sort of a contract with you for the investors? I don't know much about these things, but I imagine that would be part of it."

"Oh, sure," Jill said smoothly. "Honey, if you're really that interested, your timing is perfect. Paolo is just about ready to get started and the window for investors is closing. I'll be glad to get the information together for you to look at this afternoon."

"Okay," said Jill. "Are you doing this as a broker, Taylor? Or just an individual? Seems like you're doing a lot of work. You should be compensated for that."

"Oh, don't worry." Taylor's eyes sparkled with humor. "I'll get my share, you can be sure of that. And I'm excited that you're interested, baby. We can have a lot of fun at this, along with making money. Think of the Hollywood luminaries you will meet at my LA parties. Always interesting, and I'll be so happy to share that with you."

"Yup, sounds like fun all right," Jill said, standing up with her empty mug. "Are you done, babe? I'll take your cup."

"Yes, thanks, hon. I'll get on gathering that paperwork for you now."

"Thanks, babe." Jill walked downstairs, turning the conversation over in her mind. Taylor seemed perfectly comfortable talking about her project. Could it be she had nothing to hide? But then what were those phone calls about, especially the one to the Cayman Islands? She couldn't wait to hear what Vivian might uncover.

At least then maybe I'll be able to settle the Taylor questions. And I'd better settle another issue immediately, as much as I can—call my broker and place stop orders to slow the hemorrhaging. Jesus, what a day. I should've relaxed more in New Orleans!

She started to put the cups into the dishwasher and then paused, looking at Taylor's. After a moment, she took out a gallon freezer bag, dropped the cup in, and sealed it. *Why not?* she thought. *You never know.*

Going into her office, she emailed Vivian with the information she'd uncovered and told her to look for the cup's delivery.

Chapter Twelve

Dory padded sleepily down the hallway to the stairs, reciting her morning mantra: "Coffee, coffee, must have coffee." In the kitchen, she found a note from Serena by the coffee pot. She was already in the studio, but she'd listed a cornucopia of goodies available for breakfast. Checking in with her stomach, Dory simply grabbed an apple and took a bite. Then she paused, looked at it, and reflected on how good it would be with raisins and syrup on a waffle. She toasted two frozen ones and built her breakfast, then settled on the breakfast barstool. Looking gloomily out to the backyard, she pondered how to continue reconstructing the disaster that was her life.

Desultorily, she checked her email, and the phone rang. "Good morning, Sunshine!" Charles's cheery voice came booming through. Dory winced and literally growled into the phone, making Charles laugh.

"Oh, don't tell me, did I wake you?"

"Not exactly in terms of my body, which is vertical, thank you. But in terms of my brain, you're dead on arrival. How can you be so cheerful at this God-awful hour?"

"Well, I'll tell you and this might wake and/or cheer you up. I studied your contract and there's no truth clause, thank God. And, I talked to your insurance agent."

"Oh, thank you, Charles. I hadn't gotten to that

yet."

"I know. This is one of the lucky things about living within the gay community—we all know each other, which helps communication. Anyway, I talked to Jeff and asked about your policy. You're well covered, unless the bills go over a million, upon which you're on your own. Have you talked to your publisher yet?"

"No, not yet. I'm still getting my ducks in a row so I have something coherent to say to him. But this helps a lot. Thanks, Charles. I'm considerably more awake than I was five minutes ago, and I even feel better. You're a pal!"

Dory hung up the phone and started up the stairs to get dressed, when the doorbell rang and startled her. *Who could be here at eight in the morning?* It was too early for a delivery. She drew her robe around her and went to the front door. Peeking out the sidelight, she caught her breath. Robby's truck was in the driveway.

Joy and hope warred within her as she flung open the door, along with trepidation. Joy and hope won out, even though one look at Robby's flinty eyes said clearly that Daddy was here. Nonetheless, her trepidation also was matched with the thrill she got every time Robby exercised her authority. She just loved it when Robby dommed her; she couldn't help it.

"Oh, thank you for coming, darling," she said, opening the door. "I'm so glad to see you. Please come in." Closing the door, she couldn't resist. She turned and flung herself into Robby's arms, bursting into tears. Robby stiffened, but then wrapped her arms around her.

"Well maybe you will be, or maybe not," Robby replied. "We need to talk."

"I know, I know, honey." Dory sobbed, wiping

the tears from her face but remaining glued to Robby's chest. "I made the biggest mistake of my life..." She went to continue but couldn't, as she was overcome with hiccups.

With a big sigh, Robby rested her head on Dory's soft hair. "You always get those hiccups, don't you? Doesn't matter if you're overwhelmingly happy or sad. Well, you know what to do." Dory bent over from her waist, taking deep breaths as the hiccups slowed.

"Would-would-would you like some coffee?" she managed to ask when she could talk again.

"No. No coffee, no daily niceties," Robby replied sternly. "We need to have a serious discussion. Is Serena not here?" she asked, looking around.

"No, she's been cloistered in the studio working on a new series. Uh, shall we go into the living room?"

They sat at each end of the sofa, facing each other, Dory with her eyes cast down.

"What am I going to do with you, Dory?" Robby said in exasperation. "This isn't the first time you've messed up, throwing my life into turmoil, but this is the worst. I had to ask myself how long I can live with that. What will you do next?"

Dory erupted with a stream of apologies. "I so love you," she said. "The worst part of this has been my fear of losing you. God, please don't leave me, Robby. I know I fucked up royally and I'll do anything to make it up to you. Please forgive me."

Robby interrupted. "I don't know, Dory," she said gravely. "A relationship is based on absolute trust. No matter what, I always knew you would tell me the truth. But you've lied to everyone, including me." Her eyes flashed. "What the hell do we have without trust? Tell me."

Dory sat, quietly crying. "Nothing. I know. I'm so sorry..."

"Damn right, nothing! Less than dating, less than hooking up, even. At least then no one expects anything. How could you do that to me, to us? And what in God's name made you think you'd get away with it?"

Dory responded in a rush. "Please listen to me, Robby. I know, I made the worst mistake of my life. It's hard to explain why, but I'll try. I wanted so badly to be published, partly so you would be proud of me"—Robby muffled an exclamation—"and partly to catch up to you. You were so successful. I thought the book was good but no one was interested in it. When that publisher wished it was a memoir, something in me just...snapped. It was like I was in a fever. Simply by doing that, I could get the book published, establish myself, and make you proud. But I'd had a pretty boring life, not like you and your cases, so I knew I had to spice it up a little. I also knew you wouldn't go along with the strategy, but I was sure I could get away with it because it was a first book, you know? It probably wouldn't sell, so all this would never come out and no one would be hurt. When Robert accepted it, I was so happy and excited, but also a little scared. I almost told you the truth the night you took me out to dinner to celebrate."

"I remember," Robby said slowly. "I felt like you wanted to say something. But when you changed the subject from the book I thought you just didn't want to revisit painful times."

"I felt like a complete fraud and I didn't want to talk about it," Dory said. "I rationalized that it probably would make a little bit of money, if I was lucky, and then fade away and no one would be the wiser. But it got even worse when the book became successful and I didn't know what to do. It's been gnawing at me for months and I've been just miserable inside. In a way, it's almost a relief that it's about to come out. But the worst part of it was keeping it from you, the very person I'd always confided in and who helped to guide me when I was confused."

She stopped and looked down, afraid to look at Robby. The silence went on so long that at last she looked up pleadingly. "Please understand, Robby. I'm begging you. Please forgive me. I didn't mean any harm."

Robby's expression was no longer cold, but confused and still very, very angry.

"You never do. But you don't know what you did to me, do you? I was shattered by this. You are like my shadow, my second self, and suddenly you were this stranger who lied to me for months, for years, who slept with me and made love to me…" Her voice broke and she angrily swiped at a tear on her own face.

"You betrayed my trust," she said harshly. "You betrayed everyone's, in fact: your publisher, who's also your friend, for God's sake, and your readers who believe in you. How do I, how do we, get past that? Who the hell are you, really? I just don't know."

Dory studied her hands in her lap in complete despair. "I know," she whispered. "I know. I don't deserve your forgiveness, but I'm asking for it anyway. Robby, I'm still the Dory that you know and love. Or loved, anyway." She wiped her face. "It's true I made an impulsive, terrible mistake, and I'll do anything to make it up to everyone. I've already started trying to make amends and repair the damage I've caused.

"Darling, please listen to me. I know I screwed up

royally, and that I'm scatterbrained and occasionally incredibly stupid, although nothing like this before. But I love you, I adore you, I can't imagine my life without you. I swear I will never, ever disappoint you again—at least not on this scale. You know how I am…I can be impulsive and do dumb things unthinkingly. But I'll never make you doubt me for who I am, ever again.

"And that is, I am yours, totally. And I am basically a completely ethical person, I promise I am. I am all the things you thought I was. I just failed miserably when tested, and for that I beg your forgiveness. Do you want me to kneel to you? Because I will. Anything, to feel you open to me again.

"Please, Robby. Can you find it in your heart to give me another chance?"

Robby was a study in expressions as she listened to Dory. Anger, doubt, conflict, and puzzlement raced across her face, followed by a look of stony resolution. Dory sucked in her breath as she awaited her judgment.

"I won't lie to you, Dory," she said. "I'm not all there, not yet, and I don't know if I can ever again be the same with you. You have done so much damage, I think you have no idea. You've gotten into scrapes in the past, but this…" She shook her head gravely. "This is beyond a dumb mistake or a neglectful act." She scraped her hand through her hair as Dory held her breath.

"But I'm willing to give it a try. Maybe we can repair it, I don't know. Do you understand?" She reached over to take Dory's chin in her hand and looked seriously into her eyes. "I really don't know. I can't guarantee anything. We can try, but I have to tell you, if we do get past this, you can expect to be on a tighter leash until I feel I can trust you again."

Dory exhaled, trying not to burst into fresh tears. "Oh, thank you, honey," she said. "I do love you so. And I'll work so hard, I promise you, to make it up to you." She paused, not sure if she should say more.

"And?"

"Please may I come home?" She held her breath again.

Robby looked at her, considering. "Well, I suppose if we're going to work at it, we might as well do it under the same roof. Besides, Killer misses you and, to tell the truth, so do I."

Dory felt her heart expand and couldn't keep the radiant smile off her face. "Oh, thank you, darling! I'll be right out." She leapt up.

"Uh, Dory?" Robby said, a tiny smile hovering at her lips.

"Yes, sweetheart?"

"Don't forget to get dressed."

Killer was a golden blur out the door when he heard and saw Dory's car come up the driveway. He danced around it barking joyfully and, when she got out, leapt into her arms.

"Whoa, Killer! Remember, you're not a lap dog," Dory said, laughing as she disentangled herself from the ecstatic dog.

"He has never known that he grew," Robby said. "He'll probably always think he's still a small puppy."

"And so he will be," said Dory resignedly. "He'll always be our puppy." She picked up her bag and rolled it up the walk, lifting it up the stairs into the hallway, where she paused. Robby had gone ahead, but turned when Dory didn't follow.

"Ah, this is awkward, but where should I put my bag?"

Robby just looked at her. "Do you have to ask?"

Abashed, Dory hung her head. "I'll get settled in the guest room," she said. When Robby said nothing, she thought, *Silence indicates consent*, and headed up the stairs. She put the bag on the bed in the room across from the one she'd shared for years, and crossed it to look out the window at the neighborhood. Conflicting emotions raged within her: sadness, disgust with herself, hope, and above all, gratitude to be home. *I'm not really "home" yet, but I'm in the house. And here I can fight to rebuild my relationship and my life.*

Killer came in and nuzzled her leg. He looked up at her quizzically and then looked at the door across the hall, whined, and looked back at her. Dory sat on the bed and he put his front paws in her lap. She hugged his shoulders and ran her hands over his soft hair. "I know, Killer, it's confusing," she said softly. "But it'll be all right, boy, you'll see. You'll see.

"From my lips to God's ears," she whispered to herself, and then set about unpacking.

The following morning, Dory awoke to Killer's cold nose and an empty house. Robby's truck was gone. Wondering where Robby was, Dory poured her coffee and carried it to her computer, where she settled in and began the tasks Annabelle had given her.

First thing was to finally get back to the reporter, Gwen Fanning, before she forged on by herself. She had to control the message, and Fanning was the first likely loudspeaker. She took a deep breath, picked up her phone, and selected the number on her recent calls list.

"Hello, this is Gwen Fanning," came the voice

she'd been avoiding.

"Gwen, good morning. This is Dory da Silva. I apologize for being so long getting back to you, but my trip to New Orleans mightily distracted me. Would you like to meet?"

"Dory! At last. Yes, New Orleans can be delightfully distracting, can't it? But I really do need to talk to you and I certainly would like to get together. How about brunch today?"

"Since I've only had coffee so far, that sounds good," Dory answered. "How about the Buttered Biscuit in an hour or so?"

"Deal."

Dory hung up, heart racing and armpits moist. *Well, here I go. Resurrection, one way or the other.* Mind racing, she headed up to change for yet another of the most important meetings of her life.

Fifty minutes later, she settled into a booth at the Buttered Biscuit, studying the menu. *Why do I even bother? I always get the Dump.* The Dump was a delectable small iron skillet loaded with home fries, crumbled bacon, onions, and green peppers, topped with melted cheese and a perfectly done egg. *But on second thought, I'm not sure my stomach is up to that this morning.* She ordered a bagel and cream cheese and a side of fruit, and sipped the strong coffee as she waited.

It wasn't long before she spotted Gwen Fanning coming up the walk. She was a diminutive woman with short spiky black hair, dark intelligent eyes, and an angelic face. Her appearance worked well to mask her strong personality and quick wit, and worked to her benefit when she was interviewing an unsuspecting subject. But Dory had heard all about Gwen, who was well known in the lesbian community as an up-and-coming reporter. Ambitious but not vicious, she had begun with the local gay magazine, for which she still occasionally freelanced, and then graduated to the city's third-ranked publication. Dory could only hope that her approach would appeal to both Gwen's better nature and her ambition. She waved to her as she entered the cafe.

"Good morning." Gwen smiled as she slid into the booth. "So glad to be able to talk to you at last. How was New Orleans?"

"Oh, wonderful," Dory said. "I really needed the getaway, which was why I was so neglectful to my messages. I apologize. I'm glad to meet with you, too. I'm hoping that we can help each other."

Gwen's eyebrows rose with her quick glance at Dory. Gwen placed her order and they fell silent as her coffee was poured.

"Really," she said, as she poured cream into her cup. "That's interesting. How can I help you, and vice versa?"

Dory sat back, taking a deep breath. "Okay, here goes," she said, watching her companion closely. "I have a confession to make, to you and the whole world, and I'm hoping you'll be one of my conduits. I'm offering you an exclusive on my story."

"Really," Gwen said again, putting down her cup. "This does sound interesting. Tell me more."

"Well, I wrote the book, as you know, but not exactly truthfully."

"'Exactly?'" Gwen echoed, leaning forward. "I'm sorry, I'll stop interrupting. Do go on."

"I had a book that I knew in my bones was good, but I was getting nowhere with it, until a publisher suggested it would sell as a memoir. So…"

Gwen drew in her breath and her eyes got wide. "You mean, *Quitting* is not a memoir?" She took a sip of her coffee and said, "I have to admit I'm not completely shocked, but I'm still surprised. I was beginning to wonder why things in the narrative didn't quite add up. What are you going to do?"

Dory heaved a heavy sigh. "Whatever I do, it's going to be nasty, I suppose," she began. "But I'm going to come clean. I've been living with this Sword of Damocles over my head for a year, and the more success the book achieves, the worse it gets. So I want you to tell my tale. I'm hoping you might couch it in the changes in publishing and, with everyone now being a writer, how it is much harder in some ways for a writer to get published." She rushed on, noting Gwen's skeptical look. "I know, I know. There are many more outlets for an author these days. But hear me out.

"Everyone thinks they can write a book. You know as well as I do that that's not realistic, but publishers are inundated with manuscripts. If you don't have some connection in a publishing house, the work you spent years on just sits in the incoming slush pile until some assistant looks at it. If it's not a mass-audience type of story, it probably won't go anywhere. Even if it's a niche story sent to just the right niche publisher, chances of it moving on aren't terrific.

"Then, even if you get published, the work to get your book out there is largely up to you. The days of the publisher holding your hand, doing all your publicity, and arranging book tours for you are over, unless you're a big name. But you do have an advantage with a publisher: their mailing lists and Facebook pages, editors and layout staff, and a whole lot more.

“Or, you can self-publish. But to do that, you need capital to invest in advertising beyond what you can do for yourself for free on social media. You need someone who’s expert in all the platforms, who knows people who know people, like the right bloggers to promote you. I didn’t have a few thousand dollars to invest in such a person. I was despairing of ever achieving my dream of being a published writer.”

Their orders arrived and Gwen tucked into hers, but Dory left hers untouched.

“Yes, I know,” said Gwen, thoughtfully. “Being a writer is not the romantic dream people think.”

“Exactly. So you languish—one languishes—in obscurity for years, working hard and trying repeatedly to gain a foothold. Then, one day, someone in a position to know offers you an off-the-cuff comment that’s a clue to that very foothold. And you might take that path, even knowing the risk. Well, I did take that path. I told myself that the book probably would go nowhere, but at least I’d have a publisher who would look at my next works, which would be entirely on the up-and-up.

“But to my surprise, the book just took off. I was thrilled and terrified at the same time. To tell you the truth, I haven’t really enjoyed the success that much. I’ve felt like a complete fraud. Well, I guess I’ve *been* a complete fraud and I want to end that now. Do you think you can help me to explain all of this so that I don’t look like a worthless human being? A weak one, maybe, but not worthless?

“I’m hoping that you will provide the broad view, beyond the sensationalism of exposing”—she winced—“a literary fraud. It’s painful for me to even say it. But I think if you do present the whole story, it also might give you a much more meaty tale and be of broader media interest."

Gwen gazed at her thoughtfully. "Interesting proposition. I appreciate you coming to me. That does make a difference.

"I know that publishers have deliberately done this in the past. The publisher of the runaway best seller *Papillon* is just one case in point. But I don't know if that's still true. I'd have to research it. But there's no doubt there are still fee agents, vanity presses, and book doctors who bleed writers dry by promising to improve, represent, and publish their works, and then don't follow through.

"But these things don't really apply to you. You weren't a hapless victim, you decided to go ahead with it all by yourself. How can you spin that positively?"

"I know," admitted Dory. "I'm not saying I'm a victim, at all. I'm not. I'm just a weak human being who got swept away in events she didn't expect. I never thought it would hit the big time, not in a million years.

"But what I also didn't consider was that it would bother me like an itch you can't reach to scratch. My conscience has been a subliminal scold every day, never letting me rest. And other than the fix I'm in, I'm just exhausted by my own betrayal of myself. So, *laissez les bons temps rouler* now—out with it.

"I'm hoping that people will forgive me if I explain that it's not all fiction. The events I described are real—well, with some literary license that happens in any book. They just didn't all happen to *me*. Some did, some didn't. I'm hoping that my readers will take away the larger purpose of the book and what it says about human nature and society in general. It has some good points to make, I think."

"Well, it does, I agree. And you have one thing in your favor. People do tend to forgive a truly contrite penitent. It makes them feel good about themselves. And if they really enjoyed your book, they might continue to support you, who knows? So, what are you planning?"

"I am going to contact all the readers on my email list personally and fess up," Dory said firmly. "And I'm going to post the story publicly. But I can coordinate that with your story release. I'm not asking for a whitewash, Gwen, by any means. But I would like you to let me see your article before you release it. Are you willing to do that?"

Dory could practically see the thoughts going through Gwen's head. She hoped Gwen could see the opportunity, and that she appreciated Dory's clear regret. Either Dory could release the news herself and Gwen would be just another reporter in the pack following the trail; or they could coordinate, and Gwen could still be honest *and* have a scoop that would raise her own profile.

"Okay, I can do that," Gwen said. "As long as you know up front that I'm not going to pull any punches. There are a number of approaches I can think of for this story, offhand. It could be the struggling writer, or the ethical questions involved and whether Americans' judgment of such things is stricter or looser than in the past. I mean, compared to other, uh, indiscretions like *Papillon*, your case is very mild, and you are divulging it yourself, which means something. That counts with the public. Well, we'll see how it goes."

"Oh, good." Dory breathed a sigh of relief and finally took a bite of her bagel. "I would far prefer to work with you than to have you arrayed against me, to be honest. And I've read your work. I like your reporting. It's educated on the issues, and balanced. I particularly liked your series on the school cheating scandal. You couched that in terms of the pressures on teachers and students alike to perform well on standardized tests, and you presented what was lost because of that—the time to learn the whole story, to give the children the context of what they were being taught, as opposed to just facts suitable for a multiple-choice test. I guess what I'm trying to say is that you seem to look at the whole picture and do real journalism, and I appreciate that."

"Well, thank you," Gwen responded, seeming pleased. "That was a great story to cover, very satisfying. And this could be sort of like the reaction to that scandal. People were divided. Some understood and supported the use of standardized tests to provide a level playing field with which to judge school districts' performance. Others disliked what they saw as real education declining in the pursuit of the good scores needed for continued school funding. And others hated that the poorer-funded schools' challenges to provide a good education for their lower-income students weren't acknowledged at all. There was no gray area, just black and white, just the score. Just for an example, and I'm sure there's more.

"I do hope we can work together. We'll have to see how it goes. Let's start now, shall we?" she said, pulling her recorder out of her purse. "Tell me about your struggle to be published. How long was that? How many houses rejected or ignored you?"

Dory nodded, satisfied with the still uneasy alliance she had forged. *First step done. Now, to go home and write my mea culpas for the social media.*

Chapter Thirteen

Dory was deep into her writing when she was surprised to hear the home landline ring. "Oh, probably another trash call," she grumbled. "So much for the Do Not Call list." But the area code was right, so she answered, and was even more surprised when she did.

"Hello, Robby?" said a voice that was vaguely familiar.

"No, she's not here," Dory answered, puzzled. "May I ask who's calling?"

"Oh, is this Dory? Hi, Dory, sorry, I thought I dialed her cell. This is Jessie."

"Jessie? Wow, hi. How are you?" As she spoke, her mind reached back, capturing the image of Robby's former partner. And capturing the lingering jealousy she'd always felt about her. *Jessie. For heaven's sake. Why is she popping up now, after all these years?* Something unpleasant stirred within her before she quickly pushed it down.

"Oh, I'm fine, thanks, Dory. How about you?"

"Good," Dory lied. "Is there something I can help you with?"

"Oh, no," Jessie said. "I was just trying to catch Robby up on some things I uncovered on the case we're working on. I'll try her cell. Sorry to have bothered you."

"No problem," Dory said smoothly. "Bye. Have

a good day!"

"You, too," Jessie replied, and disconnected.

Dory stared into the middle distance, phone still in her hand. Jessie. What case? Why hadn't Robby mentioned any of this to her? *Oh, duh,* she wryly thought. *Uh, because we haven't been speaking? But wow. Jessie. Again.*

She just couldn't help herself. Her imagination wandered, bringing up images of Robby meeting with Jessie, telling her all—the thought made her grind her teeth—and having a cocktail with her. She shook her head vigorously to dispel the thoughts. *Oh, for God's sake. We weren't separated that long! That's just a little unlikely, don't you think?*

Still, the memory of her lover's former partner couldn't be shaken. She knew that Jessie and Robby had always shared an understanding that Dory never would. Their bond, achieved over years of working together, backing up each other in risky situations, and enduring dull stakeouts, was complete. She wouldn't have minded that at all if Robby's partner had been a nice, heterosexual, happily married man. But Jessie was of the sisterhood and, in Dory's opinion, a hot little number, too. What she lacked in stature she more than made up for in a neatly packaged, curvy body, blessed with a cute face, a riotously awful sense of humor, and, of course, an authoritative personality. Dory had always wished she couldn't stand her, but alas, she couldn't help but like her.

Everybody liked Jessie. *Curse her.*

Dory grimaced, hating the gnawing doubt growing in her heart. How had Robby and Jessie hooked up again? She was retired, so what was this case? And should she ask about it, or just leave it alone until Robby told her on her own?

Oh, but she knew herself. She wouldn't be able to leave it alone. She'd have to bring it up. She just hoped that when she did she wouldn't blow it by being anything other than casual. But her Italian passion was stirring, she knew. The relationship around which her life revolved was in trouble, and another woman had just entered the circle. A very threatening one, to boot, and Dory could just feel her protective instincts gathering force. *Careful, baby. This is no time to blow it. This is the time to be sweet and humble.*

Ha, she thought dismally. *Like that's my nature. But I'm smarter than that. I am. I can do this.*

From my lips to God's ears. She allowed herself that one final thought, then firmly put it all out of her mind and returned to writing her contrite, hopefully career-saving messages to the world.

Robby pulled up to the Big Steer Steakhouse at 4:30. She settled into a window booth with a good view of the expansive room. She ordered coffee, leaned back, opened a paperback book, and five minutes later spotted Charlene's entrance. Charlene looked around quickly and, not seeing Connie, nodded briefly to Robby, then sat in a booth by the front window. Robby rose and casually wandered out to the parking lot, standing as if she was waiting for someone. Her gaze sharpened when a car entered the nearly empty lot and a woman got out. She watched her enter the restaurant and slide into Charlene's booth, then walked over to the car.

"Aw, bless her heart, she rented from a cheap

one, of course." She chortled, looking at the rental company name emblazoned on the tag's frame. She took a photo of the plate and the VIN plate in the window, then returned to the restaurant. Pleased to see the booth behind Connie vacant, she slid in to enjoy—and record—the conversation.

"Connie," Charlene said, coldly acknowledging her presence.

"Greetings," Connie cheerfully replied, clearly feeling in complete control of the situation. "Ready to part with some cash?"

Charlene leaned back and looked at her speculatively. "Let's have a little conversation. I didn't sit on the bench for years to just roll over at the first cheap shakedown to come my way. I want to know a few things before we go any further."

Connie's eyes narrowed as her good cheer disappeared. "Now see here," she began. "I don't think you're in any position to negotiate—"

"Oh, but I am," Charlene coolly replied. "I'm retired, you know? I can do anything I want. I can run for office, or not. I can have you arrested for extortion, or not. And of course, you know I must have many friends in the police department. So, why don't you get down off your high horse and answer a few questions for me?"

"Talk about high horse!" said Connie, but her bravado had vanished. "What do you want to know? Seems like I've got all the knowin' necessary here."

"What's your daughter's name, if you really have one, and where does she go to college?"

"You don't need to know anything about her," Connie said defensively. "She's none of your business. You leave her in peace."

Charlene shook her head. "Huh-uh. She was your justification for the piss-poor excuse for blackmail you have. But I can relate to wanting your child to do better than you. So I want to know. If I give you one red cent, and I do mean *if*, it will go straight to her, not you."

"Shit, what would you know about having a child?" Connie sneered. "You never had one, did you, you and your queer friends? You don't know what it's like—"

"Oh, spare me! You don't know the first thing about me or my life, so don't presume to assume what I'm like or what I've done, what I know or don't know. Just answer the question or get the hell out of here."

"Now, now." Connie's tone had changed, clearly alarmed. "I think we got off on the wrong foot." Charlene snorted. "I'm just asking for some consideration in light of past favors I did for you. That's fair, isn't it?"

"I repeat, you got your cut of my pay back then. You're just a common blackmailer now. I don't owe you a thing. You're threatening to make public work I had to do to survive when I was young, work that wasn't illegal in any way. What makes you think you'll get away with that?"

Connie shifted nervously in her seat. This was obviously not the cakewalk she had expected. "Still, you've put a lot into this campaign. I've been looking into you, so I know. You really want it. Why would you risk losing it when you don't have to?"

"Do I look crazy?" Charlene smiled grimly. "Don't you think I know that you'd never stop at this? You made the mistake of thinking I'm an easy mark, but I'm not. I'd advise you to think about it, long and hard. You have a lot to risk, including prosecution and jail time. If you really have a daughter, how would she feel about that?"

Deciding bravado was the better part of caving completely, Connie jumped up. "Well, I'd advise *you* to think about it. Don't think just because you're so high-and-mighty that you can cow me. Maybe we're at a stalemate here. You think on it, Judge, you think on it. I'll give you twenty-four hours and I'll be back in touch."

"No," said Charlene. "I'll call *you*, and I'll decide when and where we meet. I'm not going to be yanked around by the likes of you. If you want to talk again, you text me at this number." She gave her a slip of paper with the number of a prepaid phone she'd bought. "Take it or leave it," she said firmly.

"Well, no need to be so hostile," Connie said plaintively. But she took the paper and walked out.

Charlene collapsed back into her seat, heart racing. She watched Connie drive away, followed by Robby. A few moments later, her phone rang.

"Good job, girl," Robby said with admiration.

Charlene smiled weakly. "Funny, you know, these sorts of things are far less stressful when you're hearing them from the bench than when you're embroiled in the middle of it. What's the next step?"

"I've got her in my sights and I'll find out where she's staying. I'll pass that info on to Jessie, who will be able to do things I probably shouldn't to get more information. We'll follow up on that fast. I'm expecting that we'll have a lot of what we need to counter her threat by tomorrow afternoon."

"Jessie? Your old partner?" Charlene asked with

surprise. "I didn't know you were still in touch."

"Well, we weren't, but I bumped into her in New Orleans, of all places, and we caught up. She's a PI now. I might just join her. I'm thinking about it."

"Really? And what would Dory think—oh, sorry, none of my business. Good for you. You do what you want to do. We're old enough to have earned that right, right?"

"Right," Robby said. "And don't worry about it, Charlene. Dory and I have had our bumps before and I know we'll ride this one out, too. You'll know all about it sooner or later, I'm sure."

"Oh, don't I know it." Charlene sighed. "Dory has that passionate Italian nature, which has certainly kept your relationship alive and…interesting…for years, hasn't it?" She laughed. "And we all love her for it, but I know it can be bumpy for you sometimes. Well, you know, we're all on call for both of you if you need us, right?"

"Right," Robby reassured her. "Oh, she's turning. Think I found her lair. I'll talk to you later."

"Thanks, Robby," Charlene said, and disconnected. She leaned her face onto her hand for a few moments, just staring out the window. *Good grief, just a couple of weeks ago we all seemed to have such placid lives. How things can change. But one thing's sure: If I'm going to change anything, it'll be because I want to, not because someone else is forcing me to. Screw that.*

She picked up the check, paid at the counter, and marched out to her car. If Connie thought she was going to roll over, boy, she had another think coming. With Robby and Jessie on the case, she felt confident she'd know all she needed to, to decide just how vengeful she felt about this attempted blackmail. She wasn't a judge anymore, but she still had plenty of pull. She'd just wait to find out what the details of Connie's life were, and then decide.

Robby watched Connie enter her room and turned the car around to the manager's office. Her appearance and attitude convincingly implied to the young clerk that she was still on the force, though she never said so, and a short conversation produced Connie's registration information. She called Jessie from her car to let her know she was on her way.

Jessie grinned when she walked in. "Right on time. We've still got it, girl, knowing about how long it might take. So, what have you got to tell me?"

"Well, I've got an address in California and license and credit card numbers," Robby replied, stretching out her long legs. "Geez, you know what has changed? How stiff I get sitting for a long period of time. Good grief, it wasn't even that long. I think I'd better start doing some stretches in earnest."

"I know what you mean. And you can add a sore hip to that, too. But hot dog, now we can get going and wrap this thing up in short order. Hungry? Shall we order?"

"Sounds good," said Robby. "I've been off my feed lately and I'm hungry. But the amount of calories I consumed in New Orleans probably more than made up for any recent shortfall."

After they ordered, Robby asked, "How was your trip to New Orleans? I never did ask, were you there alone?"

"No, it was a junket with someone I'd been

seeing," Jessie replied. "But that weekend was the last hurrah for us. I sort of knew it beforehand, but we'd planned the trip some time ago so I didn't want to spoil it. We had fun. But when we got back, she left a message about getting together again and when I called back, I got her voice mail. I left a message that I wanted to talk to her, and I haven't heard a word since. So I think she knew, and she's big on avoidance. I broke up without even having to have a conversation about it. A little weird, but I'm not inviting drama."

"Hmm, that's a new one," Robby said. "Sorry to hear it, though."

Jessie shrugged. "No biggie. So, how are you and Dory doing? Oh, by the way, I hope I didn't make any waves for you. I called your landline by mistake and she answered, and sounded real surprised to hear from me. I take it you didn't mention we bumped into each other in NOLA?"

"No. We've had sort of a rough time lately, haven't been communicating very well. But that's okay, don't worry about it."

"Ah, I remember that used to happen with y'all with some regularity," Jessie said. "But it never lasted. Hope it's true this time, too."

The waiter arrived and Robby changed the subject as they dug into their steaks. "Thanks. So, what do you do in your free time, other than go to New Orleans and break up?"

Jessie laughed. "Having your own business is a tricky thing," she said. "It's really hard to get the boss to give you a day off! So I don't have a lot of free time, actually. While I don't handle many cases—just the ones that interest me—I have good people who consult with me, most retired PD like us, and I keep up with all the cases. And remember how difficult it was to be single, at least after we matured out of our heady adrenaline- and estrogen-soaked days?"

"Well, sort of." Robby laughed. "What's it like now?"

"Oh, man, let me tell you, it sucks. You know, the internet was supposed to make everything easy, and there are meet-up sites for every age and disposition. But it's the internet, you know? And everyone lies on the internet. So, you finally wade through all the faces you've seen repeatedly for the last six months and see a new one. She's kind of cute and her interests seem to match yours. Hurray, you think to yourself, and you contact her.

"Well. It can go any number of ways from there, but usually down. Either she turns out to be a complete loon, or you make it through the emailing and maybe phone calls and then meet. And it turns out that her photo on the site was from her own ancient history. Now, I'm not fat-ist, or size-ist, or whatever they say today," she clarified. "I'm no raving beauty myself. But really? Why would anyone want to immediately disappoint someone they want to impress? Why not be honest?

"And there are virtually no bars anymore." She continued lamenting as Robby started to grin. "Oh, I know, I'm on a tear here. But it's frustrating as hell. Used to be you could go to the bar and have a drink, meet your friends, maybe meet someone new. Not anymore." She shook her head. "I just don't know. I may just give up and become a lesbian hermit."

By this time, Robby was laughing outright. "Thanks, friend, I needed that," she said. "Yeah, relationships are tough at times, but I didn't think things were as grim as what you're describing. Good grief."

They ate their dinner and continued to compare notes and strategies on the Connie case, their past cases, and laughed more about Jessie's disastrous-sounding love life.

"Well, keep your eyes peeled for me, girlfriend," Jessie said, finishing her drink. "You might come across a hot number for me. I'd better get going and get my research started. I'll call you in the morning, okay?"

"Sounds good." Robby reached for the check.

"Oh, no, this one's mine," Jessie said, grabbing it. "I'm the gainfully employed one, remember? That you're paying, actually. So it's my treat."

Robby thanked her, let her pay, and left appreciating the value of a long, enduring working relationship. She and Jessie were sure to help Charlene out of her jam.

Chapter Fourteen

Robby drove home, humming along with the radio's songs and smiling to herself. Jessie's stories were amusing and she was grateful that that wasn't anything she needed to worry about. Being in a relationship could be a challenge, and lord knows she and Dory had had their share—the temper that girl could have!—but the rewards were worth it.

At least, that's what she thought until she opened the door. The moment she walked in, the air felt electric and her guard rose. She looked around cautiously, then thought, *What? Don't be ridiculous,* and tossed her backpack on the hall chair. Dory emerged from the kitchen, mug in hand, but for some reason her bright smile made the hair on the back of Robby's neck prickle.

"Hey, babe," she said. "Where have you been all day? Are you hungry? I made dinner."

"No, I've had dinner," Robby answered.

"Oh, really? Where?" Dory asked, too casually. "What did you have?"

Robby leaned against the wall, studying her lover's face for clues. Something was off, and she suspected Jessie's call related to it.

"What are you really asking, Dory? Isn't it really 'where was I and who was I with?' Well, I'm not sure that concerns you for any number of reasons, not the least of which being that I've never given you any reason for concern, but particularly now."

Dory blushed and looked down, but then looked up again with fire—a small fire, but a fire—in her eyes. "Well, can't I be curious?"

In spite of herself, Robby felt a smile tugging at her lips as she looked down at the little spitfire she'd shared so much of her life with. "Well, as it happens, I was at the Big Steer with my old partner, Jessie."

"Jessie, really. So, you're still in touch?"

Now Robby really did grin. "Oh, baby, give it up. I know you talked to Jessie, so you don't need all this subterfuge."

Now Dory blushed deeply. Crimson-faced, she looked down and muttered, "Well, I was just wondering, you know."

"Yes. Well, not for quite a while, but in fact, I ran into her in New Orleans, of all places."

"New Orleans?" Dory looked up, startled. "And you didn't tell me?"

"Well, I didn't have much of a chance, since you unloaded your bomb before I could, and then that was the last thing I was thinking of."

"Oh," Dory said in a small voice. "Yes, I see. Well, how is she?"

"Oh, she's fine," Robby said dryly, rather enjoying her discomfort. "And if you must know, we're working together on a case for Charlene."

"Charlene? Wow, it's one surprise after another. What on earth are y'all doing for Charlene? Something to do with the election?"

"Well, indirectly," Robby replied. She briefly filled her in and then her face settled into a stern expression. "But Dory, you have no business giving me grief about anything right now. We're still not good, baby. You don't get to stamp your little foot, metaphorically speaking, and try to rule my life like nothing's happened, do you understand? In fact, if I really get to thinking about it, it's going to piss me off." Her eyes and voice grew cold. "So back off, you hear?"

Dory dropped her eyes and said not a word as Robby stalked off. Dinner that night was separate, each of them working on her computer while Killer wandered between the two, whining softly.

Robby felt fueled by her righteous anger and spent a productive evening on her computer. She had agreed to explore Connie's alleged daughter, leaving Connie to Jessie. Birth records produced Connie's daughter, Danielle, and Robby signed up for a free week's subscription to Intelius to start tracing her life. *I might have to keep that resource, who knows? Although, if I work with Jessie, I'll bet she's already all signed up to all the databases she needs.*

Danielle turned out to be a student at UC Santa Barbara, majoring in psychology. Her LinkedIn page indicated she was an honor student, well-liked and active in her college community. Her resume, for a college kid, was an impressive demonstration of a healthy work ethic, evidenced through regular summer jobs, work-study jobs, and even volunteer activity. It was her Facebook posts that pointed to financial trouble. One asked for any information available on scholarships and other financial aid. "I know there are weird scholarships out there," she wrote. "Like for kids of left-handed Ukrainian wallpaper hangers. I'm looking hard for awards and loans. Let's crowdsource this, please! Any leads will be most appreciated. I don't care if it sounds weird—let me know!"

Yikes, yeah, Robby thought, checking the cost of UC tuition. *Over thirty grand a year, even for a state resident. Didn't college used to be free in California?* She leaned back in her chair, drumming the desk with her fingers. So Connie wasn't just a fraud after all. She really did have a daughter. This didn't excuse her attempted blackmail by any means, but it might cast a different light on the matter. Charlene would have to decide that.

She thoughtfully powered down her computer and turned off the office light. Really, the whole situation was starting to look more pathetic than threatening. A mother who might be fighting for her daughter's future—she'd have to see what Jessie turned up on Connie herself—and a girl struggling to make a life for herself without much support. *Life really is shades of gray, isn't it?*

She made her way into the bedroom and then stood under the driving rain of a hot shower, her face to its force. She was depressed, troubled, and the water helped sooth her roiling spirit. She slipped naked into the bed and looked over at the pillow next to her head. How had everything gotten so screwed up? She missed Dory, she missed their unspoken communication and closeness. She missed her warm body snuggled up to her. She missed feeling sure about things in general. Nothing seemed the same. Even Killer had seemed depressed all night, pacing back and forth from room to room.

She dropped off into an uneasy, shallow sleep state, peopled by dreams of shadowy, threatening people and helpless children, in a world that was cold and lonely.

⁂

Dory decided on a long soak in the tub in the guest bathroom, where she dismally contemplated the state of her life. It made her want to sip on a tall, cool glass of wine, but instead she sipped on a long, cool glass of lemon-lime seltzer.

Oh, God, how did I get here? she thought, tears clouding her eyes. *I just spent an entire day writing apologies to all the people who have supported me. How could I have been so incredibly stupid? And then, I picked this time—good God, of all times—to show my ass to Robby. Okay, I understand it. I'm feeling exposed and vulnerable and threatened. Dammit, I said I was smarter than that, but I'm not. My own weaknesses got me here, and they're making things even worse, which I didn't think was even possible.*

Oh, God, please, help me through this, she prayed, eyes closed. *I don't know that I can do it on my own. And if I can't fix this, what's left for me? No career—but that's not the big thing. No Robby. God, I just can't live without Robby.* Her tears flowed freely as she prayed. *Please help me.*

She splashed water on her face, then climbed out of the tub wearily, wrapped herself in a thick towel, and stumbled to the guest bedroom. Slipping into her nightgown, she fell into the bed and pulled the sheets over her. The bed seemed to embrace her, the soft support of the pillow, the crisp caress of the sheets, and she quickly fell into a deep but restless sleep.

Dory woke around 2:00 a.m. and could no longer stand being away from Robby. She stole silently across the hallway, and saw Killer's ears perk up in the dark as his head raised toward the opening master bedroom door. He whined softly as Dory crept into the room, wagging his tail when she stopped to cradle his face in her hands.

Standing at the side of the bed, she looked at her sleeping lover. This was the woman with whom she had shared such a large part of her life, who was absolutely her life's center, to whom she had pledged her eternal love and loyalty. She squeezed her eyes shut and sent a silent prayer to the gods, lifted the covers, and crawled quietly into the bed. Her hand reached out to Robby's exposed shoulder and, pausing for an instant, she softly touched it, and then began to softly stroke the soft skin of her arm.

Robby stirred and, awakening, stiffened as she realized she was not alone. Dory began to speak in a low voice.

"Remember, darling, how we met? You were the cutest butch at the party and I just couldn't take my eyes off of you. And when I found out that you were a detective, well, that did it. I was lost. I just had to meet you. So I just screwed up my courage and walked over to introduce myself...and tripped over someone's foot. 'What an impression,' I thought as I sprawled on the floor at your feet. I was mortified.

"But you jumped into action, leaned down and lifted me bodily off the floor—literally—into the air, and asked if I was all right. I looked down at your kind eyes and felt your strong hands holding me tight, and fell for you hard. Harder than I fell to the floor."

She heard a muffled chuckle from Robby and her heart leapt with hope. Softy, she continued tracing their life together.

"Remember our first vacation? It was to Hilton Head, in a really nice condo on the beach, and Jill and her current flame—who was it, anyway?—were next door. We walked and biked on the beach, feasted on fresh seafood, gawked at the yachts in the harbor. Remember the yacht that came in with the two gay boys resplendent at the wheel, with the poodle running up and down barking at us on the pier? We were ready to trade places with the mutt.

"And then the time we went to Venice, and traded our lovely fourteen-foot-ceilinged room for the attic room so the honeymooning young couple could have ours? We got the better part of the deal, it turned out, with free access to the roof. We bought wine and bread and cheese and watched the sun go down behind St. Mark's Cathedral, and woke to the sounds of a medieval city coming to life. To this day, that was the most romantic setting of my life, even though we were in twin beds. Hell, that didn't stop us anyway."

Another chortle. She plowed on.

"And then remember how we were sick at the end of our trip to Paris, and the bathroom was downstairs, with the light on a timer that kept plunging us into darkness? And we got to Amsterdam and had to go through customs to catch our flight home. We were late and just decided we had no alternative but to be ugly Americans and butt into line in front of a huge group of Chinese people, thinking 'They're too polite to object.' Ha! We know better now. But we did make our flight, barely.

"And then we were on the plane and the nice man in front of us without a seat partner gave me his seat so I could lie down. And every time I woke up, I—"

"I know, I know," Robby said. "Your head kept

popping up in front of me saying, 'The drinks are free. Drink! Drink for me!' and then you'd disappear again."

"Yeah." Dory laughed into the darkness. "I couldn't stand the idea of wasting free booze. That was the easiest transatlantic flight in history, I'll bet. I was only awake for a little of it."

She turned to her lover and moved closer, wrapping her arms around her. When Robby didn't pull away, she snuggled close. "Robby, darling, I love you more than I love myself. I know it's hard to believe sometimes because I can be a brat, but I really, really do. Please, sweetheart, I—well, I just simply can't live without you. Won't you please let me back into your life? I swear I will never, ever disappoint you again." She held her breath, waiting for Robby's answer.

Robby heaved a big sigh, then turned toward her and wrapped her in her arms. "Oh, baby. I know. I don't want to live without you, either. For one thing, it would probably be so boring. I never know what you're going to do next."

Dory had started to softly cry again and then started to laugh at that, which of course brought on her hiccups.

"Oh, lord, there you go again," Robby said. "Go ahead, get up and bend."

When Dory had them under control and had snuggled up again, Robby said, "You know, you have the cutest ass in the world. I can't help it, I just can't stop looking. I always want to spank it."

Dory giggled. "Yes, and don't I love it."

"But I'd better hold off on that for a while," Robby said. "I'm a little afraid I'll remember how furious I've been with you and get carried away."

"Oh, honey," Dory said contritely. "I deserve it.

If that would help you get some resolution to all this awfulness, I would welcome it."

"Ha! You don't fool me, girl. It wouldn't work. I know you'd enjoy it too much. No," Robby said thoughtfully. "There does need to be some punishment for what you've done. I know you have a lot of that coming, however you deal with your public. You'll have to fill me in on that tomorrow."

"Yes, of course, darling," Dory murmured. "It's painful, but I think I'm making good progress. Annabelle is helping me and it's going to be a full campaign of apology, trying not to lose all of my readership."

"Well, tell me about it in the morning," Robby said, stifling a yawn. "So, I know you'll be paying the piper. But there's some paying to do to regain my trust in our relationship, too. I don't know what it will be yet, but you can be sure it's coming."

"Yes, Daddy. Of course, and I accept whatever you decide. I know it will be fair compensation for the grief I've caused you. And I'm sorry for my little snit this afternoon. I was just feeling so vulnerable, and most of all scared that I'd lost you, or was losing you. And then Jessie appeared again, and I was always a little jealous of her. I'm sorry."

"I know, babe. But you know there's only one woman in the world for me."

"I know, but that doesn't always keep me from shooting off my mouth…"

"Oh, don't I know it," Robby said. "But enough now, baby. We're both worn out. Let's get some sleep and start again in the morning, okay?"

"Absolutely," Dory said, snuggling back into her lover's arms. Robby sighed and rolled over, and Dory spooned her happily. As Robby's breathing deepened again in sleep and Killer softly snored by the bed, she smiled and let herself relax into the deepest sleep she'd had in months.

Killer's cold nose and soft whine woke her the next morning, unnaturally early. "Well, anything before seven is unnatural," Dory grumbled to herself, looking enviously at her sleeping lover. "Too much water last night, eh, Killer?" she whispered to him as she sat up. He stepped back, wagging his tail energetically, and looked at her expectantly. Yawning, she struggled into her robe and slippers and followed him down to the kitchen, opening the door for him to the early birds' songs.

She left the door open to the chorus as she took out the coffee and brewed the first pot. Pouring a cup, she went back to the open door and leaned on the jamb, enjoying the peace of the morning. A feeling of great contentment washed over her as she watched Killer sniff around his domain. She was home, bless the gods above. She had gotten home again, the place she loved with the woman she loved, and the world was right again.

"Oh, and of course, you, too." She laughed as the dog bounded back inside. He barked joyfully in response and she shushed him immediately.

"Oh, don't bother, I'm up," came the voice behind her, and she turned into Robby's arms. She rested her head on her shoulder and squeezed her with her free arm.

"Coffee?" she asked.

"Yup, please," Robby sleepily replied. She took a cup from Dory and the two returned to the French doors. Dory pulled the covers off the deck chairs and they sat together in comfortable silence, sipping and watching the world wake. Finally, Robby looked over at her.

"It's good to have you home, babe."

Dory looked at her, eyes suddenly glistening, and just said, "Yeah." They clinked their cups together to toast the moment.

"So, what's up now?" Robby asked.

"Well, I have, have, *have* to make arrangements to go to New York to meet with Robert," she replied. "Boy, not looking forward to that. But the longer I wait, the worse it's going to be. And I feel terrible that he's going to be completely blindsided by all of this, but it's just accelerated so fast that I really haven't had time to forewarn him. Well, except for the last year, of course.

"Oh, God. But I'm meeting up with Gwen Fanning this morning and think she'll have the article to share. That will inform my conversation with Robert."

She shook her head. "I'll just soldier on and hope to heavens it all turns out well." She got up and paused. "More coffee?"

"No, thanks, I'll wait until I'm dressed and ready to go," said Robby.

"Okay. Oh, and Robby?"

Robby looked up.

"Thanks," Dory said simply.

Robby smiled and raised her cup in a salute.

Later, Dory parked at the Buttered Biscuit and

took what had become her usual booth to await Gwen's arrival. She leaned back and gazed sightlessly out the window at the cars splashing through the rain outside, until the waitress came with her coffee.

"Thanks, Ariadne," she said, smiling up at the spiky-blue-haired young woman with tattooed arms. "By the way, did you pick your name or were your parents big fans of the Greek gods?"

"Oh, no, not my folks!" The waitress laughed. "They might never have even heard of the Greek gods, for all I know. No, I picked it in my Goth days, as a symbol of the maze that life is. Profound, right? But actually, not that bad. Ariadne was the guide in the labyrinth. So now that I'm so much wiser," she said, tossing her head mockingly. "I figure it's even more suitable."

"Well," Dory said, smiling. "You carry it well. I always get her mixed up with Arachne, the Web spinner and, well, you have that great tattoo on your arm."

"Oh, yeah." Ariadne laughed. "Wow, glad you mentioned that. I like confusing people. But no, that's a whole 'nother story. You keep coming in, you'll have my life history. Hey, you could put me in one of your books."

"I just might, don't count it out," Dory said as Gwen slid into the booth.

"Hi, Gwen. Coffee?" Ariadne said.

"Definitely," Gwen answered gratefully. "Great day for ducks out there, isn't it? And a Monday, to boot."

"Yes, I know. It was even worse in the dark, when I was coming in. People in Atlanta just don't like driving in the rain, and it shows. Coffee, coming right up."

"I wish I could just hook it up to an IV," Gwen grumbled as she carefully propped her dripping umbrella up against the side of the seat. "I don't operate at my usual speed on these low-light days. I think in a future life, I'll be a solar battery. Or a robot with one strapped to me."

"I hear ya," Dory said. "It was hard getting up this morning, for sure. So, what's been happening? Are you done with the article? Are you shopping it? No pressure, but my life's sort of hanging in the balance here."

"Oh, no you don't," Gwen replied, giving her the hairy eyeball. "I didn't get you into this fix, you did. Don't shoot the messenger."

"Yeah, but it's the message that's giving me an ulcer. When do you think I can see it?"

"Well, how about now?" Gwen handed her an envelope. "I'll email it to you, too. Let me know what you think. I'll consider any thoughts you have, but I have to tell you, I'm ready to go with this."

Dory sucked in her breath and tore open the envelope as Ariadne placed Gwen's coffee before her. "You ladies ready? The usual?"

"Yup, the usual for me," Gwen said.

"Not me," said Dory. "I think for now I'll just settle for coffee and juice. Check with me again in twenty minutes. I'll either be throwing up or starving."

Ariadne looked at her, puzzled, as she refreshed her coffee, then shrugged and moved off to her next table.

"Oh, it's not that bad, Dory," Gwen reassured her. "As promised, I didn't pull any punches, but I did find a good cosmic couch for the story to rest in. You go ahead—well, you already have, haven't you?—and read it. I'll catch up on the news on my tablet."

Dory devoured the manuscript in short order, then went back and re-read some passages as Gwen's breakfast was delivered. "Well?" the waitress asked Dory.

"The Dump, please, Ariadne," Dory responded. "And a bowl of fruit."

As her order was being filled, Dory flipped through the document again and then gave Gwen a direct look.

"Well, I knew you were a good reporter," she said. "But I think this might be the best thing I've ever read by you. I suspect you're on your way to greater things, Gwen. Thank you. This is beyond balanced. Actually, it's generous in its treatment of me."

Gwen grinned. "Thanks, I think it's good, too. I really sank my teeth into this one. The story opened the door to such a wide social field that I could've gone any which way with it. Lucky for you, I found the overall social context much more interesting than your individual story. But in the end, I don't know if that'll help you much. People will focus where they want, and that's usually more on the drama than the intellectual questions involved."

"Yes, probably." Dory sighed. "But I do appreciate it, anyway. Have you been shopping it?"

"Oh, yeah!" Gwen grinned. "I made a deal with *Vanity Fair*. And the gods must really like you. It turns out that their editorial calendar will be perfect for an article of this type in two months for the July issue, which means—"

"Right! Yes, it means I have time to prepare my publisher for the disaster to come. Oh, you don't know how much that means to me, Gwen. You probably don't know it, but he's a friend. I've been agonizing over how to buffer this for him. This gives me a little time. I'll get right on it."

"Well, I wish you luck," Gwen said. "That won't be a pleasant conversation, I'm sure. But coming to know you a little bit, I have hope that you'll manage to turn this around. And if I've helped at all, I'm glad of it. Now, have your breakfast and tell me about your next book. I do reviews, you know."

Chapter Fifteen

Dory woke early Tuesday morning to bird songs and Killer's cold nose. "Oh, Killer, for God's sake, have a little mercy." Delighted to have a response, the golden terror jumped on the bed and snuggled so unmercifully against her back that he almost knocked her to the floor.

"All right, all right! Good grief," she exclaimed, feet seeking out her slippers. As usual, Robby was already up. "I'm up, I'm up," she grumbled to the dog, now standing on the bed, tail wagging wildly. He grinned at her and jumped down, heading to the hall and looking back to invite her along. "I'm coming, I'm coming," she said. "At least let me pee first, would you?"

That taken care of, she groaned when she looked in the mirror. Killer appeared at the door, as if to block her from crawling back into bed. "Why is it, Killer, that you can get up in the morning and look just as fabulous as you do all day, while I..." She gestured helplessly at the mirror. "Well, you have hair all over. Beautiful hair. And I brush you. Hmm. Maybe after I brush my mop." She whacked at her hair with the brush and stood back to inspect. "Nah. Nothing's gonna work. Never mind."

Pulling on her robe, she padded sleepily down the hall mumbling her morning coffee mantra on the way to the kitchen. Robby was there, already at work on her laptop at the breakfast bar, and greeted her with a small smile and cocked eyebrow.

"Good morning, Sunshine," she said. "Ready to face the day?"

"What does it look like?" Dory mumbled in return. "God, you're always so awake, even when you just open your eyes. How do you do that?"

"Natural excitement. Can't wait to see what'll happen next. Must be a holdover from my cop days. Or Killer's influence."

"Well, I can wait, at least on this particular day," said Dory, happily inhaling the fragrant steam before taking a big gulp. "Today's the day I talk to Robert."

"Yes, I remember, the Gibbs of the publishing world," Robby said, wincing. "You sure he wasn't ever in *NCIS*?"

"No, but at times it sure seems like he could've been in the Marines," Dory answered, climbing onto the barstool, cup cradled in her hand. "Robert's fair, but he's pragmatic and he doesn't take any shit. It helps that he's a writer himself, not just a businessman, but that will never distract him from his publisher role and the bottom line. I really don't know what's going to happen."

"What time is your flight again?"

"Eleven o'clock. I'll be going directly to the hotel, and then our appointment is at four. Before this, we'd always adjourn to the Algonquin's Blue Bar to debrief the day, but I don't think that's likely this time."

"Nope, think you're right. Well, good luck, baby," Robby said, sympathetically but bluntly. "Call me to fill me in when you're done."

"I will. The important thing all along was that I never wanted to blindside Robert, but I guess there wasn't any way I could avoid doing that. I feel terrible about him. This has all moved along so fast. There have been so many moving parts to all this that I couldn't possibly control, as badly as I wanted to. I'm hoping against hope that he'll hold his fire until he's had time to process the news. That's usually his MO—he doesn't shoot from the hip. That might give me some time to do some vigorous, proactive PR, like on talk shows. Annabelle is looking into that. How do you think I should approach him?"

"Professional but very, very humble, and sorry beyond belief," Robby suggested. "And what you're doing to make it better."

"That's what I was thinking, too. Accent on the sorrow and the positivity. So I'll be gone for a few days, baby. I'll be at the Marriott Essex as usual. Killer will keep you good company."

"Yup, okay, have a good trip. I've got to get going. I'm meeting Jessie to discuss another case."

Dory's eyes popped open. "You are? Are you coming out of retirement?"

"No, don't think so. But I do want to keep my hand in. I was a little surprised at how good it felt to be working again, on this thing with Charlene. A little of that in my life can only do me good, I think."

"Just be careful, my love," said Dory. "And I promise, I've gotten over my craziness about Jessie. But you know, I still really do think she has a crush on you even though she's never acted on it. We need to find her a girlfriend."

Robby smiled. "See if you can rustle her one up in the big city." She kissed Dory and went out the door whistling.

Dory watched her truck leave from the front window, sipping the last of her coffee. Then, sighing, she rinsed out her cup, put it in the dishwasher, and headed upstairs. *Time to do battle,* she thought grimly. *Well, the one thing I want to have coming out of this is at least a little of my integrity restored so I can rebuild it. It'll be hard, but by God, I'm going to do it.*

She had already pretty much packed, so she put the last items in the suitcase, went down to the kitchen, and whistled for Killer. "Time for you to take me for a walk, big guy," she said as he skidded around the corner. They cruised around the riotously blooming neighborhood, Killer sniffing as many blades of grass as Dory would allow, and returned home. She carried her luggage to the garage, then showered, dressed, and bade Killer goodbye.

She paused at the kitchen door to the garage and fondly looked at her light-filled home. "It'll be good again," she whispered to herself. "I can do this." With a final pat to Killer, she squared her shoulders and began her journey of atonement.

Dory looked out the window as the jet circled Manhattan. The view never failed to impress her and she was constantly amazed at how it seemed to change each time. It would seem that the city had no more room for any additional skyscrapers, but then behold, another army of cranes appeared to elevate another to pierce the sky.

The aircraft swooped above Flushing Bay, as usual seeming to threaten to simply ditch everyone in the water, and landed with a bump. As they taxied to the gate, Dory gazed pensively out the window at nothing, tensely anticipating the next most-important meeting she might ever have. *Another one*, she thought wryly.

Robert had sent one of his assistants to pick her up, and the two chatted aimlessly as they rode the expressway into the city. Dory checked in at the JW Marriott Essex House, a grand old hotel that she loved, right across from Central Park. She dropped her bags in her room, lingered with the view for a moment, and then took the elevator down for the short walk to Robert's office.

She greeted his secretary warmly and accepted a chilled bottle of water. Moments later, the door opened and Robert emerged beaming, giving her a hug and ushering her into his office. She felt a pang of real guilt as he guided her to the couch rather than to the chair opposite his desk, but she hugged him back and steeled herself to say what must be said.

"It's great to see you, Dory. Happy May Day! How was your flight? How's the new book coming? Are you at the Essex again?" Robert asked as they settled on the sofa. "It's getting on in the afternoon and it's five o'clock somewhere. Would you like something a little stronger to drink? Or do you want to wait as usual?"

"Water's fine and the flight was, too, Robert, thank you. And yup, I just love the Essex. It's really good to see you, too, but you might not be as enthusiastic about me after you hear what I have to say."

Robert's eyebrows arched skyward. "You're not quitting us, are you?" He walked to the richly paneled bar on the side of the room and poured himself an amber drink, straight up.

"No." She sighed. "I'm perfectly happy with you. You just might not be with me."

"Good grief, girl, out with it. What could be so

terrible?" He settled back on the couch and sipped, looking at her curiously.

"I did something incredibly stupid, Robert. When I was looking to be published I hit all the usual walls—"

"Until we found you, that is." He laughed, but it didn't mask the anxiety in his voice. "Not that my having known you forever before counts."

"Yes. Yes, but there was one more publisher before you who made a comment that changed my life and, ironically, brought me to you."

"Who?"

"Doesn't matter. It's the comment that matters. He said, 'You know, if this was a memoir, I'd publish it in a minute.'"

Dory let that statement hang in the air and watched Robert's expression change as he understood. Slowly, he put his glass down on the side table and leaned forward, his face darkening.

"Please tell me you're not saying what I think you're saying," he said in a slightly strangled tone.

"I'm afraid I am," Dory said quietly, and proceeded to tell her story. Robert listened, his body language growing ever more tense as it progressed, finally getting up to pace to the window. He stared out as she finished, then stayed there silently for long moments.

Dory let the silence linger, then spoke to his back.

"Robert, I know how serious this is. I can't apologize enough. I betrayed not only my own ethical code, but you, who placed your trust in me, and I can't decide which distresses me the most. I've been in an agony of indecision about it for the last year.

"I just wanted you to hear it from me and to tell

you that I've started to fix it."

Robert turned at last to look at her and she held her breath.

"Fix it," he said slowly. "Fix it. You just told me my number one seller is a complete fraud, but you're going to fix it. Oh, and please do tell me, Dory, how are you going to do that?" He walked over to his desk and sat stiffly in his chair, elbows on the desk and hands clenched as he settled a piercing stare upon her.

Dory gave a tiny flinch but then sat upright herself, hands folded in her lap.

"Thank you for not exploding, Robert—"

"Oh, don't thank me yet," he said icily.

"I do appreciate that. We've known each other for a long time and I also know that this, uh, revelation, probably upends your image of me. I want you to know first of all that I'm still the Dory you know. Just maybe a little stupider—or a lot stupider—than you might have thought. I hope you can listen with an open mind, and even more important, if possible, an open heart."

Robert eyed her skeptically and remained silent as she explained.

"Okay, so that's the story of how I got to this awful spot. The problem got worse and worse as time went along and the sales went up. In fact, at one point when we had drinks at the publishing convention I almost told you, but my nerve just failed me."

"The fix," Robert said in a monotone.

"Yes, yes, the fix. Well, first, what prompted the fix. So, I was being interviewed by a reporter for a local magazine and she started getting suspicious about my timeline."

"Oh, God. The media have a hold of this? And you're just now coming to confess to me? Dory, have you completely lost your mind?"

"I know, I know, but hear me out, please. This has all accelerated very fast in the past few weeks, so in truth I didn't have a lot of time to regroup and strategize what I'd do."

"Weeks? What *you* would do?" Robert finally exploded. He rose to his feet and glared fiercely at her. "Who the hell do you think you are? The only person on the planet? What about me and the publishing house, all the people who work here who depend on you? What are you, the center of the universe?"

"Please, Robert, please let me finish. I know it's awful. I know I've done a horrible thing here. But I'm trying, I really am, to make it better, or at least okay. Please let me continue."

Robert stared at her with an intense emotion that she didn't want to think was hatred. She nervously watched him walk over to the side table, pick up his glass, and drain it in one gulp. He sat on the sofa opposite her again, to her relief, but sat stiffly.

"Go on."

"I met with the reporter and told her the truth…"

Robert closed his eyes.

"…and struck a deal with her, that I'd give her an exclusive to the story if she would hold off until I could arrange a coordinated plan. I'm going to confess what I did and try to explain to my email list and on my social media pages, timed with her article's publication."

"Do you know where she's publishing?" Robert asked, returning to the bar.

"*Vanity Fair* picked it up," Dory replied, and braced for the next storm.

"*Vanity Fair*," Robert echoed as he walked back to the sofa. To Dory's surprise, he didn't erupt again.

Instead, he grew quiet.

"Yes," she said hastily. "She showed me the draft and she actually really did a great job with it. She focused it around the evolution of the writing and publishing professions, aligned with the public's changing expectations of both the news media and the entertainment media. Or maybe I should say, what the public will accept from the two. And she talked about writing from the omniscient point of view, and tried to couch my narrative in that perspective. After all, everything in the book is true, it just didn't all happen to me, personally."

Robert groaned. "Yes, that option occurred to me right away. But there's no doubting that you didn't really present it that way, either. It's not omniscient, it's first person. Oh, God, da Silva."

Dory plowed on. "She also told my story of being refused by multiple houses and having it suggested that a memoir format would be accepted right away. She doesn't pull any punches that it was morally ambiguous to do, to say the least."

Robert snorted.

"But she does present it in the context of the struggling artist trying to gain an entrée to the market, and what a massive challenge that is these days. She even briefly tracks the writer's career choices back to the Middle Ages patrons. Anyway, she also does present me in my entirety, as a complete person, to indicate that this is not normal behavior for me."

Robert got up and refilled his glass, a little higher this time, and glared at her, his eyes narrowed over his glass. "You're going to get me drunk before you're done, aren't you?"

Dory risked a small smile. "I'll try not to. So, I

met with Annabelle…"

Robert's lips twitched just a little. "I had a feeling that her fingers were in this strategy somewhere."

"Yes. She had the idea of the massive release of information, by the article, my posts, my emails, the works. And she absolutely insisted that I respond to every communication. Well, other than death threats, of course."

Robert winced.

"Do you think I really might get them?" Dory asked, eyes wide. "I sort of dismissed it, but you never know, do you?

"Anyway, I will probably be spending the better part of six months at least, just troubleshooting to get past this. That will include appearing on talk shows to deliver my apologies in person, which of course will advertise *Quitting* even more. Alongside the good reviews it's gotten, people hopefully will be even more curious to read it.

"And she is investigating talk shows I can go on, after the article is published, to apologize and explain. But perhaps the biggest part of the strategy that Annabelle suggested was…" She peeked at Robert and took a deep breath. "To offer my next book at half price to my mailing list."

Robert gasped.

"Just for a period of time!" Dory hastily added. "And since it's fiction, any doubts about me will not apply. An 'if you liked me before, you'll love me now' kind of thing. The idea is that when I post the offer on social media, it could massively increase my mailing list and therefore my readership and the market for this and subsequent books. Annabelle thinks that people love to forgive the true penitent—after they give them a hard time, which is what the talk show appearances are about—and will come around. I'll probably take a hit, but she doesn't expect it to be permanent."

"And you expect me to underwrite this?" Robert asked, aghast.

"Well, no," Dory responded. "I'd carry the load from my payout on previous sales, which is why it has to be time-limited. I can't subsidize it forever. But I did hope that maybe you and I could figure something out to build on Annabelle's ideas that might be a little less costly to my budget.

"I know that I'm really rebuilding my entire writing life here, Robert. I am committed to doing that, and I will, no matter how long it takes.

"But even more than that, I don't want to lose my friendship with you," she said, eyes moistening. "We were friends long before you became my publisher. You're part of my life. I might not deserve it, but I'm asking you personally to please forgive my monumental blunder. What you decide to do as publisher is up to you and the business gods, of course, but please consider our relationship separately.

"There, that's it. That's all I have to say."

Robert gazed at her soberly, returned to the bar and took out two cold bottles of Perrier. Uncapping them as he walked slowly back to the sofa, he handed her one, which she gratefully sipped. Her throat was dry as the Sahara from nerves and her long exposition.

"Well, Dory, you can bet the business and personal aspects will be separate, for sure," he began. She nodded.

"But they are linked, of course, which is probably the only reason why I haven't thrown you out of my office and called my lawyer to begin legal proceedings against you, to separate my house from your tainted reputation with immediate and surgical precision."

Dory nodded again, her expression miserable.

"Jesus Christ. I hope Robby has taken you over her knee and blistered your ass. You deserve that and more. And thank you for not telling me how other writers have recovered from cluster fucks like this. That would have sent me completely over the edge. That was a very wise choice, if it was conscious.

"I know that writers borrow heavily from their own experience in their writing. Hell, I do, too," he said, raking his free hand through his hair. "But to blend fact and fiction and then present it as fact? You absolutely vaulted over the line.

"What to do? My mind is simply reeling. Annabelle has done her usual good job of trying to turn a turd into a gem, but I'm not so sure it'll work. And I could just kill you for not coming to me sooner. I am completely furious with you for presenting this whole disaster to me as a *fait accompli*, you ungrateful little brat!"

His voice rose with his ire, finally let loose.

"If we weren't friends, I'd have your ass in a sling right now. I can't believe you did this to me."

He stood again and paced distractedly around the office, tracing a path before the plate glass wall of windows overlooking the park and the city. Wisely, Dory kept silent as he paced.

"Okay, there are so many questions to be answered. First of all, you impersonated people. How many? Will they sue you for misappropriation? Me? What do you think? Won't they think my pockets are deeper? Will they come after you and/or me legally for a share of the royalties? I'll have to bring in our attorneys, thank you very much, at a zillion dollars an hour. And don't think I'll carry this financial load alone. I hope you've been saving the very ample proceeds from this book because, honey, you'll likely spend every cent of it just to fucking survive.

"To be frank, I'll have to ask our legal and insurance teams what our exposure is, whether we actually will have to sue you to make sure the house is covered."

Dory blanched.

"Yeah, you're getting the picture now, huh? This isn't Little League, Dory. You're in the Majors now.

"I don't think we have a truth clause in your contract. My God, I never thought I'd need it, with you."

He looked at her sorrowfully and she dropped her eyes, studying her clenched hands in her lap. She could handle the anger, but the disappointment was devastating.

"On the personal side, well, I just don't know, Dory. I've always known you're not the most level-headed person on the planet, but I loved you in spite of or maybe even because of that. But your stupid impulsivity in this threatens my reputation and livelihood. Not to mention my employees, who depend on me for their living. And your decision to just go it alone to fix it, without consulting with me, makes it far, far worse.

"It's going to take me a long time, if ever, to trust you again," he said gravely. "I'm sorry, but that's how it is."

Dory nodded slowly. "I understand, Robert. That's the absolute worst of it all," she began, but stopped when her voice quavered. She collected herself and continued. "Of course you need to protect yourself and your company. And I just want to repeat that I will do everything in my power to make this right. Including giving you my next book, which is even better, if you still want to be associated with me. I think it's the best thing I've ever written and it's almost done. You can keep the royalties. It's the least I can do."

Robert's eyebrows arched as he looked at her in a mixture of disbelief and speculation. "Well, I have to say that I don't know what to say, Dory. Part of me wants to say 'Are you fucking kidding me? You're asking me to publish another book of yours now? Do I look completely insane?' You are damaged goods now, dear, don't you get it? You'll be lucky if your writing career is not over completely."

He leaned back again. "But on the other hand, you'll also be in the spotlight for a while, and as P.T. Barnum is supposed to have said, 'There's no such thing as bad publicity.'"

Dory raised her eyes and looked in his, a spark of hope flaring in her chest. "Yes, there will be a lot of publicity," she said. "I'm going to make sure of it. I'm going to throw myself on the mercy of the public and take my lumps, and I'm hoping that my honesty and penitence will win the day. And besides that, offering my new book at a huge discount shouldn't hurt. And I really do think, Robert, that the reviews will be very good."

"I want to see it as soon as possible," said Robert, and barked out a short laugh when she reached in her case and tossed a manuscript into his lap.

"It's not quite done, but I'd hoped you'd say that," she said. "I should have it finished in the next couple of weeks and I'll email you the rough draft after I at least spell-check it."

"Okay," Robert said slowly. "I'll consider your proposition." He eyed her narrowly. "You're absolutely sure that everything in here is the truth, the whole truth, and nothing but the truth, right?"

"Absolute fiction, not based on anyone or anything." Dory laughed in relief. "I swear."

"Well, we'll see," he said, getting up. "When will your talk shows begin?"

"Hopefully, right after *Vanity Fair* comes out," Dory said, also rising. She looked at him hopefully. "Can I say anything about the new book?"

"Uh, no," Robert replied, but then he hesitated. "Well, let me think about it. I'll call you after I talk to our legal and insurance people, not to mention our publicist, Carmen. I have to do that anyway, to develop a statement for the media. But if Carmen thinks a united front will go over and work for all of us, maybe. But only maybe."

Dory flung herself into his arms in a big hug. "Thank you, Robert. I really mean it, thank you. I'm sorry to be such trouble. I never intended it."

Robert sighed. "I know, Dory. I know. Doesn't make it any better, though. I'll talk to you later."

Dory left the building and walked back to the Essex with a spring in her step. There was hope. And "where there's hope, there's life," Anne Frank said. "It fills us with fresh courage and makes us strong again."

She would prevail. She *would.*

Dory sipped her coffee looking moodily out at the backyard. The work to assemble the *Mea Culpa* Project was going well, and Annabelle had miraculously and quite expeditiously booked her a slot on the morning show *Perspective* on July second, the day after *Vanity Fair* would come out. Then she would be ready to go. She would just have to drop in the all-important offer to her emails and posts, given Robert's blessing. Everything was just hanging in the balance.

What about Robert? What I can say going forward has everything to do with how he's going to handle this. As if the gods had heard her, the phone rang. Picking it up, she felt a chill down her spine when she heard Robert's voice.

"Well, good morning, prodigal child," he said. "I imagine you're already preparing for your appearance on *Perspective*?"

"Yes, emotionally and psychologically," Dory replied. "As well as all my social media work. But you have everything to do with what I'm going to say. Have you reached a decision, Robert?"

"Yes, and I want you to know that you owe me the karma of a lot of lost good nights' sleep," he said. "But I spoke with all our legal, insurance, and publicity people, and at least for the first two, we're covered. That is to say, you're pretty much on your own, kid, if anyone comes after you for damages."

"Yikes. Well, okay."

"I spent most of my time talking with Carmen, our publicist, and of course, even more reading over your manuscript."

Dory held her breath.

"And I have to say, with some reluctance, that it's wonderful."

Dory exhaled and weakly collapsed against the armrest of the chair next to her. "Thank you."

"Oh, yeah, that's your saving grace," he said. "I think it could hit the top of the charts for you again. You are unbelievably lucky, you know?"

"Oh, trust me, Robert, I know."

"Well, lucky that this scandal hit when you had another work ready to go, and lucky that you're talented. I'll give you that. And Carmen also believes in the 'no such thing as bad publicity' maxim, so we're going to go for it."

"Oh, Robert," Dory said. "How can I ever thank you? And I just pray that someday enough time will have passed that you can forgive me. Your friendship means so much to me."

"Well, just sell a million for me. And yes, let's let time pass, Dory. We do have a lot of history and that should mean something. Good luck on the show."

"Thank you, Robert," she said, and hung up. She stood at the window, heart beating fast, feeling as though she was holding her future in her hands. But it felt like a galloping wild horse, muscle and sinew fighting her for its head to lead her into chaos. It had felt that way for weeks. She was in full-out stress control mode, and the effort was getting to her.

Chapter Sixteen

Jill's hand clenched on the phone as Vivian responded to her questions.

"Well, Jill, we'll discuss all this in full when we get together, but I can tell you right now that Taylor has some common markers for a scam artist," Vivian said. "She's built a social consensus with her alleged LA investors to back her up, which got Atlanta investors interested, and she's apparently using scarcity tactics, like mentioning that there's only a few investment units left."

"Yeah, that sounds familiar."

"I've been looking into the producer that you named and don't see any previous festival submissions by him so far. Have you been able to find out if he has any agreements with any known actors for this film?"

"No," Jill replied. "She talks big names, but I've never heard her say anything definite."

"How about any more about Paolo Brocca, the director? He does exist, but I haven't been able to find any connection so far to LA. I might just call his company and see if they have any present work going on with someone there."

"Nope. To tell the truth, I haven't been pumping her too much. I don't want her to get suspicious. But I will raise the topic again. She says the investment window is closing, though..."

"See?" Vivian said.

"Yeah, I know, but maybe that will let me press her a bit without her suspecting. I'll see how it goes."

"Okay. You also should try to find out the distribution market, if you can. They might intend to go direct into DVD, Blu-ray, or electronic distribution instead of theaters. If so, they should have an agreement for a market to guarantee a minimum revenue from the film, no matter how it performs. That would be good, and it also would back up any borrowing they might do. It's sort of collateral.

"The main thing is, of course, you never want to invest more than you're willing to lose. Do they have any accredited investors other than you? That is, a person with either a minimum net worth of a million dollars or an annual income of over two hundred thousand dollars? How about a completion bond?"

"Oh, God, there's so much involved." Jill moaned in frustration. "Well, I'll do my best. Did you get the cup I messengered to you?"

"Yes, I did," Vivian replied, and Jill could hear the smile in her voice. "It's a little unusual, but I am already getting the prints checked out. You're certainly are doing good due diligence."

"Well, thanks," said Jill, pleased. "I thought it might be worth a shot."

"Just something to think about, Jill," Vivian added. "If Taylor turns out to be not a good investment alley for you and you're still interested in indie films, there are other mainstream vehicles you could take. You could be an angel investor making bulk investments in films, like through Film Angels in LA, or Get Real USA. Or Indie Vest Services matches investors with specific indie film makers.

"I'm going to get back to work. I'll explore her

Kickstarter account for one, and continue her full specialized background search, especially of civil case histories, as I told you.

"Oh, and there's one other thing you maybe should think about. If Taylor is planning a quick hit and run, we might be short on time to find out what we need to know about her."

"Good point. I'll keep it in mind and redouble my devious methods. And thank you, Vivian. You're a workhorse," Jill said. "A very *glamorous* one," she added. "But a workhorse nonetheless. And I couldn't be more grateful. Talk to you later."

Jill was a distracted driver as she headed for her gym. *I've got to get through this. I've never been good with sustained pressure. Maybe I should just toss Taylor. Why go to all this trouble? It's not like I'm planning to marry her.*

"Hmm, marry her," she said thoughtfully, as the germ of a plan grew in her mind. *Wow, if Taylor is as greedy and underhanded as I'm beginning to suspect she is, what would be the best vengeance? Oh, and it's more than the money. If she embarrasses me in front of the whole community, I'll be madder than a wet hen. I'm going to rip her jet-black hair off and find out if the roots match, and then I'll go on from there. I'll sue her to kingdom come until she's a pauper.*

A slow smile spread over her face, growing larger as the plan grew. *But what if Taylor senses a bigger payoff than a simple little scam? Like marriage to someone she thinks is a real moneybags?*

The longer she thought about it, the more gleeful

she became.

Oh, yeah. Perfect. And the big reveal, if she is crooked, can be done in public. Does that seem too vengeful? She chewed on her nail, contemplating the thought. *Nah. If she's up to what she seems to be up to, all bets are off. This could be fun. I'll start laying the groundwork when I get back from the gym. Hopefully, it won't take too long to lure her in. Bet Vivian would help me. And, even if Vivian finds out she's pure as the driven snow, it'll be time to break it off anyway. If I can even imagine that she's guilty, I don't need to be with her. Nor she with me, actually.*

"Hey, Viv, long time no talk," Jim said, answering Vivian's call.

"Yes, I know," she responded. "How is my favorite sleuth at the National Crime Information Center? When are you coming down to Atlanta to visit again? Or actually, there's a chance I might be coming back up there to DC with a client in the near future, depending on what you have to tell me."

"Oh, bonus! That would be great. Well, I don't know if this is what you're looking for, but I did get one hit on the cup's prints. Which was pretty weird, too, I must say. I don't often get a cup couriered to me to lift prints first and then identify them."

"I know. See the lengths the poor private sector PI has to go through?"

"Yeah, well, I don't know how poor you are, but I have to confess, it was kind of fun to do that again. It's been a while. Anyway, yes, I got a hit from a few years ago. These are the prints of Miss Teresa Stoddard."

"You don't say," Vivian murmured. "And how did Miss Stoddard end up in the NCIC database, pray tell?"

"Oh, nothing very serious. Check kiting, but it crossed state lines, so she came to our attention. I know you'll be amazed to hear that she skipped bail and disappeared before making her date in court."

Vivian laughed. "Uh-huh, imagine that. So, what was the date of said crime? And nothing since then?"

"Uh, let's see, it was in California ten years ago, but it spilled over into the Nevada jurisdiction. No, nothing since then. I have to say, though, this one's a knockout. Whatever she's doing, I'm sure her face is helping her along. I'll email you the info."

"Thanks, Jim. I'll wait until I see it, but I have a feeling I'll be seeing you up there sometime soon. Let me guess—she's a very dark brunette or black-haired woman with blue eyes?"

"Check," Jim answered. "Well, it'll be great to see you, sweetheart. Let me know if it pans out."

"Will do. Thanks, Jim, I owe you. Think about your favorite restaurant in town and I'll take you there."

"Oh, you always did know the way to my heart, girl. Take care."

"Bye, Jim."

Vivian gazed absently out the window at the fragrant wisteria in bloom as her email reloaded. *Boy, wouldn't it be great if it was Taylor? Everything could be so much easier and quicker.* A moment later, she had opened Jim's document and a huge smile lit up her face as Taylor's face looked back at her.

She started database diving in earnest. The civil suits database produced the tawdry details of the case that landed Ms. Teresa Stoddard so much attention. She called the attorney of record and persuaded him to dig out the old case records. He described a history of extra-legal antics that had progressed to juvenile delinquency early on and then, after high school, assorted low-paying jobs. She had managed to stay off the authorities' radar until her mid-twenties, when she and her older boyfriend were caught in the check scam.

The lawyer gave her Taylor's last known address and she logged in to Transunion's TLOxp database. That helped her track Taylor's moves from California to Chicago to New Orleans, and then to New York City. As she cross-referenced the addresses with each city's demographic database, she noted Taylor's apparently rising comfort of living. "Now, how did you do that, Taylor, or whatever your name is?" she muttered to herself.

Then she pulled up IRBSearch, one of the detective's best friends. IRB and similar databases like Transunion's, IQ Data, and MasterFiles could cost a bundle in monthly fees, but their massive data banks were up-to-date and comprehensive. *You get what you pay for,* she thought grimly. *The cheaper services usually have old information, and well-sourced data can show relationships among people. Now, that's what I'm interested in. Who has Taylor been hanging out with in the past?*

Interestingly, the trail grew cold in New York. The car that had so neatly allowed her to be followed was sold and no new vehicle was registered to Teresa Stoddard.

"Okay, so you changed your name in New York, or maybe even before," she said, and turned to IRB's advanced search function. Taylor's rebirth strategy had a few obvious faults, among them that she never did change her Social Security number and she was addicted to reading fashion magazines.

"Love you, Publishers Clearing House!" Vivian chuckled in a brief coffee break from her work. As she sipped, she used those two items alone to follow the credit cards of Catherine Harris and Olivia Robbins. Facebook and LinkedIn gave details of her increasingly fabulous life. Auto Data Direct detailed her vehicle history, indicating an only recent expensive taste in cars. "Hmm, how did you graduate so fast from a Mustang to an Audi, girlfriend?" Vivian wondered, marking down the registration dates.

Vivian followed up on the discovered contacts for the rest of the afternoon. For those affiliations that weren't otherwise obvious, the CLEAR search function gave her still more names, and she relentlessly followed each trail.

With the fading light of late afternoon, she leaned back in her chair, exhausted and hoarse from dozens of conversations. Some were more illuminating than others, but together they stitched a fabric of the quintessential con artist moving swiftly through an environment, reaping its riches, and then moving on in another persona. Taylor was quite the chameleon, seeming to fit in everywhere there was some profit to be made. Some whose lives she had touched had made initial moves to bring her to account, but for one reason or another—primary among them that she'd disappeared and they concluded the cost and time involved wasn't worth it—they gave up the search.

Ah, but they didn't have the fury of a Jill to impel them. She had to smile, if wearily, to think of Jill Hunt. She looked forward to giving her this rewarding news, but beyond that, she just looked forward to seeing her. She was a pistol, no doubt. Vivian admired her drive and humor and intelligence, and always came away energized from their meetings. No one had caught her interest in such a way for a very long time.

Wonder if this could go anywhere, she thought, rising from her chair into a long, luxurious stretch and preparing to leave. Whether it did or not, she concluded, she hoped to remain linked to Jill Hunt, even if only as friends. People like her were hard to find. Still, she didn't know much about her, did she? Would it be too weird to look into Jill?

Switching off her office light, she picked up her briefcase and headed out, contemplating the fine lines between information gathering and invasion of privacy.

Chapter Seventeen

"Is there smoke coming out of my ears?" Jill took a hefty swig of her martini and eyed her speechless friends. They had a lot of catching up to do since they got back from NOLA—how could it have been a month already?—and were doing just that at Two Urban Licks, their usual hangout.

"Uh, well, you look like there should be, but not yet," said Charlene sympathetically. "Why are you suspicious? And what precipitated it?"

"Well, I took a little license with Taylor's phone in New Orleans," Jill said, grinning. "I couldn't help but wonder who she was calling almost daily in LA, and was particularly interested in an unfamiliar area code that turned out to be in the Cayman Islands."

Dory's eyes widened at that, and Robby's lips tightened into a frown. Pensive, Charlene asked, "Did you ask her about them?"

"Hell, no!" Jill guffawed. "I figured I'd just do a little checking on my own and if it appeared harmless, then I'd indirectly ask. I put my old pal Wallace on the case. Well, actually, an associate in her agency, Vivian. Ah, now there's an attractive woman," she dreamily added.

"Oh, you're incorrigible, Jill," Charlene scolded. "You're still with one woman but looking at another? Again?"

"Hey, I'm not dead," Jill objected with mock

injury. "And besides, if Taylor is up to something, which I'm beginning to be really suspicious about, what's the harm of looking?"

"Ah, Wallace," Robby said, smiling. "Now, there's a redoubtable person camouflaged as a harmless little woman. A great one to have on your side. So, tell us about this Vivian, and what you've found out."

"Well, not a lot so far, really. I'll catch up with Vivian shortly, I'm sure." She waggled her eyebrows and her friends laughed. "I'll expect to know more then. But I've also been hearing disturbing noises around town about Taylor. Some of the people who were interested in investing in her movie project before we left town have dropped out, and no one is being particularly specific about why. But they're uneasy, which makes me uneasy. Even more so, actually, because I feel like I've been her conduit to potential funding sources here that she would never have had access to without me. That's why I'm so mad. The very thought that she might've taken advantage of me and could embarrass me just makes my blood boil. Nobody takes a Hunt for a fool."

"Well, hold on, Jill," Charlene said reassuringly. "You know, innocent until found guilty, remember?"

Jill snorted. "Yeah, well, if she is guilty, she's going to be one really sorry girl, I can tell you that."

"Yeah, yeah," Robby said. "But I hear you, girlfriend. Let me know if you need any help. But if Wallace and this interesting-sounding Vivian are in your corner, sounds like you're set."

"Ah, yes, Vivian." Jill smiled. "Now, I know Taylor's a knockout, but so is Vivian, in a very different way. Taylor has that jet-black hair tumbling down her back and those icy blue eyes, and she gives you—well, gave me—a feeling of danger and adventure."

"Yes, dear, and that's precisely what attracts you, other than the obvious, isn't it?" Charlene rolled her eyes.

Jill shot Charlene a look. "But Vivian! Now, Vivian is a class act. She could have gone to one of the Seven Sisters. I'll bet she did, but I'm not totally sure about her background yet. Hmm, maybe I should ask Wallace. Anyway, she's a little shorter than I am, maybe about five six or five seven, and she looks a little like Catherine Bell, remember her? The actress who played a lawyer on the series *JAG*? She's as gorgeous, too. Medium-length dark hair, sort of an olive Mediterranean complexion, calm dark eyes. Elegant. Subtle jewelry. A really good listener and clearly a very sharp mind. Wow. Just the total package."

"Not that you noticed much," Dory said. "Shoot, I'm surprised you don't have an x-ray of her teeth!"

"Oh, great teeth." Jill giggled. "Wonderful smile that really warms her eyes and face. You know," she said thoughtfully. "I fell in rapid lust with Taylor and went after her great guns without knowing much about her. It bothers me now that I don't. I won't make that mistake again, especially for such an unknown quantity. What was I thinking?"

"Oh, I don't think you were thinking much at all at the time, honeybun," Robby said. "You know how you can get carried away by your enthusiasms."

"Yes, I know," Jill admitted. "It's part of my charm."

"Uh-huh," Robby said noncommittally. "So, what are you thinking?"

"Well, that I might have dodged a bullet is what I'm thinking." Jill quickly riled up again. "At first I thought that a few of my friends might've just taken a hit in the recent market dive."

"Oh, yes," Charlene said. "Are you all right, Jill?"

"Oh, it hurt, for sure, but I will be, thanks for asking," she said breezily, trying to not let a flash of worry cross her face. "Anyway, I thought that might be why they'd backed off, but I've heard some disquieting reactions, or I guess I should say impressions, of her, and their financial advisers aren't very encouraging. It's made me rethink everything. And coupled with those phone calls—and oh, there was the text, too."

"What text?" asked Dory, enraptured with the tale.

"I saw a text from someone named Cisco who seemed to be coordinating her stuff in LA, who asked how it was going with 'the subject.'"

"Subject? That's a different word to use," exclaimed Dory. "What the hell?"

"Yeah, that's what I thought, too," Jill replied grimly. "Really odd word to use. The only one worse might be 'mark.' So my antennae are tingling on full alert these days. Anyway, that's my story. What's up with you guys?"

All eyes turned deliberately to Dory and then Robby. Dory blushed and even Robby squirmed in her seat, and she turned to Dory.

"Oh, guys, it's a long story, and not a happy one," Dory said. "I'm so embarrassed to even tell it. I'm afraid to, in fact. I don't want you to think badly of me. But even so, you have to know, because it'll be public knowledge sooner or later. Probably sooner."

"Oh, lord, Dory, what have you gotten yourself into this time?" Charlene burst out, surprising even herself with her bluntness.

Dory looked down at her fingers, spread out on the table, and told her tale. When she finished, she looked up at her friends pleadingly. "I'm so sorry, you guys. I never thought I'd deceive anyone like this, least of all my closest friends. I really thought the book would just languish in sales and nothing would come of it, but ever since it sold well I've been living in dread. I am so sorry. All I can ask is for your forgiveness, and promise I'll never do anything like that again."

The table was quiet for a moment and then Robby said, "As you might guess, that's what's been going on with us. We're working it out. Won't be easy, but we will."

Charlene sighed. "Life is like that, isn't it? I've seen more cases before me involving people who wound up doing something they never thought they'd do. I'm sorry you've been going through this alone, Dory. I'm sure all of us would have loved to help if we could." She looked around to nods. "And we still would. I imagine you're going to have to soldier through this pretty much by yourself, but if we can help, we will. We still love you, sweetie. We know you're not perfect. Neither is any one of us. So, what are you going to do?"

Dory hiccupped and wiped at the tears threatening to spill.

"Oh, lord, there she goes," Charlene said, laughing and handing her a tissue. "Chill, girl. It'll be okay."

Dory thanked them in a shaky voice and then told them of her meeting with Annabelle and the reporter.

"Oh, good girl," said Jill. "You want to have the best experts on your side and Annabelle sounds great. And your approach to the reporter was a perfect win-win. Go, fight, win, girl! And if you need any help at all, moral support or financial, you hop on the phone to me PDQ, you hear?"

"Yes, I hear," Dory said, looking around at her friends. "You know, I just love you guys."

"Us, too, sweetheart. Us, too," Charlene said, smiling at her.

Jill turned her eyes to Charlene. "Okay, your turn, Char. What's been happening with you? How's the election going?" Her eyebrows arched as she watched her friend go pale. "What? What on earth? Something's up. Now what?" she exclaimed, looking around the table. "Is everybody dealing with drama these days?"

"It would seem so," Charlene quietly responded. "Well, yeah, it's my turn. And Dory, this should make you feel better. Remember in New Orleans when the fortune teller said we all had secrets? Well, I have one, too, that I never told anyone about."

Jill's and Dory's eyes widened and they leaned forward in their seats.

"When I was in college I was utterly broke all the time. I worked multiple jobs but usually had barely enough for tuition and lodging. Food was usually ramen, except for when I worked in restaurants and managed to score one good meal a day. So, I had to do some, uh, extracurricular work to make ends meet."

"Extracurricular?" asked Dory, round-eyed again. "You mean..."

"No," Charlene hastily replied. "I never did anything illegal. I never could have passed the Bar background check, or certainly the one for judge, if I had."

"Oh, right," said Dory, sounding just a little disappointed, which made everyone laugh.

All eyes turned back to Charlene and she forged

on. "I was a party girl. I'd go to kegs and bachelor parties and dance for dollars, come out of a cake, whatever the boys needed to whoop it up. I had a number of referral sources, like the college secretaries who knew the social goings-on. But I never prostituted myself. Still, it wasn't my most sterling employment, so I kept it a secret all these years.

"Trouble is, the past came back to haunt me. One of my referral sources was a woman who tended bar in the town. Somehow, she seems to have kept track of me and she's trying to blackmail me now to keep my secret."

"No!" Jill gasped. "Oh, that bitch. Call the police, right, Robby?"

Robby paused. "Well, I'm sort of involved in this now, too."

"What? You are? Do tell," Jill said.

"My old partner and I are investigating this woman, Connie, for Charlene. Our hope is that we can find out enough about her to make her call it all off."

"Good grief," Jill said. "What else could possibly—oh, I know better than to even ask that. You always find out 'what else' could go wrong. My God, we've all been in a whirlwind lately, haven't we? Have you found anything out? Oh, wait a minute, this calls for another round."

She signaled the waiter and put in the order.

"Nothing yet, but we're on the trail," Robby reported.

"And I'm so grateful," added Charlene. "You're right, Jill, it makes all the difference to have experts on your side. I'd pretty much decided that I'd chuck the election if I needed to. I wasn't going to have that kind of threat hanging over me for the rest of my life. But maybe I won't have to now."

"Damn straight," said Dory. "Living the up-front life is the only way to go. I am a fervent believer now."

The drinks arrived. The group toasted to an end to trouble and inspected their menus to order dinner.

Charlene glanced speculatively at Jill. She couldn't help but wonder about her real status. She seemed edgy, off-kilter. While she'd always been the least tranquil of the four, there seemed to be something more—beyond Taylor—eating at her. Charlene thought of her gambling in New Orleans and her seeming dismissal of the recent market downturn, and just had to wonder. She had inherited wealth, but she had always been pretty free with it. What was her status now?

And was Jill still hiding something? Maybe not just from her friends, but from herself, too? Charlene frowned, sinking into thought amid the background noise of her friends' voices. She had been in law practice and on the bench long enough to know how devastating addiction could be, and gambling was as fierce as any chemical addiction. Jill always was a risk-taker, something she suspected Taylor had quickly tapped into and encouraged. And she was emotionally volatile at the best of times, often swinging from a high to a low. Add to that that no other addiction had as high a suicide rate as gambling—twice as high, in fact, with about one in five gambling addicts trying to kill themselves—and it was clear that Jill was wandering in potentially dangerous territory. She had been seriously down in the dumps before she met Taylor and her

Svengali ways, and now she seemed too tightly wound in merriment, almost a little manic. *Worrisome,* Charlene thought.

Finally, there was something just wrong about Taylor. She was too smooth and secretive. *I need to feel like I'm doing something about this. Maybe I should ask Robby about checking into Taylor. Oh, lord, that's not the first time I've thought that. When am I going to actually do it? Tomorrow. I'll do it tomorrow.* Feeling better, she turned her attention back to the menu.

Later, Jill glanced down at the speedometer and gasped in surprise. "How did I get up to eighty? Thinking about that potential snake in the grass, Taylor, that's how. What is she up to? I can't wait to hear from Vivian tomorrow. Oh, yes, Vivian..." As she slowed her car, she consciously tried to calm herself at the same time. "I need a clear head to think about what to do," she said to herself. Thinking of Vivian calmed her and made that easier, so she indulged for a while. She thought of her in her trim business suit, then tried to imagine her in jeans and a shirt, then a bathing suit, then a sexy peignoir, then... "Oh, cut it out, girl," she scolded herself. "You'll be speeding again before you know it."

The following morning, Vivian stared absently at the red light that kept her from completing her journey to work. It was maddening; her building entrance was *right there*, but the guy in front of her had blocked two lanes as he tried to turn left in the busy morning traffic. "Come on, come on," she urged him. "Courage. You can do it!"

As she waited, her thoughts turned to Jill. It was pretty clear that she had both taken to Taylor in a major way and similarly been taken *in* by her. It hadn't taken much discussion with her client to spot the behavior of a con with her mark. *Classic,* she thought. Taylor paid attention and listened to Jill, mirrored her words and actions, flattered and shared supposed confidences with her. That made Jill believe Taylor trusted her, which honored Jill and further strengthened their bond. She borrowed money from her and paid her back promptly, proving her trustworthiness, so Jill felt guilty that she even suspected Taylor. *And it doesn't hurt that she apparently is a tiger in the sack. Man, she's got all the bases covered. If this movie isn't a quick scam, I'm a monkey's uncle. Or aunt.*

The hesitant driver finally turned and Vivian breathed a sigh of relief as she entered the parking lot. As she parked and walked into the office, she returned her thoughts to Jill. She was interesting in her own right. She was no dummy, but sometimes intelligent people were the easiest to scam. The slow ones had to be led to the brink over and over again before they fell. And Jill's character, although she couldn't be sure of this yet, seemed like the classic gambler. She would respond to Taylor's adventurous proposition, the glamour involved and the potential gains. As a fellow fearless thrill-seeker, Jill would have a hard time separating out her emotions from her own self-protective instincts. But they were still there, for sure, or she would never have come to Wallace and Vivian for help and advice.

Hmm, she thought as she settled at her desk. Lots of cons were enlisted from Narcotics Anonymous; addicts were among the best talkers and hustlers. *Wonder if she has any hint of that in her background? Although I'll bet she's got it pretty scrubbed clean.*

Vivian thought more about Jill as she sipped her coffee and booted up her laptop. *What an interesting woman. Full of energy and fire, blunt and honest, maybe a little too much so.* She had to smile at the recollection. *And a heart of gold, from all I've heard. Probably a vulnerable center to all that bluster.*

There was a clear spark of interest there when they met. That was interesting, too. Vivian, for all her social grace and attractiveness, was not a social butterfly. She liked people who were transparent, and too few were. Everyone seemed to have an agenda, or enough baggage to have cemented their view of the world. She liked more open-minded people, and she liked those with courage. Most people ran in the well-worn path that was created for them and they assumed, or that they developed themselves from the treadmills of their life.

Who am I to be critical? she thought. *I could be describing myself. Maybe I gravitated to those people as a way of living vicariously.* She grabbed another kind of that *joie de vivre* when she switched careers, dropping out of her boring financial specialty to pursue a PI license. But while she was still attracted to the rebel, the outsider, she looked less for extremes as she aged. *Except for my last girlfriend, the biker.* She laughed to herself. *Her age was right, but her approach to life was just like her bike—hard and fast. Boy, was that a mismatch. No wonder I took a couple of years off. The peace was a blessing.* But the peace had become a little stale, she had to admit. It would be nice to have a companion again.

"Well, Jill and I will meet again and just see where it goes from there," she said aloud.

Booting up her computer, she sipped on her coffee and considered which gold mine of a database she should consult first. "Well, start with the easy ones," she muttered, and pulled up Facebook. No incriminating Taylor photos there, but lots of photos with celebrities, all possibly photoshopped. Thanks to Jill, she had the date of birth, driver's license number, and Social Security number that were the keys to unlocking the mysteries of Taylor Smith and her multiple personalities. The information in public databases was usually stale, but her driver's license record showed one suspension, which she might have to investigate.

She began her snooping with enthusiasm, particularly attentive to any indication of civil cases, fraud, or judgment recovery. She pulled up Transunion's TLO, entered Taylor's information, and watched the graph fill with detailed connections between her associates, court filings, businesses, and other noteworthy factoids.

"Hmm, interesting. She lived and worked in New Orleans for a time." She noted the name of the business, Phoenix Enterprises, to start a separate check on that, then noted links to New York City and Atlanta. Each led to a different company name but, interestingly, all had Cayman Island registrations. She spent the next two hours following their footprints and discovered another commonality: a board member named Cisco Navarrez. His post office box address in Los Angeles wasn't very enlightening, but a cross-check by his name was.

Mr. Navarrez seemed to have friends on all the continents, but they were concentrated in South America and Europe. His companies' names were generic enough to not indicate any particular activity but hinted at financial services. She began sleuthing among the Cayman Chamber of Commerce, banks and financial markets, and began to detect a trail between Mr. Navarrez's enterprises and companies in Buenos Aires, Lima, Luxembourg, Bonn, and Geneva.

Oh, boy, shell fishing, for sure. Just what are all these shell companies hiding? They all had an agent in common, a law practice in Georgetown with one of the vaguest websites she had ever seen. Essentially, whatever you needed in the Caymans, they would hasten to serve you. She cross-checked that with Taylor's Cayman number and, son of a gun, they were the same. She called the number.

"Good afternoon, Georgetown Law Offices," a female voice with a pleasant Caribbean lilt announced. "How may I help you?"

"Hello," Vivian said. "This is Vivian Rhodes, with Wallace…Investments," she hastily amended. "We are based in Atlanta, Georgia, and have a new client who is interested in investing in the region. Do your services include acting as an agent to assist in the legalities involved, and perhaps refer us to a financial institution?"

"Oh, definitely. Let me put you through to Parrish Diamond. He is the partner in charge of our foreign clients. One moment, please."

Twenty minutes later, Vivian had received an emailed PDF file on all of Georgetown Law's services, which verified her initial impression. She also had a personal referral to a bank manager whose institution's website offered the pleasures of "enhanced asset protection from lawsuits" and "an open door to attractive offshore investments."

"Uh-huh," she muttered to herself. "And a greased pathway to money laundering among other things, I'll wager."

Interestingly, Mr. Diamond could not offer any references. "Confidentiality, you know," he smoothly stated. "But I can assure you, we have many satisfied clients in the US, whose names you would undoubtedly know."

"I'm sure. Let me just ask you, are you familiar with Mr. Cisco Navarrez? I believe I remember him mentioning you, which is why I called your firm."

Diamond hesitated just a millisecond before apologetically denying any acquaintance with a Mr. Navarrez. "But you know, we have so many clients. It's possible he is one of our newer clients, handled by another partner."

"No, I doubt it," Vivian said. "He would be established. I thought you handled the foreign clients?"

"Oh, yes, I do," Diamond hastily said. "At least, certainly our established ones. I'm sorry that I cannot help you with Mr. Navarrez."

"Well, thank you anyway," Vivian said politely. "I'll be happy to review the material you sent me and discuss it with my client. Have a good day."

She hung up and rapped her knuckles thoughtfully on her desk, then turned back to her computer. Selecting the database with the best link to law enforcement, she typed in "a/k/a Cisco Navarrez" in the search bar.

"Holy smokes," she said, eyes widening as the

results scrolled on her screen. Then she did something she hated to do—went on both the Dark and Deep Webs. A few minutes later, she sat back in her seat.

"Oh, Jill, honey. I think we might be just in time, girlfriend."

She picked up her cell and pushed the speed dial. "Hey, Jill. Yeah, good to hear your voice, too. Listen, I think we should meet. Just found some info that positively scorched my eyeballs. Got some time to meet and talk?"

Chapter Eighteen

Vivian and Jill walked into Murphy's restaurant in the Virginia-Highland neighborhood, having sidestepped the freshly released middle schoolers hanging out at the adjacent park. They settled in at a porch table and ordered iced tea. Vivian took some papers out of her leather case and leaned forward to eye her companion seriously. "Jill, we might have stumbled into some serious shit here."

Jill's eyebrows arched as she squeezed the lemon into her tea and took a sip. "Okay, lay it on me," she said. "I'm sure whatever it is can be addressed by my army of retainers."

"Well, yeah, maybe, at least for the legal stuff, but it's the extra-legal activity that worries me. Taylor seems to have fallen in with some shady characters pursuing lucrative but highly illegal activities. To begin with, she seems to have been a small-time con, but then she met Cisco Navarrez. He's probably not any kind of kingpin, either, but he has some unsavory connections that I certainly wouldn't want to have anywhere near my universe."

"Yikes, really? Like who? And what kind of activities?"

"Like cartel activities. Like at least money laundering, which seems to be Mr. Navarrez's particular choice of vice. He's the front, the agent, but I checked out his various corporate entities on the Dark Web and their trails went to some creepy places. I looked a little further on the Deep Web—"

"I don't know what on earth you're talking about, Viv," Jill interjected. "I have heard of a Dark Web, of course, but don't know much about it. Isn't it for illegal activity?"

"Some. Maybe mostly, although legitimate sources are using it more to take advantage of its encryption, like journalists in censoring countries, and even Facebook, to reach such places. Interpol even offers a technical training program on it, for cybersecurity and simulated Dark Net market takedowns. So, the Dark Web is sort of 'invisible,' but it's massively larger than the regular internet we all know. That's also known as the Clearnet or the Surface Web, because it's not encrypted. But the Deep Web is even more mysterious and potentially dangerous. One Reddit user posted that he found a website advertising a hitman whose service charges went up based on the type of target. The lowest was for civilians, then police, politicians, and the highest was for kids."

Jill gasped.

"Truly evil people are on the Deep Web. ISIS recruits there. I don't go there if I can help it. And Mr. Navarrez is on it. There have been stories of people who were directly contacted by someone from a website they simply clicked on, as if they could actually see the person and communicate with him or her whether they wanted it or not. It's like getting grabbed up through the monitor. I wonder if Taylor has any idea what she's mixed up in."

Jill's fair complexion had gone a little paler at that story. "Oh, cripes. I see what you mean. Okay, we have to get out of that orbit ASAP. What do you suggest?"

"Well, it's up to you, really, since you're the link to Taylor. Whatever you do, I'd advise you to tread very, very carefully. I don't know if or how much Taylor knows about her associate's connections, but either way, it's not looking good. And then again, we have no proof that Taylor's planning anything other than what she's claimed. Innocent until, you know?"

"Yeah, but not until the noose is tightening around my neck. I need to think. But careful, yes, to say the least. Gee, when I got a little suspicious I thought Taylor would be at the most an annoyance to get rid of. This does change things a bit, doesn't it? Boy, can I pick 'em."

She looked at Vivian in dismay. "You know, I'm not a complicated person, really. All I want is to have a good time and do some good. I don't suppose that sounds all that deep, but I'm a pretty basic person. And, come to think of it, what else is there? I want to love someone who loves me back, and for sure that doesn't seem to be Taylor. Well, to be honest, I never expected that from her, really. I guess I've just been drifting along for quite a while now. Maybe I deserve all this for my lack of attention."

"Oh, bite your tongue. You haven't done a thing in the world wrong, so don't start taking its ills on yourself. You're a good person, don't sell yourself short."

"Well, thanks," Jill said. "I appreciate that. But yes, I feel like I need to do something, but it's all so catawampus that I'm not sure how to proceed."

"Well, I have a friend, Jim, with the National Crime Information Center in DC, who got me Taylor's original identity. He might be able to help us in a number of other ways," Vivian said thoughtfully. "Including a referral to the FBI. With even the limited amount I've been able to uncover about Taylor and particularly Navarrez, I'm thinking they might be interested in them as potential conduits of information to other people the FBI really wants. For all I know, they're already working on it, but I think it'd be nice to have their resources on our side.

"So, let's just go on with the investigation," Vivian suggested. "The more we know, the better. I'd just continue as you have with her. I don't think this'll go on much longer. We can decide on a course of action at any time. In the meantime, I've had some success finding people who have known Taylor in her previous iterations. Why don't we set up a meeting with them somewhere central, like Washington, DC, to discuss their experiences? And, maybe Jim could set up a meeting for us with the FBI to see if there's any interest there."

"Good thinking," Jill agreed. "The sooner the better. I'd put my travel agent on it, but it might be safer if you do it. No chance of Taylor finding out by accident."

"Okay, I'll get to work on our DC trip," Vivian said. "I'll catch up with you later. Call me if anything new emerges."

Later that night, Jill climbed the stairs to prepare for bed. Hearing Taylor speak as she approached the bedroom door, she paused and unabashedly eavesdropped.

"Well, it's going slower than I expected," Taylor

was saying. "But I'm still aiming for a half million and I'm getting close." She fell silent for a moment and then snapped "Well, I can't push the river, you know? You'll just have to wait."

Jill had heard enough. She turned and silently made her way back down the stairs and to her office, closed the office door again, and called Vivian. "Well, something new has emerged," she said tautly, and filled her in on what she'd overheard. "Let's go to DC now."

A short time later, her phone buzzed with a text. *Airline reservations in place, 4 p.m. tomorrow Delta 1453. See you at the gate.*

Chapter Nineteen

Jill sipped her Irish coffee as the jet glided over the national monuments of Washington, DC. "You mean, all of them are coming?" she asked Vivian.

"Yup. I mean, who would refuse an all-expense-paid weekend at the best hotel in DC?" she said. "And if that wasn't enough to attract their attention, intimating that we might be able to exact some revenge for them certainly did. It was the photo of Taylor that did it. They all knew her by a different name, of course."

"Yeah, to them DC is no big deal, but I'm sure hearing about Taylor piqued their interest. It's going to be fun meeting them all."

"Oh, and I'll bet this is just the tip of the iceberg," said Vivian. "Just wait until the authorities get involved. My sleuthing is good, but I don't have nearly the resources they do." She started to laugh. "But I am glad that I at least did have that buddy at the NCIC who could run her fingerprints. I still can't believe you did that. It was genius. That broke it open and made our work a lot easier and quicker."

"Well, sometimes impulses work out," Jill replied, pleased. "I wonder if she even remembers that little slip-up that put her prints in the national crime database. The charges were dismissed. I'll bet she doesn't. Okay, so who are we meeting?"

"You're going to know some of these names, for sure." Vivian ticked off a number of names linked to the country's most well-known families in politics, industry, entertainment, and finance.

"Wow, let's see, that includes New York City, LA, Atlanta and New Orleans, at the very least. She's really had a who's who of marks, hasn't she?" Jill said. "I have to sort of admire her, in spite of my spite. She might be a devious devil, but she certainly has a degree of skill, you have to admit."

"Oh, yeah," agreed Vivian. "It'll be very interesting to see what her total take has been, and where she has it stashed. My guess is the Caymans, of course, thanks to your phone-number-napping. But it'll probably be years, if ever, before her ill-gotten gains can be restored to her victims."

"And I'm just grateful to not be one of those." Jill smiled at Vivian and took her hand, looking in her eyes. "I owe that to you, my dear, and I look forward to showing you my gratitude in the days to come. And I hope that, once this wraps up, we can still see each other. You are great company, you know?"

"Why, thank you! And back at you, boss."

The final approach announcement came over the speakers and, as they prepared for landing, Jill smiled to herself.

A woman of substance. Gosh, would Vivian even have me? She's an accomplished woman and a real grown-up. My record's not so great in either of those categories. But she's a little quiet. She might like a little wildness in her life. Well, not wildness. Well, tempered wildness. Oh, who the hell knows. I just hope we can hit it off. I'm going to give it a shot.

An hour later, the limo delivered them to the door of the Willard International Hotel and they were ushered to their rooms overlooking the city's monuments. Vivian confirmed the other guests' arrivals, and the concierge reminded them of the private breakfast to be held the following morning. All the invitees had confirmed their attendance.

The two stretched their legs with a pleasant sunset walk along the Basin and then repaired to their rooms to freshen up for dinner. They dined on the patio of a small Greek restaurant, finishing the delicious meal with the sweet, sticky wonderfulness of baklava and strong coffee.

"Oh, my lord," Vivian exclaimed as they walked arm in arm back into the hotel. "I forgot to specify that I wanted decaf. I wonder if that coffee was leaded or unleaded?"

"Oh, don't worry about it," Jill responded, squeezing her arm affectionately. "It'll be all right. You might have the best night you've had in ages."

Vivian looked at her curiously. "Well, it's been really nice so far," she said. "But you might want to check with me again at three a.m. if I'm awake."

"I might," Jill said with a laugh, and they parted at her door.

Vivian unlocked her door and reached for the switch as she walked in but stopped when she realized the room was already alight with a low, subtle glow. Cautiously, she walked the short hallway past the bathroom and peeked at the bed, her breath catching in her throat.

The lamp was on its lowest setting, providing a warm, intimate illumination of the bed, covered in rose petals. On the table by the sofa was an ice bucket with a bottle chilling, and a small envelope next to it. In wonderment, she walked over and glanced at the bottle—an excellent Bollinger Brut champagne—and opened the envelope.

I can think of a number of ways to make this pleasant evening even more memorable. Call if you're interested. It was signed simply "*J.*"

Vivian smiled. *Ah, the coffee comment explained.* She fingered the heavy stationery stock and walked to the window, pulling aside the drape to gaze at the giant monument glowing in the night. She turned and looked at the bed and its fragrant decorations. She picked up the note and flipped it over.

The pleasure of your company is requested in Room 1501, she wrote, and slipped it under Jill's door with a soft knock. Rushing back to her room, she put on her silk kimono and opened the bottle of champagne. When the soft knock came on her door, she peeked out, then opened the door, only her bare arm visible with a glass of champagne.

"Do come in," she said sexily.

Smiling, Jill took the glass and stood aside as Vivian closed and locked the door, then took her by the hand over to the table. She picked up her own glass and they clinked them together in a toast.

"To beauty, inside and out." Jill looked Vivian directly in the eye as they sipped.

"The city and the hotel, or me?" Vivian laughed.

"Oh, there's a case to be made for all of the above." Jill put both glasses on the table and took Vivian in her arms. "But the most breathtaking of all is in my lucky arms right now." She kissed Vivian softly, then led her to the bed and slowly lowered her upon it. "May I tour, lovely woman?"

Vivian settled herself comfortably among the soft petals, then picked one up and gently caressed the face above her with it. "Oh, yes, let's do," she murmured, and surrendered herself to Jill's kisses and the night.

"Good God, how many dozens of flowers did you have to order to get all these petals?" Vivian asked, laughing, as she tried to scoop them all up and throw them away. "Although, it is a great shame to dispose of them."

"Don't know. I just ordered several gallons of rose petals, I didn't strip them. Why on earth are you doing that? Isn't that why God invented vacuum cleaners?"

"Oh, it's a little embarrassing, you know?" Vivian said, but she paused in her mission. "Well, you're right," she said reluctantly. "It would take too long to get rid of the guilty evidence anyway."

Jill laughed outright. "Like the maid would care. And besides, I think we already gave up the game when the room service attendant delivered our breakfast this morning.'

"I did notice his eyes widen a bit when he brought the tray to the bed," Vivian said, getting a little pink at the memory.

"Oh, baby, I'm not sure it was the rose petals that popped his eyes. More like it was sultry you lounging against the pillows."

"I doubt it, but water under the bridge," Vivian said briskly, recovering her equanimity. "I'll get ready, we'll have our breakfast meeting, and then let's go see that agent Jim referred us to. I think we should have plenty of time before our flight home."

Two hours later, their ears ringing with stories about Taylor-by-other-names, they had checked out and left their bags with the concierge. Their Lyft driver skillfully made her way through the morning traffic and cheerily wished them a good day as she deposited them at the FBI building door. They passed through security and gave their names to the receptionist, only waiting a few moments until their agency contact arrived.

She was a slim woman, looking to be barely five feet five inches tall, but she carried herself with such assurance that no one would likely disrespect her. She held out her hand and shook theirs with a firm but not overpowering grip.

"Good morning. I am Special Agent Deborah Foster of the Fraud Division. Thank you for coming in. Please follow me."

She led them to a small conference room and offered them refreshment, which they declined.

"Well, welcome," she began. "Jim outlined your situation, so I've also invited a Treasury agent and a colleague from the DEA to join us this morning. Frankly, your friend Taylor is of great interest to us because of her, ah, interesting colleagues. She may be just the entrée we've been looking for to link and therefore close a number of cases."

At that point, two other men entered the room and were introduced as the DEA and Treasury agents. Both wore sober business suits and plain ties, the type of garb to attract no attention unless one was looking for a federal agent. *Well, except for the sunglasses,* Vivian thought. *Why always sunglasses?*

"Pleased to meet you," Jill said. "And I'm glad to help. But I hope you'll understand when I ask, is there any risk to us in this? I have to admit, when Vivian told me what she'd found, I was a little chilled."

"Perfectly understandable," Agent Foster said. "And no, I don't think you have any cause for concern. We have been looking for one central actor, if you will, to connect a Mr. Cisco Navarrez to several of his colleagues in the illegal activity being followed by a number of agencies. I suspect that Ms. Taylor may have enough information to bring Mr. Navarrez to a bargaining position and, if that is accomplished, we may have further doors open to significant actors on the international stage. However, your role in bringing her to our attention will be private and anyway is unlikely to arouse anyone's interest, and you will have no further involvement in her case."

"Well, that's a relief, I don't mind telling you." Jill sighed. "So, what do you want to know?"

"Oh, this worked out well." Jill smiled contentedly as she sipped on her martini and viewed the scenery passing thirty thousand feet below.

"Yes, I'd say so, too. I don't know yet how the whole scenario will work out, but it'll be good to have it settled at last, won't it?"

"Oh, I have an idea for a scenario," said Jill impishly, looking sideways at Vivian.

"Uh-oh. I'm getting to know you well enough that I recognize that look as an invitation to something wild," Vivian said cautiously. "Are you hatching some sort of plan?"

"Oh, yes, ma'am," Jill exclaimed, eyes gleaming. "Well, I was thinking about what would be the best vengeance if she did turn out to be crooked. If what she prizes above all else is money, we'll just have to deprive her of it *and* embarrass her at the same time. If she's as devious as all that, I'll just have to make her think twice before she ever tries it again."

"What do you have in mind?"

"A wedding," Jill said triumphantly. "A big, splashy, invite-everyone-who's-anyone-in-Atlanta wedding and somehow unmask her right there, in front of everyone."

Vivian stared at her, open-mouthed. "Wow, you really go all out when you get mad, don't you? Seriously? Are you absolutely certain that you want to spend all that money on this?"

"Oh, definitely. She's up to no good and she had the nerve to target me, a Hunt! So sure, I have no problem throwing money at such a delightful comeuppance."

"Okay...if you say so. Seems just a little extravagant, but I guarantee you'll capture the social drama prize for quite some time if you do that."

"Yes, that's just what I'm thinking, too. I. Just. Can't. Wait!" Jill raised her glass to Vivian's soda water and beamed as they toasted to success.

"Oh, before I forget, there's something I'd like you to do for me, if you would," she added. "I'd like to add you to be able to access my bank and brokerage accounts to make sure that Taylor's sticky little fingers don't finagle my cash out some devious way. I don't think she can, but you know more about the world of electronic banking and fund transfers than I do. Would you do that?"

"Sure thing, no problem," Vivian assured her. "As always, better safe than sorry."

Chapter Twenty

"Okay, Charlene, it's true. Connie does have a daughter, and from what I've been able to gather, she's had a struggle raising her. But it seems she did a good job at it anyway."

Robby leaned back in the chair, sipping her iced tea. They were sitting on Charlene's deck, waiting for the cool, late afternoon temperatures.

"How you want to deal with this is up to you," she continued. "But I have to admit, I went into this thinking the absolute worst, and I've become a little more lenient in my attitude. It's not that what she's trying to do is okay by any measure, but I at least understand it a bit more."

Charlene looked quizzically at Robby. "Well, tell me about it."

"Jessie really went to town and investigated Connie, including contacting her past friends and acquaintances. I looked into the existence of this alleged daughter.

"So, Connie worked at that hotel bar for ten more years after you graduated, until the early eighties. She then got married to a long-distance truck driver named Chuck Brewer and moved to California with him. He seemed like an upstanding kind of guy and they had two children, a boy and a girl. Connie worked full time and kept their home, probably more or less as a single mother with him gone so much. Still, they seemed to get along well enough until the kids' tween years, when the boy started acting out, just getting into trouble in general.

"It's an old story. He fell in with the wrong crowd and before you know it, he's in front of a judge for possession. According to friends who knew them back then, Chuck and Connie took a tough love approach to him. Chuck took another job as a dispatcher to stay at home, even though that was a hit to their income. Connie doubled down to compensate, taking a part-time night job tending bar again.

"Things seemed to get better, according to reports, and the boy straightened up, started doing better in school. As a reward, Chuck took him camping in the national parks, and that's when it all fell apart."

"Why? What happened?"

"Do you by any chance remember the Trail Stalker murders?"

"Oh, God, yes, I do. It made national news. What does that have to do with Connie?"

"The murderer was convicted after killing four or five women in the same area and he's still in San Quentin's death row for that. But before the women, there were two other murders that DNA evidence later linked to him. Those two were Chuck and his son."

"Oh, no!" cried Charlene. "That's terrible!"

"Yes," Robby said soberly, leaning forward on the table. "It was. As you can imagine, Connie was devastated and she just lost it. She started sampling the wares at the bar herself, got fired from there and later from her day job, and things went downhill from there. Her daughter Danielle was only twelve at the time and the school reported signs of neglect. Danielle was taken by DCFS and sent to live with an aunt. This is a recent picture of her, from her school website."

Charlene took the photo and inspected it closely. She saw a young woman working in a laboratory coat, with dark curly hair and bangs that framed her similarly dark smiling eyes. She looked up at Robby, waiting for her to continue, an odd expression on her face.

"What?" said Robby. "You look funny."

"What am I supposed to do with this?" Charlene replied hopelessly, dropping the photo in her lap. "Am I supposed to feel sorry for her? To ignore what her mother has done, or tried to do, to me?"

"Certainly not, I would never expect that. What she's done is abhorrent and you have every right to be outraged. But you wanted to know her story, so that's what I'm giving you.

"After an expected period of adjustment, Danielle thrived with her middle-class aunt's family. She excelled in school and showed a real talent for science.

"Losing Danielle apparently was the wakeup call Connie needed, and she started the long climb back up. She went through a state rehab program and sobered up, got a job as a hotel cleaning lady and a room at a budget hotel. It took her two or three years, but she saved up enough for an apartment and Danielle moved back in with her. She continued to do well in school and, when she applied to several colleges' nursing programs, she got in with partial scholarships. But that funding fell with the state budget cuts."

Charlene nodded slowly, anticipating Robby's next words.

"So this is what I think happened. Connie was desperate to help Danielle finish her education and, unable to do anything to help her financially, she cast about for someone who *could* help. You apparently were just one of a number of people she either approached or researched. Given the amount of time that had passed, she never thought in a million years that you'd even consider helping, so she made up this crazy blackmail scheme. It's pathetic, really."

Robby stopped speaking and leaned back in her chair. The two friends sat in silence, looking out at the garden, listening to the birds' songs and the fountain splashing into the fish pond. Charlene tried to focus on her surroundings as she processed the story, moving from anger, to shock, then dismay and comprehension, and finally deep thought. It was a lot to take in.

Finally, she sighed deeply and looked over at her friend.

"Thank you, Robby. What a story. I have a lot to think about. And please thank Jessie for me, too. Both of you uncovered a lot of information in a very short time and I so appreciate it. I owe you both, well beyond Jessie's fee."

"Nah," said Robby. "That's what friends are for, right? And I have to admit, I've enjoyed being back on the job again. It's been a while since I flexed my investigative muscles, and nothing has really captured my fancy since I retired. Jessie's interested in my joining her, and I just might do it. Anyway, it's all thanks to your coming to me. Which if you hadn't, I also would've been royally pissed off at you, you know?"

Charlene smiled and nodded. "Back at you, girlfriend. Speaking of which, how are you and Dory doing, or should I ask?"

"Better. We're going to get there. It might just take some time, and she has some big, big hurdles to get over, other than me and us. But you know, one step at a time."

"Right. That's all we can do. Would you like more tea?"

"Thanks, but no, I'd better hit the road. Good to see you, Char. Don't be a stranger. Call anytime."

"I will, promise. Thanks again, Robby. What's the saying? 'A good friend is a blessing from God'?"

"Somewhere in the Bible, I think," Robby replied, giving her a big hug. "I'll leave that to you. I'm not that familiar with it, but I like the sentiment."

Charlene walked her through the backyard to her truck in the driveway and waved as she drove off. Then, deep in thought, she walked back to the pond and sat on the stone wall, watching the koi. *A blessing from God. Oh, that could apply to so many things.*

She sat there for a long time, watching the fish cruise the small pond in their flashes of gold, blue, black, and white, occasionally rising to nibble at the water before her in hope of food. She smiled, looking at them, then closed her eyes and raised her face to the sun. She thought about her life, its ups and downs, the lucky chances and hard work that had gotten her through. She thought about the people who had challenged her and helped her. She thought about the children she never had, nor missed very much, really. She'd never felt compelled to have a biological family of her own. Instead, she had dispensed the love in her heart in every decision she made from the bench in search of real justice, as well as on the beloved friends who were her created family. And on pets, of course, the current one being Aristotle, the enormous Maine Coon cat who ruled her roost.

Aristotle! Oh, lord, it's time to feed him, she thought, startled to notice the cooling temperatures as the afternoon waned. She walked back into the house and was instantly greeted by the thirty-pound soft-coated monster rubbing up against her legs and shepherding her into the kitchen. As she put his food in a bowl, Aristotle's rough tongue insistently licked her calf, only pulling away when she stepped back to put his bowl on the floor.

"You're a lucky cat, you know it?" she rhetorically asked him as he bent to his dinner. As if hearing her, he looked back up and swished his bushy tail a couple of times, as if to say, "I know, thank you, and now don't bother me, please."

Charlene stood gazing at the pampered cat and thought of Danielle. Her own life was so rich, she had to admit, everything she wanted and more. What fortune had blessed her so and given Connie so many trials? What must Danielle be thinking at this moment, wondering how or if she would reach her goals?

"'To whom much is given, much is expected,'" she murmured to herself. "Dear Luke, you got it right." Aristotle, finished with his repast, came back to give her a couple of appreciative rubs, then padded off to the open bay window to lick his paws and watch the birds roosting in the trees.

Squaring her shoulders, she picked up her throw-away cell phone and dialed the texted number in its history.

"This is Charlene. Meet me tomorrow, same place, at three o'clock. And don't be late."

Picking up her own phone, she dialed Robby. "Hey, sweetie, I've come to a decision," she said. "Can you meet me at the Big Steer again tomorrow at three? I'm meeting Connie again, and I'd like you to be there. Are you still a Notary, by any chance?"

"Sure thing, Char," Robby said. "Yes, I am. And I'm curious, of course. What are you going to do?"

"Well, I think I'm going to pay a little karma forward, but on my own terms. Thank you, love. I'll see you then."

After a restful night, Charlene got up early, put on her robe, and fed Aristotle. She brought her yogurt, berries, and granola to her office computer and typed as she drank her coffee and ate. With an occasional glance at LexisNexis, she was done in an hour, printed the document out and edited it. With a few corrections and additions, it was final and the signature lines were inserted. She went to her bedroom, changed into her gardening clothes, and headed out to the yard to do what she loved best. She was out there all morning until her lunch break, and anyone who saw her might have commented on her serene expression.

Later, showered and dressed, she drove to the Big Steer, and found Connie waiting on her, early.

"Hello, Connie. I see we're both ready to settle this. There is one more person joining us—oh, here she is."

Robby entered and sat by Charlene at the booth as Connie eyed her suspiciously. "Who are you?" she demanded.

"My name is Robby Martin, formerly a detective with the Atlanta police department." Connie paled. "And as of this moment, perhaps your worst nightmare. Or perhaps your salvation. Your choice."

Evidently deciding to go on the attack, Connie began to bluster. "What the hell do you think you can do?" she sneered. "A *former* detective means squat. What are you going to do? Bore me with your stakeout doughnut stories?"

Charlene reached across the table and gently rested her hand on Connie's arm. Startled, she snatched it back, and for just a second a look of fear flitted across her face. Her eyes darted from Charlene to Robby.

"So, a former judge and a former cop. Big firepower, huh?" she said. "Don't make me laugh. Come on, let's get this over with so we can all go on with our lives."

Robby settled back on the seat and Charlene leaned forward, speaking so softly that Connie had to lean forward to hear her.

"Connie. We used to be friends once. Casual friends, of course, but friends. I didn't see you as any lesser than I was, that's for sure. God knows, I was barely scraping by myself in those days."

"Yeah, but that was then and this is now," Connie retorted. "You've come way up in the world, haven't you, Judge? What would you know of hard times now? Do you even remember?"

"Oh, trust me, I do remember, daily. And even more so when I was on the bench. I would see people come before me and think more often than not, 'There but for the grace of God go I.' No, I never forgot, Connie. And that's why I wanted to meet with you today.

"You've been as horrible as I think you could imagine being, trying to browbeat me into meeting a real need that you have. I know what's happened in your life, and I'm sorry for it. But that doesn't give you the right to hold me up. It might give you the right to ask me for help, but not to steal it."

Connie's eyes shifted uneasily, and she was clearly nervous.

"Oh, right, I'm so sure," she said, shifting in her seat. "What, you would give a rat's ass about me?"

"Well, it's more complicated than that," Charlene replied quietly. "It's everything, really. It's the good fortune that I've had, that I worked my ass off for, but with good fortune as well. I'm grateful for that. And from what I've heard, your daughter Danielle is cut from the same cloth."

Connie started up, almost out of her seat. "Danielle? You leave my daughter out of this," she screeched. The few diners in the restaurant turned to look and, glaring at them, she sat down again. "Don't you dare threaten me or my daughter, you…you…"

"Rich bitch? Is that what you think, Connie?" Charlene's eyes narrowed as she looked across the table. "Do you think I'm here to threaten her? Or you, for that matter? I don't need to. You might recall from what I said last time that I have no dog in this game. I'm settled. I don't need to run for office. I have a reputation that I don't think the likes of you can damage.

"But that's the thing. I don't think what I'm seeing is the real you."

Connie's knuckles were white as she clenched the table. A riot of emotions rushed across her face as she stared at Charlene, then Robby, then back to Charlene. She began to tremble, all her bravado seeping out of her wasted frame. She shook her head furiously as her eyes began to fill with tears.

"What do you mean? What do you want? I don't have anything to give," she said. "Dear God, if I did, do you think I'd even be here?"

Charlene's expression softened as she watched her nemesis dissolve before her. She had seen this before, when the menace brought about by desperation evaporated into sheer despair. Robby, however, remained stony-faced, looking hard at Connie, who refused to return her look.

"No, I don't imagine you would," Charlene said softly. "And that's just the point, isn't it? So tell me, Connie, what do *you* need? What is going on that you would take such a desperate gamble? I know already, but you have to tell me. And you have to make it right. You know that, don't you?"

Connie positively crumpled in her seat. Her thin shoulders shook as the tears coursed down the lines of her careworn face. "I…I…" She tried to speak but couldn't. At last, she did look at Charlene fully in the face, and contrition washed over her own.

"I'm sorry. I am, I'm so sorry. I just couldn't… think of any other way. My daughter…she's all I have, and she's such a prize, you have no idea. She's bright, so smart, and funny, and good. And she has a strength that's amazing to me, she makes lemonade out of lemons. But we have no hope left. She's going to have to leave school and her future will be as bleak as mine turned out to be. I just couldn't let it happen. I just had to try." At last, unable to go on, she fell silent and looked pleadingly at Charlene before dropping her eyes.

Charlene reached out again and took Connie's hand. She jumped, but this time she didn't pull away, just looked at Charlene, completely puzzled. She looked at Robby then. "I'm sorry to you, too. I've been a completely miserable person for months now, dumping on people who didn't deserve it. I don't even know you. I shouldn't have been so awful. And I'm not just saying that because you probably still have friends who could in fact come in and arrest my ass."

Robby, surprised, barked out a laugh. "Yes, ma'am, yes I do," she said. "But I'm not doing that just yet. And maybe not later, either. It all depends on this fine woman here."

Connie turned her gaze back on Charlene, bringing herself under control. Withdrawing her hand from Charlene's, she said, "Well, you've got me by the short hairs, Charlene. All I can do is apologize. What are you going to do?"

Charlene's lips curled into a little smile. "By the short hairs. Oh, Connie, now I remember the real you." She started to chuckle as Connie looked on in growing amazement. "That's one of the things I always liked about you. You were earthy and practical and honest, and you never beat around the bush. And you did care about me, I remember that. You knew the straits I was in and you helped. Yes, I gave some of the money to you, but you didn't have to get involved in my troubles at all. You were nice to me at a time when a lot of people...well, looked down on me. And I appreciated it.

"And I'm glad you apologized to Robby, because it's her and her friend's doing that brought me up to date on your life. It's been hard, hasn't it?"

She looked sympathetically at Connie, whose eyes filled again. She just nodded and looked down. "It has," she acknowledged in a whisper. "There were many times when I just didn't want to go on. And if it hadn't been for Danielle, I surely wouldn't have."

Charlene nodded. "I understand. So I'll ask you again, Connie, what do you want?"

Connie looked up and her eyes flashed. "Oh, God, there's only one thing in this whole world that I want," she declared. "I want my daughter to have the chances that I didn't have, so that her daughter can grow up without the pain she's experiencing, can have a normal life. Whatever that is," she ruefully added. "I want to see her happy with someone she loves. I want to hold a grandchild someday. I want…I want a good life for her. I don't care so much for myself, but that would make me happy."

"And what would make that happen, Connie?" Charlene asked, pinning her with an intense look.

Connie sighed. "The root of all evil. Money, of course. That's what put all this nonsense into motion."

"Well, I don't know about that," said Charlene. "In my opinion, money isn't the root of all evil. It's the lack of money that's the root. Well, not for everybody. But I've seen more than my share of basically good people parade before me for things they'd done that they would never have imagined they'd do."

"Preach, sister," Connie said.

"I've been blessed, Connie. And as you noted, I never had any children…"

Connie blushed furiously. "Oh, I'm real sorry about what I said. I don't think that way at all, really. I really had the devil speaking through me. Whether or not anyone has kids is none of anybody else's business. In fact, how anyone lives their life is no one's business, if they're not hurting anybody."

"Right. But no problem, actually. We all give in our own way. But I haven't had as many obvious opportunities to give as a parent might have over the course of a lifetime. Once again, you have Robby to thank for a comment she made that made me think hard about that. So I'm going to forgive you for trying to shake me down, Connie."

"Oh, thank you, Charlene," Connie said, voice trembling. "I really am grateful. It was such an unbelievably stupid thing to do…"

"And trust me," said Robby. "You are so bad at it." She glared at Connie. "You. Will. Never. Try to do that again, understand?"

Connie blushed again, abashed. "Yes, ma'am. You can be sure of that."

Charlene sighed. "Well, okay, as you said, let's wrap this up."

Connie moved to slip out of the booth. "Thank you—"

"Oh, no, we're not done, not by a long shot," Charlene said firmly. "Sit back down."

Connie stared, bewilderment and some fear returning to her face. "What?"

Charlene pulled some papers out of her bag and handed a set to Connie. "I have some documents here that I want you to sign. Robby will notarize our signatures."

Warily, Connie took the papers and started to read them. As she proceeded, her expression changed from defensiveness to incredulity to shock. When she finished, she looked at Charlene in wonder.

"You would do this? Really? Why?"

Charlene looked her dead in the eye. "Because 'of those to whom much is given, much is expected,'" she replied. "Because I've been given much. Because you gave me much when I really needed it. And because the sins of the mother should never be visited on the daughter. And, finally, because the Connie I knew is still there in you. I've just seen her and I want her back."

Connie's shoulders shook again as she wept silent tears, still staring at Charlene in wonderment.

Robby sighed. "Oh, lord, there she goes again. Waterworks. Do you think if she bent over from her waist, like with Dory's hiccups, she'd stop?" Charlene mock-glared at her. "Oh, okay, just kidding. This is just getting so intense, you know?"

Charlene turned back to Connie. "But don't neglect the first part of the document, right, Connie? The part where you acknowledge what you tried to do and swear to stick to the straight and narrow for the rest of your born days. And in return, I will pay Danielle's school expenses until she graduates and is gainfully employed helping others. Deal?"

Connie nodded and clutched Charlene's hand. "Oh, yes, deal. Yes. You're an angel, and after what I tried to do to you."

Charlene snorted. "No, no angel, I can assure you, my friend. Just a human trying to be what that could really mean. And besides, I like to invest. Danielle looks to be a good investment in the future."

"Would you like to meet her?" Connie asked.

"Someday, maybe." Charlene smiled. "Maybe at her graduation. Now let's sign."

Chapter Twenty-one

The evening twilight's peace was interrupted by the purring of powerful engines carrying the party guests to the valets at the immense front door. The mansion was alight with lamps and candles, and the smooth echoes of a jazz combo drifted up from the back patio. The event, held at one of the most prestigious addresses in Buckhead, was a benefit for the symphony.

Inside, the guests called to each other by name as they sipped their drinks and mingled, until the art auction began and the crowd moved to the ballroom. As they did and servants circulated with fresh drinks, a figure slipped unheeded from the back door into the busy kitchen. Taylor, dressed in a blond wig, starched white blouse, and black pants covered by a white apron, deftly picked up an empty tray and confidently climbed the foyer's curving staircase, following the arrow to the bedroom designated as the coat check.

"I'm your relief," she told the young man attending the room with a dazzling smile. "Go on down and get yourself something to eat and drink in the kitchen while the aristocrats are busy buying art."

"For real?" he said, startled. "I wasn't expecting that, but thanks."

Taylor watched him descend from the balcony and returned to the room.

Pulling out her smart phone, she clicked the

scanner into its port and eyed all the small, chic purses. Picking one at random, she pulled out the credit cards and began scanning. Five minutes later, her task complete, she pocketed her phone, picked up the tray, and equally confidently descended the stairs. She put the tray back on the kitchen table where she had found it and slipped back out the door. Walking rapidly down the curving drive, she reached the street and turned left, only to stop abruptly.

"What the fuck?" she cried in outrage at the empty space where her car had been parked. She looked around and spied the tow truck pulled over at the corner, and took off in a dead run.

Out of breath, she reached the truck and jumped up on its step to pound on the window. It slowly descended to reveal the annoyed face of the female driver. "Just a minute," she said into her phone. "I have a crazy person here."

"What do you think you're doing?" Taylor screeched. "That's my car."

"Well, ma'am, we were hired by the homeowners to make sure no one violated the street parking regulations during their event. They didn't want to annoy the neighbors."

"Neighbors be damned," Taylor shouted, her color rising with every syllable as she climbed down from her precarious perch. "Besides, I was only there, what, maybe thirty minutes tops? Release my car!"

"Sorry, ma'am, no can do. You are free to contact Abernathy Towing to complain, but I can tell you it won't make a bit of difference. Here's a card with their address, to claim your vehicle tomorrow. Gates open at eight."

"Are you insane? This is an outrage! My engine

didn't even have time to cool down. What's your name? I'll sue your ass. Don't be such a bitch."

She continued her stream of enraged invective until the door began to open. She stared as the large, tough-looking woman slowly climbed down from her cab and walked up to her, definitely crowding her personal space.

"Sticks and stones, ma'am. My name is Ms. Washington, although my friends call me Bear. You can call me Ms. Washington. And I do take exception to being threatened and, in fact, that's kind of like poking a bear with a stick. Do you really want to do that?"

She stared hard into Taylor's eyes, who stepped back again and decided to try another tactic.

"Look, can't we work something out? How much is the towing and retrieval charge? Can't I just pay you now? Then we can both just go about our business."

"Well, now, that sure sounds like a bribe, ma'am. And I've already called the tow in, so we can't just pretend nothing happened here."

"Oh, come on." Taylor dismissed her comment haughtily. "I'll double the amount. You can split it with the dispatcher. Surely you both can use the cash. I don't imagine driving a tow truck and dispatching them gets you much money."

"Well, now," Bear said. "Isn't that just too understanding of you?"

She smiled again, but in such a feral manner that Taylor stepped slightly back one more time.

"Come on," she said pleadingly. "I really need to have my car. Surely you can understand that. I'm just a working girl like you. Won't you cut me a break?"

Bear eyed her up and down, then stooped to examine her shoes.

"Hmm, aren't these Ferragamo loafers?" she asked, pushing herself back up. "You must be one really high-priced waitress, honey. And the party's not over yet. What're you doing leaving now?"

"I have an emergency," Taylor cried excitedly. "I have to…meet my aunt at Piedmont Hospital. She texted me that my father's had a heart attack."

"Is that right?" Bear said, rocking back on her heels and putting her thumbs in her waistband. She eyed Taylor again, her smile returning. "Funny you didn't say that right off, now, isn't it? I don't suppose you'd let me see that text?"

"How dare you?" Taylor shouted, freshly outraged. Who was this low-class broad to question her about anything? "I'll report you to your supervisor. I'll report you to the police, tell them you tried to shake me down."

"Aw, honey, sorry, that won't work either. For one, my supervisor has my in-process report right now, and my dispatcher has been on the phone all this time listening to our pleasant little conversation.

"Now, lady," she said, advancing steadily as Taylor retreated even farther. "I suggest you get on your very expensive phone and call a car service before Bear really loses her temper, you self-absorbed, stuck-up, privileged rich bitch!"

Taylor gasped, mouth agape and completely speechless at this utter disrespect. Bear smiled dangerously at her again, wheeled about, and hoisted herself back up into her cab. She gave Taylor a one-finger salute as she pulled off into the night.

Taylor remained immobile in the pitch darkness, not believing what had occurred. Everything had gone so smoothly until that fat bitch came along! She snatched out her phone and pulled up Lyft, disappointed to see so few drivers near the house's address. She prayed no one would leave early and see her standing in the street, then paced restlessly until her ride arrived.

Shit, what will I tell Jill about the car missing? Oh, hell, I'll just say it's a recall or warranty issue. What a pain in the ass. And that driver! She shook her head furiously. The nerve of that low-class bitch, talking to her that way. People just had no respect for their betters anymore. And she sure didn't like it that at least one person had, in fact, seen her. *Oh, no matter. Who would listen to her, anyway?*

Relief flooded her as headlights approached. "Smith?" said the driver, peering out the side window. "What are you doing down here in the dark?"

"Never mind that." Taylor gave him Jill's address. "Just take me home." She settled into the back seat, still agitated. *What a cluster fuck this night almost turned into,* she thought. *It was supposed to be an easy job while Jill was out of town. But calm down, girl. It's okay. All's well that ends well. No one saw me—except for that bitch, and she doesn't count—and the profit from tonight should be considerable. I'll get Cisco on it tonight. And actually, between that and the investors I already have, it's a good time to quit the scene. Jill's starting to ask too many questions and her rich friends aren't coming through the way I'd hoped. Tonight should take care of that. It's time to shut down the movie and move on.*

She looked at the night outside and willed herself to calm down. It would be fine. It always was.

Back home from her weekend in DC, Jill stared pensively out the window at the gray morning sky lowering over the yard in her Buckhead home. Rain coming. Maybe into her life as well as her geography. She shivered slightly. Tension was building within her about this whole Taylor situation, combined with her market losses. She felt jittery with nerves, but determined, utterly focused on bringing this drama to a close. But to do that, she had to create a little—well, a lot—of drama. She was far more looking forward to that fun, she decided, than nervous about pulling it off. Knowing Taylor's greed for sure now, she expected it to go pretty smoothly. She smiled a little grimly when she heard Taylor's car pull into the garage, bringing her home from the gym.

The stage was set. The stemware and mix for her favorite dirty martini were chilling in the freezer, the lights were lowered, and Jill welcomed her at the door.

"Hey, baby," she said, putting her arms around Taylor. "How was your workout?"

"Good, good," Taylor replied, smiling and returning the hug. "How was your afternoon?"

"It was okay," Jill said. "I looked over the paperwork you gave me on the movie..."

"Oh, good!" said Taylor, smiling broadly.

"And I still have a few questions. We can discuss that over dinner, if I can keep my mind on business."

"Oh, really?" Taylor responded, giving her a sultry smile.

"Yesss," Jill replied, kissing her on her neck as Taylor exposed it to her lips. "Umm. Uh, where was I? Oh, yes, dinner," she said, heading for the kitchen. "I made reservations at Chops on West Paces, for that nice corner table we like."

"Yay," said Taylor. "Sounds great. Are we celebrating something?"

"No." Jill said, returning with two frosty drinks. "I just thought maybe I hadn't been paying enough attention to you."

"Well, gee, I hadn't noticed, but if this is your response, neglect away, darling!" Smiling, Taylor took a sip. "Yum. Okay, let me take a quick shower and get dressed, and I'll be ready to go."

"Okay," Jill replied smoothly, watching her ascend the stairs to the bedroom. When she was out of view, she pulled out her phone, closed the library door, and sat in the comfortable chair by the window. Watching the light fade in the carefully groomed yard, she dialed Vivian's number.

"You still working, girl?" she asked as Vivian answered.

"Oh, sure," she replied. "You have things you want to know, right?"

"Sure do. And I'm working on that little plan I told you about. But it means I can't meet tonight. I'll tell you about it tomorrow. When can we meet then?"

"How about breakfast? The Landmark Diner on Roswell Road? Nine o'clock? Seems we have a lot to tell each other."

"Perfect. Nine it is. See you then." Jill hung up the phone and gazed out at the gathering twilight. *Odd how life goes on,* she mused, sipping the savory liquid. *I don't feel any older than I did at thirty.* A smile crooked her lips as she imagined her friends hooting at that in agreement. *"Or act it!" they would say, even though at times it hits me hard.*

Like now. How on earth did I get mixed up with someone like Jill? Honestly, sometimes I behave like a rank adolescent, really. She doesn't share my passions, except physically. But, well. She chuckled to herself. *Of course she does that very well. But hell, there's so much more to life than that. And I don't think she reinforces my better nature. Actually, since we met I've been even more reckless with my money than before. Although I certainly can't blame that all on her. It's like my stock and casino enthusiasms are self-perpetuating. The more I enjoy the adrenaline hit from a win, the less careful I am.*

She rose and walked out of the library to the kitchen, then out to the deck to enjoy the closing of the day. The birds were winging on their sunset flight, something she looked forward to every day, and their good nights rang out in a serenade to each other as they roosted in the treetops. The neighborhood, always pretty quiet, was becoming enveloped in the evening's peace. The smell of newly mown grass, damp with the gathering dew, merged with the scent of the thousands of flowers abloom in Atlanta. She breathed in the fragrant air, reveling in the gigantic garden her city became with the return of warm weather.

You know, this is what's real. All the rest is the crazy manmade window dressing that I get so constantly distracted by. I need to back off and regroup. I can't be a crazy ditz all my life. I'm almost sixty, for God's sake. Maybe I should grow up. About time, too.

But first she had to take care of the Taylor problem. Looking out into the dusk with considerably less equanimity than she had before, she felt her anger rising. When she heard the French doors open behind her, she gathered herself with an effort of will and forced her facial expression to be bland. Taylor stepped out, wearing an electric-blue raw silk sheath that matched her eyes and showed off her long legs, managing to be glamorous while still subtly casual. *Perfect Buckhead society lady,* Jill thought with just a touch of derision.

"I'm ready," Taylor caroled. "And feeling mighty fine after that martini, thank you very much. Shall we go?"

"Yes, let's do," said Jill. They walked to the garage entrance door, where Jill picked up her car keys from the china dish on the Demilune table and held the door for Taylor as they both walked to the car.

Let the games begin, Jill thought grimly. *I'm ready and rarin' to go.*

The valet looked discreetly but admiringly at Taylor's stiletto-heeled long leg emerging from the car as he held the door and extended a hand to help her out. She gave him a brief smile as she swept past, pausing only for the doorman and Jill to catch up. Taylor always did love a grand entrance.

"Welcome back, Ms. Hunt," the maître d' said, smiling warmly.

"Hello, Geoffrey," Jill replied. "Is our usual table available?"

"For you, always," he said. "But it will be just a moment or two. Would you like to wait in the bar?"

"Certainly."

He led them over the dark chocolate-and-white marbled floor into the warmly paneled bar, softly lit by copper Art Deco wall sconces.

"Another martini?" Jill asked Taylor, who nodded in assent as she smoothed her short dress under her on the leather seat. Settling into her seat opposite, Jill placed the order and leaned back.

"So, okay, let's get the movie out of the way and then we can enjoy the evening," she said.

"Oh, it's not that dull," Taylor exclaimed. "And

oh, baby, are you ever going to enjoy the LA parties we'll be going to, rubbing shoulders with the celebs."

"Well, that's not that interesting to me," Jill said. "I already know some of them anyway."

Taylor raised an eyebrow.

"I'm more interested in the financial side right now, honey, boring but essential," Jill said. "I didn't see a lot of detail in the papers you gave me about the company name this will be generated under, or much about the producer or writer. Have they won any awards? Or if they're new, where were they trained? Did Brocca's other movies come in under budget, make money? And what are the distribution plans for the money it makes?"

Taylor's eyes narrowed, but she smiled. "Wow, babe, you are a Gatling gun of questions. And you're right, the papers I have are more marketing oriented than business detailed. And you do need to know those things, I suppose. I can assure you that this is not a risky investment—I have a good deal of my own money in it—but I'll do my best to gather that info. Although, the window is closing, honey. Are you sure you want to risk losing out?"

Jill had been playing with Taylor's fingers and rings, looking down as she spoke. "Well, I don't know, to tell you the truth. I've been thinking about another investment more lately than mundane things like money." She looked up and looked Taylor in the eye. "You, in particular."

"Me?" Taylor looked startled. "What about me?"

"I know we haven't known each other all that long, sweetheart, but you seem to have become a part of my life. And I don't want to scare you, but I've been thinking that I'd like to make that a more formal arrangement."

"Arrangement?" Taylor stared at her in confusion. "What do you mean?"

"Taylor, will you marry me?" Jill asked smoothly. She drew a small box out of her pocket and popped it open to reveal a gleaming multi-carat diamond-and-emerald ring.

Taylor gaped at the ring and then at Jill, but quickly recovered. "Oh, darling! Oh, my goodness. I had no idea. Are you sure?"

"Oh, I'm pretty sure, all right. Say yes, why don't you? I know you have decades ahead of you and I'd like to share as many of them as I can. But I don't know how many I've got, baby…" Taylor made a muffled objection. "and I don't want to waste them. We can travel, play, invest, gamble…" Taylor smiled. "and do all the things we love to do together so much more easily if we were married. And I'd be sure you'd be well taken care of, if I should go off a bridge somewhere."

"Oh, for heaven's sake," Taylor said. "You sound like you've got one foot on a banana peel, Jill, and you're one of the most dynamic people I've ever met in my life. You'll probably outlast me."

Jill smiled. "From your lips to God's ears, baby girl," she said. "But the only thing we know for sure is that we don't know for sure. So, what do you say?"

Taylor stared at the ring sparkling in the box as a smile spread across her face. Jill could practically see the wheels turning and calculators whizzing in her brain as she processed the offer. *Shoot, Taylor,* she thought to herself. *It's a no-brainer. But this is one of those moments the rest of your life is hinging on, so you might want to take care, you know?*

"Yes, darling," Taylor said. "Yes! Oh, my God,

this is so wonderful. I just adore you, you know that, and I'd just love to spend the rest of my life proving it to you. Thank you for asking, darling. I'm honored, and so happy to accept."

Jill smiled broadly, took out the ring, and slid it on Taylor's finger. "I had a feeling you might—I mean, I certainly hoped you might. So, yes, this will be a celebration dinner, after all."

"Oh, you sneaky little thing. So that's why we're here. Oh, my, I'll have so much to do! When do you want to do the deed, honey?"

Jill shrugged. "Well, I was thinking sooner rather than later. June's the month for brides, isn't it? Why wait? I can contact my usual caterers and event planners. What do you say to two or three weeks?"

"Two or three weeks?" Taylor almost shrieked. "I can't be ready in that time. I have to find a dress and contact people and..."

"Well, you don't have to worry about the actual event planning," Jill said, soothing her. "Mostly just your own immediate needs, like the dress and friends you'll want to stand up with you. Any idea how many you'll want to invite?"

"Oh, not many," Taylor replied evasively. "Come to think of it, I've lost touch with most of my former crews, and as you know, I have no family. I'll be happy to just be with you and yours, lover."

"Aw, well, okay," Jill said. "Not to worry, baby. Let's just say a summer wedding. Maybe in July? It'll be a beautiful event and lots of fun. You just worry about yourself and leave the rest to me. Now, a toast to us, what do you say?"

Taylor's eyes shone as she lifted her glass to touch Jill's.

Jill watched her and smiled as she practically read her mind. *Ye Gods, she fell for it, hook, line, and sinker. That was even easier than I thought.*

Taylor excused herself to go to the restroom, and Jill watched her walk off admiring her ring as she went. *Boy, the next two weeks or so are going to fly by,* she thought. *She thinks* she *has a lot to do! I'm going to be working this twenty-four seven.*

She couldn't resist a chuckle to herself as she munched on her olives. *Oh, boy.* The heat had definitely gone out of her relationship with Taylor—did Taylor ever have any?—and she was finding that indeed, revenge was a dish best served cold. If it came to that, she'd be downright icy. "No one takes down a Hunt," Daddy used to say, and she'd learned it well. Especially not a tacky little trickster like Taylor. Dear lordy, whatever had she been thinking?

Oh, yeah. I wasn't thinking, was I? Well, I'll make up for that now, with lovely Vivian's help.

Taylor returned just as the maître d' arrived to take them to their table. Taylor strutted into the vaulted space like Marie Antoinette, head held regally and her ring hand holding her small purse up high, the better for all to see it sparkle. Jill shook her head and prepared for an evening of pure, unadulterated acting in the melodrama her love life had become.

Yikes, and that's not the only drama, she thought as she settled in the chair and accepted the menu. *There's my diminished fortune. I'll have to address that tomorrow.* She could feel her resolve firming to fix up the mess her life had become, realizing that it had many fractured pieces. Money, gambling, foolish investments, Taylor.

That was for tomorrow. For tonight, she ordered

a fine bottle of Dom Perignon and for good measure, another martini. Alcohol improved her acting skills. Tomorrow morning she would put the action in motion.

Later that night, Taylor stood in the shower, giddy with delight. The overhead light combined with the water to maximize the brilliance of the diamond on her finger, transfixing her. She just couldn't stop looking at it. *What an amazing turn of events!* Things just couldn't be better. She'd relayed the burglary data to Cisco as her parting present. *We both have enough dirt on each other that neither of us is a threat, and I already know he has another little chippy in training to replace me, anyway.* Now she'd retire to a life of luxury and ease. Of course, she'd have to put up with Jill's annoying friends, but she could just bow out from most of those gatherings. They were used to palling around as just the four of them. She'd just occupy herself with shopping and travel, on her own if she could manage that. Shoot, there wasn't anything she couldn't manage, she thought with a smile. She was smarter than Jill or any of them, unique, a powerhouse in her own right. And Jill was older; who knew how long she would live?

She suddenly stood still under the torrent as a thought pierced her mind. Indeed, how long did Jill have? It was something to consider. She should probably invest in a life insurance policy for her, not that she'd need the proceeds. Jill was certainly healthy, but sometimes unexpected things did occur. She finished her shower slowly, lost in thought.

Chapter Twenty-two

Calm to all outward appearances, Charlene could feel her blood pressure rise as she waited at the terminals' exit at Hartsfield-Jackson International Airport. She hadn't seen Lee since returning from New Orleans and, though they had emailed, texted, and phoned, she felt the jitters of meeting a relative stranger. Except of course that was compounded because this particular relative stranger also seemed quite likely to become an intimate partner. *Yikes.*

She shook her head as if that would help clear her thoughts. *Ha! Not to be.* After a long period with no romantic relationship, she now found herself in the pleasant quandary of dealing with a budding one. She was so drawn to Lee, with her twinkling eyes, compelling personality, and downright courtly behavior.

Well, you know what they say, she thought. *It happens when you're not even looking.*

Her reverie was interrupted by a fresh crowd rising on the escalator from the depths of the train tunnel. Recognizing the broad shoulders and crew cut instantly, she waved to Lee's answering grin and subsequent bear hug.

"Oh, lordy, cher, you are a sight for sore eyes. I have so wanted to feel you in my arms," Lee said. "I almost don't know what to do. Almost."

And with that, she planted a kiss firmly on

Charlene's lips.

Charlene colored, but responded in kind. Drawing back a little breathless, she smiled up at Lee and said simply, "Welcome. Come on, let's get you home. Do you have any other bags?"

"Sounds good to me. And nope, no others," Lee replied, still smiling. She swung her bag strap over her shoulder, tucking Charlene under her other arm. "I travel light. But I did bring one nice outfit in case you wanted to go someplace fancy."

"Well, we'll see what we feel like," Charlene said. "But I suspect that going to the lake will take up most of our time and I'd be fine with being very low-key the rest of the time."

"Sounds great," Lee answered. "Just right, actually."

They exited through the gleaming glass doors of Baggage Claim to the short-term parking lot, where Charlene raised the Audi's air conditioning to the max. "Whew, it does get hot when it's closed up, doesn't it?" Lee said, adjusting the vents to blow directly on her face. "But at least you don't have the dampness of New Orleans."

"Just wait until we have our predictable early-afternoon-or-evening thundershowers." Charlene laughed. "You might think you're back home. I swear, back in the day I used to think the TV weather people could just record the forecast in May and go on vacation until September."

"Now, that would be a good gig," Lee agreed. "But things are a little more unpredictable these days, aren't they?"

"Boy, you know it. I'm so glad I live here, actually. We have the four seasons without the awful extremes you see elsewhere. Like California—I often thought I'd like to move there because it's so beautiful, but their four seasons seem to be fire, flood, earthquake, and drought. At least our extremes, like the ice storms, are infrequent."

"Yes, I know what you mean," Lee replied soberly. "Global warming is not a joke. Or should I say climate change? Hell, we can't even agree on what to call it. If I remember right, 'global warming' was adopted by the politicians because it was less alarming than 'climate change.' Or was it the other way around? Give me a break. Playing semantics while Rome burns. Literally. I wouldn't care what they call it if they'd just do something constructive about it. Oh, don't get me started."

"Right? Well, let's just let that lie for this weekend, which is designed for fun," Charlene said, and they chatted easily as she drove along.

As they pulled into her driveway, Lee said, "Wow, nice place you have here. Are you a gardener?"

"Well, yes, with a little help on the maintenance side," Charlene confessed. "I love to dig in the dirt and have the reward of blooming things, but I'm not so hot on the mowing and weeding. It's a little embarrassing, but I figure I've earned the indulgence. At least, I hope so."

"Why not?" said Lee as they entered the lovely Morningside neighborhood house. "Look at it this way: you're providing employment for someone. Oh, my goodness," she exclaimed as they entered the foyer. Tall ceilings topped the ascending stairway and columns anchored the living room's opening to the formal dining room. That in turn was open to the big gleaming kitchen and its similarly large breakfast bar, and French doors let in the abundant light from the beautifully landscaped backyard.

"Well, my dear, you sure know how to live in style."

"Would you like some coffee or a cold drink? Lemonade? And what's your place like?" asked Charlene.

"Oh, lemonade sounds good. And it's not nearly as grand as this." Lee settled in at the breakfast bar. "But I do love it. It's not in-town New Orleans…"

"What?" erupted Charlene. "You told me that my place was on your way when you were taking me around town!"

"Well, it was," Lee said, apparently a little abashed at being found out in her little white lie. "I just didn't say how far."

"How far?"

"Oh, only about fifteen miles." Lee grinned at her aghast look. "No big deal. I'm used to it. I go in and out of town all the time, visiting my clients and delivering my products."

"You devil. I'll have to remember that you edit the truth at times, I guess," Charlene said. "But tell me more about your home and about your art."

"Ah, one of my favorite topics, my woodwork. I live in a standard old cottage in the countryside, practically in the bayou I grew up in, that I bought cheap and renovated myself. Took me a couple of years, but I love it. You just don't hardly find that kind of craftsmanship in homes now. Well, except yours," she hastily added. "Whoever did this house did a magnificent job. Real quality."

"Thank you." Charlene laughed. "Yes, it would be. It was the original area builder's house, slightly updated."

"It shows. Well, my house is a small jewel, just two bedrooms, one bath. But its real value for me is the adjacent barn, my workshop."

"Ah, yes, that's what I want to hear about," said Charlene.

"Oh, I've loved working with wood since my daddy taught me to whittle as a girl," said Lee. "It wasn't much of a stretch to learning to turn bowls. I just love it. There's nothing like seeing the warmth of the grain emerge like a living thing as you turn the wood. Well, it is a living thing. But it almost dictates the shape to you, like a wood nymph inside slowly directing you to let her out."

"What a lovely image."

"Yes, it is. I always felt that way with the smooth curves of the bowls, but even more so now since I've started doing wood sculptures. I finally understand Michelangelo's comment that the marble spoke to him, and he just let the image come out of it. Of course, I've mostly done the female nude form. What could be more sensual and inviting?" Lee's eyes gleamed as she boldly winked at Charlene, who laughed in response.

"Indeed," Charlene said. "I can understand that. Well, not to suggest anything, but since you've finished your drink, would you like to see your room?"

"My room. Ah. Yes, okay, that would be fine."

Charlene hesitated for a moment and they looked at each other in unspoken conversation weighted with meaning. Lee rose from her barstool and walked around toward Charlene.

"Ah, well, I guess this is just a little awkward," Charlene said hurriedly. "But I thought it might be best to get you settled in and then just let…things develop naturally. What do you think?"

"Sounds fine," said Lee, but she closed the distance between them as she spoke. She stood right in front of Charlene, holding her gaze steadily. The closer she came, the more Charlene had to look up, until she was gazing straight up into friendly but commanding blue eyes. Lee put her fingers under Charlene's chin and inclined her head farther, then kissed her softly on the lips. Once, then again, then again. Charlene responded warmly, then returned them a little more insistently with each repetition.

They stood there in such silent communion, the only sound the quiet hum of the refrigerator as their kisses became increasingly heated. Charlene put her arms around Lee's neck and pressed close to her, opening her lips and losing herself in the moment.

"Ah, the bedroom?" Lee finally managed, and Charlene nodded, looking up in a heated daze.

"Yes, please," she whispered. "But not the guest room. I'll show you the way."

That afternoon, as Charlene went about closing up the house to go up to Jill's home on Lake Burton, Lee wandered around looking at the framed pictures in the living room. She smiled at those of the young Charlene with her family and was impressed with her legal and judicial awards. Settling on the sofa to wait, she sat up abruptly, picking up one of the small framed photos on the coffee table. "Charlene!" she called.

Charlene appeared in the doorway. "Sorry to be so long," she said. "I'm ready to go. Just need to hit the alarm and—" She stopped in mid-sentence, taking in Lee's odd expression. "What is it?" she asked, noticing the photo in her hand.

"Who is this?" Lee asked, holding the photo up for her to see.

"Oh, that's Taylor," Charlene replied dismissively. "She's Jill's latest flame. Jill is the blonde next to her and the other two are Robby and Dory. We're old friends, except for Taylor. We were all in New Orleans together. Remember seeing them? That shot was taken by our tour guide in the St. Louis cemetery."

"Taylor," Lee echoed, looking again at the photo.

"Yes, why?" asked Charlene. "We're not crazy about her, but we don't expect it to last. Jill's got a track record for going through people fast, and the age difference between them alone has us convinced she's just another short-timer. But why do you ask about her?"

"Well, I might be mistaken, but I don't think so," Lee said slowly. "Unless she has an identical twin, I knew her as Cindy. Not well, mind you, but she was running around a couple of years ago in New Orleans with the crowd my better clients are in, and I saw her at an exhibit. Never was introduced, but she's certainly easy to remember. What a knockout. But…" She paused, giving Charlene a troubled look.

"What is it?" Charlene asked, alarmed.

"Well, she just disappeared," Lee said. "And it was just about at the time that a number of those people had their credit cards hacked. No one could say for sure, but it was shortly after a big gala that Taylor was at, too, and she vanished right after that. Everyone put in a fraud claim and closed their cards, of course, but the card companies had must have eaten tens of thousands of dollars in the end."

Charlene sank into the sofa by Lee, mesmerized.

"Oh my God," she said. "You know how you get a feeling about someone?" Lee nodded. "Well, we all had that uneasy feeling about Taylor from the get-go, but Jill seemed entranced so we gave her the benefit of the doubt. But you know, the way they met was at a cocktail party here that she attended as a friend of a friend in LA, so no one really knew her. And her profession, if you want to call it that, is promoting an indie film. She was hot on the trail of investors here and, once she and Jill got together, she had a ready inside track. I'm not sure if anyone's given her any money yet, but she's been working it."

"Oh, boy," Lee murmured.

"I was thinking even before this that I should talk to Robby about her. Oh, but dear God, I never seem to get around to it. Both she and I have been sort of running in circles lately. You'll meet her this weekend at the lake. Robby's an ex-cop, retired. She and Dory have been together forever. Yeah, I'll bring it up. We already briefly talked about it in New Orleans."

"Well, better safe than sorry, for sure."

"Well, let's go," said Charlene, but her face remained creased with worry as they went out to the car.

"Welcome!" called Jill from the front door as they pulled up to her lake house.

Lee looked around in wonder at the scene. "Man," she murmured to Charlene. "I know I'm being redundant, but you girls definitely know how to live!"

Charlene laughed as she gathered her things. "It helps if you're a trust fund baby like Jill," she said. "But one of the things I've always loved about Jill is that you'd never know she was. She had a good career that she loved with a nonprofit and she's never flaunted her wealth. Of course, she has an affluent crowd that she also knows, but mostly just hangs out with them at events for good causes. Bless her heart, she's humble, a rarity among the wealthy."

"Trust fund baby, no kidding?" Lee's eyebrows raised. "You're right, I never would have guessed until now. Now, you just stay there please, little lady, and let me get that door for you. And the bags. Okay?"

"Little lady? Oh, my, we might have to talk about some of your sayings," Charlene replied. But she remained seated as she gathered her things and smiled up at Lee when she opened her door. Lee took her bag and swung it over her shoulder, extending her other hand to help Charlene out of the car.

"Oh, my God," Jill crowed in delight from the door. "Chivalry is not dead! Charlene, where have you been hiding this gem?"

"In plain sight, but in New Orleans," Charlene replied. "You might remember, peering through the window at her? Or from the paddle wheeler? Jill Hunt, I'm happy to introduce you to Lee Childs."

"Bienvenue, Lee!" Jill smiled broadly as she extended her hands. Lee smiled back shyly and shook her hand.

"Pleasure to be in such a beautiful place," Lee said. "Thank you for allowing me to come." She turned back to the car to get the other bags, and Jill smiled approvingly and winked at Charlene.

"Well, girl, it's been a while, but at first blush I think I'd have to say you've got a real keeper there," Jill said in a stage whisper. Charlene blushed and play-punched her in the arm as she slipped past into the house. Jill opened the door wide for the laden Lee and directed them up the stairs to the guest room.

"Get into your suits if you like, ladies," Jill said. "I'll be down on the dock with the others mixing cocktails. It is after five, after all."

"Thank you, ma'am. I will."

"Oh, lord, please don't 'ma'am' me." Jill laughed. "It makes me feel like an antique."

"Yes, ma'am…I mean, Jill, thank you," Lee replied.

She climbed the staircase behind Charlene, gazing at the towering whitewashed tray ceiling of the great room below. A massive stone fireplace dominated the room and above it, she was amused to see, was a big faux-antler made of laurel branches.

"Civilized," she muttered.

Charlene turned to see what she was looking at. "Yes, isn't it great? She obviously could have had anything mounted there, but she found the branches herself in the woods and had them hung. It really does look like a trophy, doesn't it?"

Lee tossed their bags on the bed. "But better. I heartily approve. And done in my favorite medium. Which reminds me, I brought a little hostess gift for her. When do you think I should give it to her?"

She pulled out a small wooden bowl from her bag, made of white ash framed in golden pecan at its top and base, with a dark walnut bark rim.

"Oh, it's exquisite!" cried Charlene. "Why not give it to her now, down at the dock?"

They both changed into their suits, with Lee donning a simple black Speedo that emphasized her broad shoulders and small waist. She whistled as

Charlene came out in an off-the-shoulder flaming red suit cut up high on her hips. "Oh, baby," she said, taking her into her arms. "Uh, do we really need to go down right now?"

"Yes, we do." Charlene laughed and wrapped a gauzy floral scarf around her hips. "Be good."

They walked down the hill to the boathouse on a broad path of carefully groomed grass around enormous natural stone pavers. They paused halfway down, arm in arm, to just admire the view of the distant mountains beyond the closer hills, reflected in the ultramarine blue of the deep lake. Lee sighed and turned to kiss Charlene on the cheek. "This is, well, absolute heaven," she said. But that gesture was all it took to elicit whoops and catcalls from the dock's rooftop deck and, smiling, they proceeded down.

"Hello, lovebirds." Dory gleefully greeted them as she walked over to Lee and gave her a hug. "I'm Dory. Sorry, I'm a hugger. Hope you don't mind. Oops, sorry," she exclaimed as she spilled a little of her screwdriver.

"No prob, you missed me," responded Lee. "It's great to meet you at last, having only seen you guys from afar. I've heard a lot about you."

"All lies, I'm sure. I'm Robby. Pleased to meet you." Lee shook her hand vigorously, butch to butch, and both of them grinned.

Taylor was last in line. She extended her hand delicately to Lee, small smile on her lips. "And you must be Taylor," said Lee, shaking her hand and holding her breath. She didn't really think Taylor would know her, but there was just a chance. She kept her facial expression neutral but grimaced inside at the weak, fishy shake.

Taylor smiled distantly and said hello, bringing her left hand up to push back her raven hair. Or just maybe, to flash her ring. "Pleased to meet you," she said, formally. "Sorry we didn't get a chance in New Orleans. Were you born there?"

"Yes, I was. A genuine native. Do you know the city?"

"Oh, not really," said Taylor vaguely. "But we sure did have a good time there. How wonderful that you get to enjoy it all the time."

"Well, you know how it is," Lee replied. "When it's always there, you don't notice it as much as someone coming from outside. But there isn't a New Orleanais who isn't passionate about our city."

"What would you like to drink, Lee?" asked Jill. "We've got a full bar. What's your pleasure?"

"A cold beer would be nice. I'm not much of a drinker, really, but I do love a good beer occasionally."

"Well, I've got a great one from a local microbrewery," said Jill. "How hearty do you like it?"

"Oh, semi, I guess," Lee said.

"Glass or bottle?"

"Bottle is fine, thanks."

Jill pulled a bottle from the refrigerator and popped the cap off.

Lee sought out Charlene's eyes and gave her a slightly pleading glance, which Charlene understood immediately.

"Why don't we take a little walk to see the shoreline?" she asked, and Lee gratefully agreed.

"Oh, thank you," she said as they descended the stairs. "It makes me really uncomfortable to be the center of attention."

"Not to worry, sweetheart, I think the spotlight

will move off you now. You'll be old news. Besides, Taylor won't allow anyone to steal her thunder for long. Lucky she didn't recognize you."

They walked quietly along the heavily mulched path, deeply breathing the pine scent and pausing to seek out the kingfisher's flight after its strident call. As the light faded, the lake water began to darken, and Charlene suggested they return to the dock to see the sunset. Climbing back up, they were temporarily blinded by the rays of the setting sun. They stood at the railing as the sun sank, Lee sipping her brew and Charlene her wine, and they watched the clouds begin to turn pink.

"There it goes. Five, four, three, two, one, good night," Dory sang out as it dipped behind the mountains. As it disappeared, its still-bright rays began to seriously paint the already pink clouds. Those at a distance from the mountain tops became a deeper pink, while those closer to the horizon deepened further with their proximity to the sun. A collective gasp rose at the sunset's peak, as the pinks turned violet, then deep purple, and the orange near the sun became blood-red, with all hues of red in between. It was simply magnificent. No one said a word.

"Oh, how I love this." Jill sighed. "I'm glad we're all up here now, too, before the Memorial Day madness when it's just too busy."

On the lake below, the boats that had come out from the coves for the sunset began to slowly motor back home. The women picked up the happy hour debris, returning limes, lemons, and olives back into the fridge and bottles to the bar shelves, and then picked up their glasses to parade back to the house. Everyone but Taylor stopped on the way back up to turn for a last look at the quieting lake and the bats swooping to feast on the mosquitoes and other insects.

"I'm going to have a word with Robby right quick, if you don't mind, babe," Charlene said to Lee.

"Go for it," Lee answered, squeezing her arm affectionately.

As Taylor led the way inside and Dory followed, chatting with Jill and Lee, Charlene drew Robby aside.

"I've been meaning to follow up on our brief conversation in New Orleans about Jill," she said in a low voice.

Robby nodded. "I was meaning to get back to you, too," she said. "Actually, Vivian, in Wallace's office—you remember Wallace?—is working with Jill and she contacted me about her as well. I think the worry quotient is rising. Vivian is familiar with Jill's financial affairs since she's been working for her to check out Taylor, and she's concerned. I'm going to meet with her in the next couple of days to get caught up on all of that. In fact, if you want, I'll give you her number and tell her that you might call, if you'd like to talk to her directly. Who knows? She may be Jill's financial saving grace, one way or another."

"Oh, thank you, I think I will. I'm so relieved you're on top of it. Especially now. What's with this engagement? I haven't been that blindsided in quite a while. I'm mystified. And I've been so caught up in my own affairs that I couldn't even follow up before this. I'm so glad you are. If there's anything I can do, please do let me know."

"Sure will, not to worry," Robby said as they

continued up to the house.

They entered the house and settled onto the couches. The last light of day softly lit the massive wall of windows and the French doors were open to the emerging chorus of cicadas and crickets.

Jill brought out a tray of hors d'oeuvres and bottles of wine. "The ribs should be done shortly," she said. "I brought scalloped potatoes and Mexican corn and roasted asparagus to go with them. And of course, a fresh baguette. Oh my goodness, I can't believe I forgot to ask. Lee, do you have any dietary restrictions?" she asked anxiously.

"No, ma'am, I mean Jill, none at all," Lee responded, to Jill's obvious relief. "I'm your basic omnivore. Except for liver."

The group feasted messily at the deck table overlooking the lake and then, groaning, went inside to shoot pool in the terrace-level playroom. It wasn't long before yawns erupted and everyone began seeking out their rooms.

Charlene closed the heavy natural wood door to their bedroom and sank gratefully onto the Stickley bed. She rolled over and lit the Tiffany-style lamp on the bedside table and smiled at Lee emerging from the bathroom. Lee went over to lightly kiss her and said, "I just can't get over the lake view. I'm going out on the deck for a little while."

"I'll join you," said Charlene, and they opened the French doors to let the night air in. Stepping out on the small deck, they settled into the Adirondack settee and, holding hands, gazed through the pines at the darkening waters. The lapping of the small waves was soothing, and a distant owl's hoot made them smile.

"This is pure northern heaven," said Lee, putting

her arm around Charlene, who laughed.

"Hardly northern! Except maybe north Georgia."

"I know, but this is so far from the bayou we might as well be in Maine," Lee replied. "I could get used to this."

"Could you?" Charlene asked, turning to her. "Well, that's nice to know. Jill makes this house available to us whenever we want it."

"Oh, yes, ma'am," said Lee. "Only I don't absolutely need the house and this setting, as gorgeous as it is. I have a feeling that you and I could be in a shack in the bayou and still be happy, making good use of the time."

"Oh, you do, do you?" Charlene smiled and tilted her head up to Lee. "Well, you just might be right, kind Lee."

Lee's response was wordless as she gently kissed Charlene. "Good night, lake. Good night, owl," she said, and rising to her feet, she picked Charlene up as if she were a feather and carried her into bed.

The last sound to emerge from the room was Charlene's happy peal of laughter, echoing through the night.

Chapter Twenty-three

June came and went. Before she knew it, Dory found herself coming groggily into consciousness as her phone alarm's sweet music gradually grew louder. Her hand automatically moved to the side of the bed to touch Robby's warm sleeping body, but met just smooth and cool sheets. She came to with a start, opening her eyes to the lovely room of the old boutique hotel. *Ah, here we are again, New York City, July 2, yet another Truth Day,* she thought, feeling her blood pressure rising with the dawn of reality. *This is it.* She wished she could just roll over and go back to sleep and reawaken with all this behind her.

She wished Robby were here with her, but that had been part of Robby's reconciliation stipulations: she had to face the music on her own.

Sighing, she tossed back the covers, padded over to the coffee pot, and turned it on. Opening the closet's tall, heavy door, she eyed its contents. She had packed several suits for this second most important day (*Or is it the third? Third, yes,* she thought. *Robby, Robert—wow, never noticed that before—and now TV)* to match what her mood might be. There was black for penitence, gray for professionalism, dark blue for an I'm-just-like-you psychological cue. Sighing again, she picked the black and laid it out on the bed.

Pouring the coffee, she turned over the likely scenarios in her mind. Her appearance on *Perspectives* this morning was the launch of what she'd dubbed her *Mea Culpa* Tour, and how it went would set the tenor of all her activity in the months to come. Indeed, it might just sink or save her career.

Well, she thought as she sipped her brew. *There's no doubt I'm penitent. I just have to convey that along with a positive attitude. Tricky, tricky, tricky, but essential.* She moved into the bath and turned on the shower to a strong, medium-hot stream, raising her face to the flow. *I can do this,* she swore to herself. *I* have *to do this, if I'm going to again have the kind of life I want to have.*

At least the most important part is in process: Robby. Thank you, God, for her good nature. Please help me today! She muttered a strangled laugh, cutting off the rest of the prayer: "And I promise I'll be good forever more!" It had always struck her as ridiculous to think that an omnipotent deity would stoop to bargaining with a mere human, and yet here she was. *Just goes to show ya, when you're desperate, all the stops come out.*

And Robert. God bless Robert's kind heart, which I'm sure helped bring around his pragmatic head. Boy, was he ever right. I am lucky, beyond belief. At least, so far.

"One more major battle," she murmured as she walked over to gaze at the skyline. "Just one more day and at least the flagrantly public part of this will be over. God, what a relief that will be. There will be more, but at least the screaming-headline part of it will pass. Hang on, girl. You've got this."

She dressed with care and applied her makeup with even more care. Of course, they would brush it up on the set, but she wanted to present as perfect an appearance as possible even beforehand. Done, she looked in the full-length mirror and nodded in approval. She was the picture of respectability, neatly groomed, and smartly, if conservatively, dressed. The palette was set and now the performance was due.

She smiled at the doorman and climbed into the cab he had hailed for her, giving the network's address to the driver. Settling back, she ignored the bustle of the traffic, closed her eyes, and attended to her breathing. She drew up the image she always used for relaxation: the sun sparkling on the lake water seen through the green shade of trees. She willed herself to relax and envisioned a successful end to the interview to come. She hoped the compensatory offer for her new book would be the help she so needed to prevail. Breathing deeply, she envisioned any negativity as a cloud that was blown away until only the peace of the sun remained. *Well, maybe a few clouds will remain,* she thought as the cab came to a stop at her destination. *But a few I can deal with. Let's get that sun back!* She climbed out, paid and thanked the driver, and marched under the network's iconic symbol through the glass doors of the venerable skyscraper.

She checked in at the desk and was escorted to Makeup, then the Green Room to await her summons on set. While there, she checked her notes from the research she'd done on the three hosts. The first was Monica, a celebrity actress well known for her liberal views; the second was Candace, a somewhat conservative lawyer-turned-newscaster; and the third was Sophia who, among other accomplishments, was a respected writer and columnist. She expected the harshest approach from the last.

And she wasn't wrong. The knock came on the door and she was led to the side of the set, walking on after Monica's introduction.

"By now you're all familiar with the best-selling memoir by Dory da Silva, *Quitting the Closet: One Woman's Path to Gay Rights.* And you might have heard that it's not quite true. Let's clear the air. Help me in welcoming our guest, Dory da Silva."

From Monica, she felt curiosity; from Candace, a cold neutrality; and from Sophia, a barely concealed hostility. That was confirmed with Sophia's first comment after she was seated and welcomed by Monica.

"So, I hear you're a liar," Sophia said bluntly.

The audience whooped and applauded. Monica jumped in. "Whoa, wait a minute, wait a minute," she cried, holding her hands up to quiet the audience. "This isn't a lynching, you know," she said. "Can we maintain some civility here? We've invited Dory on to tell her story, not leap to conclusions and summarily execute her."

Candace agreed. "Yes, I agree. Our apologies, Ms. da Silva."

"Oh, don't apologize for me," Sophia said. "I just call 'em as I see them. But you're right, Candace. Ms. da Silva has a right to explain her literary fraud, if she can."

The audience erupted into loud murmurs again as Candace and Monica glared at Sophia.

"Sophia," Monica said smoothly "I'm sure if we explored your background as extensively as people with clay feet have theirs explored these days, you'd come out smelling like a rose, right? Or might there be an indiscretion or two lurking there? But everyone still deserves at least the benefit of the doubt, wouldn't you agree?"

Sophia had the grace to look a little abashed and agreed. "You're right. I'm jumping in ahead of the game. Ms. da Silva, I apologize. Please do tell us your story."

Dory had been sitting quietly as this dialogue went on, and sat up at this invitation.

"First of all, thank you for inviting me. I am, some might say, the prodigal son, or daughter, of the week," she said, looking directly at Sophia. "I really appreciate the opportunity to try to explain."

"Yes, please do, Ms. da Silva. The floor is yours," Monica said.

"Oh, please, call me Dory," she began. "Well, the short version is that I was a struggling writer. I had a story, a good one."

"That's this book, about the struggle for equal rights in the early days of the gay rights movement?" Monica interjected.

"Yes, right. So I shopped it to multiple publishing houses, but no one was interested. Until one day, a kindly editor agreed to talk to me, and I asked him what the problem was. I asked him straight out, was this just a crappy book?

"I was so relieved when he said no," she continued. "In fact, he said it was a really good book. So of course, I asked 'Well, what is it then? Why am I getting nowhere?' He asked me how I'd developed the story, and I told him it was actually my own, but not completely. I'd taken some literary license and adopted some other people's experiences in the narrative and just written it as a coherent whole from my point of view."

"Really," Sophia said, leaning forward. "How much of it was actually yours?"

"More than ninety percent," Dory replied. "And I swear that's the truth." Candace looked skeptical.

"So the editor was quiet for a minute," she continued. "And then he said, 'You know, if this was a memoir instead of fiction, I'd take it in a second. As it is, it's just too unbelievable to be anything but bad fiction, although well written.'

"I was thunderstruck. I couldn't believe that would make such a difference. I thanked him for his time and feedback and went home to think about it. The more I thought about it, the more it seemed obvious what I should do. Since it was almost all my story anyway, I should just rewrite it that way and see what happens. To tell you the truth, I really didn't think it would go anywhere."

"So that's what you did," Candace said. "Didn't it occur to you at all that this was a type of fraud?"

Dory clasped her hands in front of her. "It did, I admit it," she said. "And it's no excuse, I know, but I was so desperate to be published. And to have someone who would know tell me that I *would* be published if only it was a memoir, it just took hold of my mind and wouldn't let me go. I was obsessed. So I decided, what the heck, I'll just see if I can adapt it. I told myself it probably wouldn't work. But it did. By the time I was done, in fact, it was a much better book than it had been before.

"So then I thought, 'What now? Well, I should submit it somewhere, just to see. It'll probably be rejected again anyway.' I wished I could send it to that editor, but obviously I couldn't—"

"Because he'd know it was a lie," interjected Sophia.

"Yes, he would. So I went to a friend who had a small publishing house, and ran it by him."

"A *friend*?" Monica gasped. "You involved a

friend in this charade?"

"Yes," Dory admitted, turning scarlet. "Of all the aspects of this mess, that might be the worst. You see, I really thought it would go nowhere. I'd sell a few books and it would vanish into the literary sphere. But at least I'd have a title to my name, which would give me some cred and help me to promote my next book."

"Credibility. How ironic," Sophia said with no nuance at all.

"Yes, I know. But then, to my amazement, it seemed to hit a social chord and just took off. And as the sales piled up and Robert's joy compounded—"

"Robert Graves, your publisher," Monica clarified.

"Yes. He was so happy with its success that it got harder and harder to fess up and tell the unvarnished truth. And then I started rationalizing: 'It has a good message. It can do some good. No one will ever know, and most importantly, no one will be hurt. Robert will even prosper as a result. I should just let it go and hope it all goes away as sales slow and then die, as all book sales do, eventually.' But then, an enterprising reporter came along to do a profile on me for a local magazine, and she started to notice that something was off in my timeline."

"That's Gwen Fanning," Sophia said. "I read her piece this morning in the new *Vanity Fair*. She did a really good job, told the truth while still cutting you some slack. You're lucky."

"Yes, I know," Dory said. "But I told her up front that I wanted the truth to come out. I didn't want to live with this anymore. That person who was so weak as to do that and to rationalize it, step by step, and then just hoping it would go away, is not me."

Sophia jumped right in. "Since the book's release

you've been hoping it will go away. So this apology tour is really because you got caught."

Dory took a deep breath. "The 'tour,' as you call it, is necessary because I am serious about being accountable to each of my readers. But even more importantly, I've come to learn that personal shame trumps any sales or popularity. I've learned the hard way that I would feel the same way and would come clean whether the book sold a hundred copies or a hundred thousand. I've been miserable. My parents raised me with good values, and they'd be ashamed of me if they were alive. Especially since they would have been so proud of me to begin with, for being published."

At this, her voice broke and quiet prevailed on the set. A camera pan of the audience showed rapt faces, some appearing cynical, some sympathetic at the last statement. Monica's expression had softened and even Candace's skeptical look had lessened.

Dory collected herself with an effort. "So, that's the bottom line. I was weak, and I failed, with every increment of rationalization. And not just in a little way, in an epic way. If it's any consolation to critics of my ethics, with whom I have no argument because I agree with them, I have not had much peace in this past year. My conscience has always bothered me, and I haven't been able to enjoy a minute of the book's success. So, when Gwen asked to meet me, I threw in the towel and confessed it all. I just couldn't go on as a fraud."

"So, what do you think will happen now? What are you going to do?" asked Candace.

Dory paused again, then faced the camera. "That's why I'm here. I'm here to ask you, my amazing readers and the American public at large, to please forgive me. I am so sorry for giving you something that is not completely true. Well, it is—all of it—but it's not all my personal experience, and I let you think it was. That's not how my parents raised me, and it's not the person I really am.

"I want to make it up to you. I am going to email everyone on my mailing list a coupon code to have my next book at half price. It's almost done and should be released in the next few months. I wish I could just give it away, actually, but I can't afford that, so this is the next best thing. And, if I do say so, it's good. And it's complete fiction, so there's no worries there." She laughed nervously.

"Thank you for listening and I hope you will forgive me. That's all I have to say. And thank you, ladies, for allowing me to be on your show."

There were a few seconds of silence and, as Monica began to respond, someone began to clap. In a moment, the entire audience, with few exceptions, was clapping. Dory looked out in wonderment, then smiled as tears gathered in her eyes. She swiped them away and started to hiccup.

The three hosts also took the temperature of the audience, then looked at each other and nodded. Monica gestured to an aide on the side and whispered to him, and he hustled off the stage.

"Well, Dory, I want to say it's been quite a while since I've heard such a frank, honest, and raw admission of guilt, and such a sincere apology," Monica said. "I wish some of our politicians were more like you." The audience roared with laughter and applauded even harder.

"So, since our audience seems to have responded to your message, I'm going to invite their comments, if you're willing to have a dialogue with them."

"Oh, lord, yes," Dory exclaimed, hiccuping. "If you'll just forgive me for one moment. I'm so sorry, I know this is going to look very strange..." She stood up and bent over.

The hosts looked on in amazement as she stood immobile for a moment, then sat back down in her seat, smoothing her hair.

"I'm so sorry," she said again in a rush. "I get the hiccups when I feel overwhelmed or otherwise excited, and that's the only thing that will stop them."

Monica started to laugh, then Candace, and even Sophia cracked a grin. The audience followed suit as Dory shrugged helplessly.

"I'm okay now, and I'd be so happy to entertain any questions or comments from the audience," she said, looking out into the crowd.

The aide appeared in the center aisle with a cordless microphone and rushed to the first hand tentatively raised.

"I think Monica said it all," a middle-aged woman said. "I don't agree with what you did at all, and you should be ashamed. But I'm glad to know that you *are* ashamed. There are so many people reported on in the media today who do the most disgraceful things and never take an iota of responsibility. But you have, and I think that speaks volumes for you. And I think your parents would be very proud of you for that."

Applause greeted that, and Dory wiped her face again.

"Thank you," she said in a low voice. "Thank you so much. That means the world to me."

The conversation continued for a few more minutes. One or two people scolded her for what she had done, but some who had read the book told why they liked it and asked what the new one was about. Dory gave an outline of the story and repeated her offer.

Shortly, Monica thanked the audience for their comments and started to wrap the segment up. She turned to Sophia and asked her directly what her opinion was. Dory held her breath. This response could negate the little headway she felt she had made in the last few minutes.

Sophia looked at her with a cautious expression.

"Well, it's not the first time this has been done, God knows," she said. "I'm sure it won't be the last. There are famous cases of people who completely invented entire stories and hoodwinked some of the most prestigious news and book publishers in the world. Some of them recovered their careers and are again successful authors.

"I really, really dislike what you did, let me be plain," she said to Dory. "You diminished the hard work of writers who strive to write the absolute truth, and that has repercussions. You feed into the 'fake news' hysteria, or at least don't counter it, and that undermines the very fabric of our culture. So shame on you."

Dory nodded.

"On the other hand, I give you props for coming clean," she said. "That takes guts. And it might be that you had to do it because Gwen is a good reporter and was going to blow your cover anyway, I don't know.

"But I believe you. I believe you simply blew it in a moment of weakness—or a week of weaknesses, however long—and that you've suffered personally for it. It's never comfortable to find out that we're not the vision of perfection we all would like to think we are.

So, I forgive you. But you'd better know, I'm going to give a critical eye to whatever you write in the future, my dear. You'd better fly right from now on."

Dory smiled gratefully.

"Yes, ma'am. I know. And I will. And thank you."

Monica turned to the camera and said, "Thank you, Dory, for joining us. We'll take a break now and return with Chef Kathleen, preparing some of the summer's best recipes with a Fourth of July flair. Stay with us."

Dory rose shakily from her seat and shook the hand of each of the moderators. "Thank you," she said. "I am really grateful for the opportunity you gave me." And to Sophia she added, "And I heard you. You were right on all counts. From here on in, you can bet your last dollar that I will be the most ethical writer you know."

Sophia smiled. "I know. That's why I said it. The whole country's watching you now, girlfriend. Go and do good things."

Dory left the building elated. It had gone so much better than she had any right to expect. The way ahead would be a hard slog, she knew. First, she had to finish the next book as fast as she could—luckily it was almost done—and then she had to do the mass social media apology and book offer, and then the most intensive of all: the rebuilding of her fan base, responding to emails, social media posts, and individual appearances. She would have to be all things to all people as much as she could be and for as long as it took for her to feel caught up again.

And write, of course, in her "spare time."

She sighed. It was all worth it. She could move on with her life now. *Hallelujah.*

Chapter Twenty-four

"A call? You're issuing a call?"

"Yes, sorry, Jill, but you know what the market's been doing," Bill Bennett, her stock broker, replied in soothing tones. "Your primary margin account is short; you need to put in another twenty thousand to cover it. And we're watching your secondary account, too. Are you monitoring the market?"

"As much as I can stomach, Bill. This is pretty overwhelming."

"Well, yeah, you know, you have that mountain of stock but with the losses, the bill's come due to cover it. And you do love those derivatives, and you don't have any stop-losses. You might want to rethink that approach."

"Now you tell me."

"It's a hard world, Jill. You know that. The lows come with the highs."

"Yeah. Okay, I'll call my bank and arrange for the transfer," Jill said, and hung up.

Jesus. This is disastrous. Well, Daddy always said 'buy low,' so maybe I need to be a little less risk-averse right now. I know I decided to cool it on that, but hard times require hard responses. This is probably a small correction, right? I only need to float for a few days, then I can cash out and recoup my losses. I just won't go all in the way I have been. Boy, that really bit me in the ass. I admit it, I've been reckless, gambling instead of investing.

"Well, let's see what's cooking," she said aloud.

She pulled up her brokerage account page and winced at the sea of red staring back at her. She opened several investing sites and backdated the feed to see what they were discussing before the current crisis. Tech stocks always looked good, the service sector had some promising candidates, and the pharma and energy sectors were generally consistent, if conservative.

"Conservative's good, but I need to make some money, quick."

Pot stocks. Hmm. Canada had recently legalized recreational marijuana and several states were already pulling in millions since their legalization. But they were like penny stocks—how to know which to buy? Instead of the dot-com boom going bust, it could be the pot-com boom and bust. She started reading, losing herself in the interesting details. Medical marijuana looked like a good bet; that was the most acceptable barrier to overcome in states resistant to changing its classification as a Schedule I drug. And there seemed to be a takeover race going on in the bigger pot companies. "Hell, there's even a pot ETF. Looks good." She put in a buy order and went back to her research.

"Asia. Everybody's talking about Asia," she muttered. "I haven't kept up, looking at those other crazy start-ups. What's Alibaba at? Yikes, over two hundred dollars now. But I just heard they're buying the Kroger grocery chain. That has to be good, and I shop there sometimes. What's their stock price? About twenty dollars, much better. And they should rise with the Alibaba merger." She placed her order.

"Okay, cool your jets, girl. You're not really thinking or, certainly, analyzing very hard. You're going by the seat of your pants the way you always do. Daddy would be in your face right now. Tell you you're acting like a spoiled rich brat instead of an adult, and he'd be right. Careless, that's what I am. I'm just so fucking careless. And look where it's gotten me. In a big mess, that's where, in just about every arena."

She rose from her desk and paced restlessly. "Hell, it's five o'clock and I could use some company. That sure doesn't include Taylor, who might be home any time now. I think I'll go down to Sisters for a cocktail. Boy, I know what they'll be talking about tonight."

Sisters was a tiny niche in the Women's Commerce Club, a full-service bar where its female members interested in the financial world could meet and celebrate or commiserate. Jill entered to greetings from an already pretty full room and caught Beverly's eye.

"The usual?" Beverly asked from behind the bar, looking sympathetic.

"Oh, yeah. Make it a double."

"That seems to be the protocol tonight," Beverly answered. "Coming right up."

Jill picked up her martini and made her way to a corner table to join some friends. "Well, I can guess what we're talking about," she said as she settled into the leather chair. "How bad has everyone been hit?"

"Oh, you don't want to know," Barbara said. "My husband is going to kill me. He told me to sell one of our bigger stock holdings over a week ago and I just forgot. I just hope he doesn't take it out of my hide."

"This is just like the real estate bubble." Mona was on the verge of wailing. "I bought three houses to flip at the top of the market and it crashed a week later. I feel cursed, I really do."

"What's happening with you, Jill?" they asked in chorus.

"To tell you the truth, I'm not entirely sure," she answered. "Denial is not a river in Egypt. I went online today and my eyes were so scarred by the sea of red that I looked away immediately. I'll need to build my nerve to do a good analysis. I did some buying, but right now, I just want to drink."

"I'm with you there," Barbara said, taking a healthy swallow of her vodka gimlet and signaling Beverly for another round for the table. "I have a feeling our cruise schedule is going to be severely restricted this year. At the very least."

"Well, if that's it for you, count yourself as fortunate," Therese said, joining the group. "I have clients whose mental health I'm seriously worried about. I've been in business a long time, but this is one of the worst downturns I've seen in a while. I can only hope the uptick will be quick in coming. And that all my clients are alive to see it.

"I'm only partly kidding," she continued. "I have one young man who uses the same accountant I do. He's a rabid day trader who had made about a million in a pretty short time. He told me just a couple of weeks ago that our CPA had suggested he take some of his profits out and put them into more conservative funds, or buy CDs, or save them somehow, just in case. He laughed about it. He is, as of today, officially wiped out. It's a tragedy."

The four slipped into silence, gloomily sipping their liquid therapy.

"Well, there is a bright side, right?" said Jill. "It's a good time to buy."

"Yes, if you have anything left to buy it with,"

Therese said. "But I am pretty optimistic, despite the terrible news today. The basis of the economy is good: inflation's staying low and employment is rising, interest rates are still low and the housing market is good. It'll probably be fine. We just need to stay the course."

"Uh-huh," agreed Jill. "It's just that my particular course, if we're talking in horse racing terms, is going to be considerably shortened. You know, I've been taking stock of my life recently…"

"Uh-oh, it's the pending sixtieth birthday syndrome."

"Bite your tongue, Barbara. I have another year to be young, I'll have you know. But your point is well taken. I've had some, er, bumps in my life recently, even before the market decided to pile on. And it's made me stop and look at my behavior. I've been pretty blissfully ignorant of, well, of everything. Not focusing on anything in particular. Just playing, going on day after day, with my mind in a sort of 'Ommm' hum. It's been that way since I retired."

"I know what you mean," said Barbara. "And my husband is starting to get on me about it. Retiring from management left me with…nothing, sort of. It's been kind of a terrible transition, to tell you the truth. I had no idea how central my career was to my self-image. And not only that, but there was the looming question every day of 'Why should I get up? I don't have to.' So I became this world-champion sleeper. I got really depressed by it all, to tell you the truth. Jerry's pushing me to find something to occupy myself. He says I'm getting gloomy and boring. And I agree. Any ideas?"

"Well, I'm not there yet, and I'm not sure I'll ever be, because I'll probably always have a few clients who just won't let me go. I'm very lucky that way," Therese said. "And I do believe it'll be a life saver to have that consistent thread in my life. I can see that it'd be a terrible shock to suddenly be cut off from a routine you've had for decades, maybe your whole life. How do you prepare for that?"

"I guess by having hobbies all along," Mona said. "But there's something missing in that, too. The reward for hobbies is ephemeral; it's just something you like to do so you do it, and you're satisfied when it's done, until you start again. But there's no visible reward other than the product, if you're making something, for example. The reward when you're working is cold, hard cash. Well, and the respect of your peers, and that's amazingly important on a subliminal level. But that money fuels your life, what you can do with it, how you can direct it, so it's far more important than just a paycheck. It's a symbol of control. It seems to me that when you lose that, you lose control over your life, in a way."

"Wow, I never thought of that," Jill said. "But I think you're right, Mona. I haven't been feeling good about myself in quite some time, truth be told. And the more I distract myself with inconsequential things, or people—not including you, ladies—the more rootless I feel. I feel like I need to take charge of my life again, actually direct it instead of floating through it. And I guess with the market the way it is, this is as good a time to start as ever. But you know what? I wonder if I can. How's that for a depressive outlook?"

"Not good, not good at all, sweetie. But you know you can," Mona said. "Everyone gets off the track now and then. Your daddy taught you well, you have the skills. You just need to exercise some self-discipline to get back in the swing of things. That's the challenge, because when you're depressed you just don't feel like you have the energy. But you do, Jill, and you can. I have faith in you."

"Well, thanks, ladies, I do appreciate it," Jill said. "Hate to break this up, but I'm meeting a friend for dinner tonight so I have to go. Keep the faith and I'll see you later."

Jill tipped the valet and moved down the winding drive toward the street. As she pulled out, she fussed with the radio to find a Sirius station to suit her mood, until a blaring horn and the sound of brakes startled her. She had pulled out right in front of an oncoming car, which just barely missed her. Shaken, she pulled over to collect herself, and selected the peaceful music of Spa to aid in the effort.

Jesus. I only had two martinis. Is that it? Never bothered me before. Or is it my mind? I've been wondering about that pretty often lately. What is happening to me? I feel like I'm just falling apart! Her eyes welled with tears, but she shook that off with an impatient shake of her head and moved back onto the road.

Still, she was feeling unsettled and blue when she pulled into the Buckhead Diner. She slid into a booth to wait for Charlene and ordered another martini. That went down easily as she checked her cell phone, so she ordered another. She was sipping on that, thinking gloomy thoughts, when she spotted Charlene pulling up to the front. She paid no attention as she came in and so was surprised when not only Charlene, but Vivian also slipped into her corner booth, facing her.

"Well! Hello," she said in surprise. "Hey, Vivian, wasn't expecting you, but as usual, you're a sight for sore eyes." She knew her powers of observation were dulled by the alcohol, but she sensed something was different about her two friends, and quickly became suspicious.

"Now, wait a minute, what's going on?" she demanded, slurring a bit as she eyed her companions. "Something tells me this isn't just the happy hour I was expecting."

"No, it looks like you've had quite enough of a happy hour already," Charlene said placidly, but skewering her with a look. "How many martinis have you had so far, Jill?"

"Oh, never mind." Jill waved her off. "You know I can hold my liquor. It's the crazy people on the road that you should be more worried about. Someone almost broadsided me coming out of the Commerce Club on the way here."

"What?" Vivian exclaimed, alarmed. "The view up the road is pretty clear there. What happened? What were you doing?"

"Oh, nothing," Jill said. "Just adjusting the radio, trying to find a station."

"Um-hum," said Charlene, calmly. "And didn't you have another close call just last week?"

"Yeah, but that was his fault," Jill said. "If he hadn't been a cop, I would've brought charges."

"Shoot, girl, you were lucky you didn't get arrested," Charlene said, more severely this time. "How long do you think you can go on like this, Jill? And what's been happening with you? You've always been a little—what's the word—well, wild, but you didn't used to be reckless. And you have us worried."

"Oh, my God, is this an intervention? Are you fucking serious? Oh, please. Where did this come from?"

Vivian reached over and took her hand. "You don't have to call it that," she said soothingly. "We just are worried, you know? And don't you owe it to us, your friends, to listen and reassure us?"

"Well." Jill huffed, slightly mollified. "I don't want you all worrying about me, that's for sure. Why are you?"

"Well, you're drinking pretty heavily lately, you know?" Charlene said.

"And I know your financial situation is not ideal," chimed in Vivian. "You shared access to your accounts with me with the Taylor investigation, remember?"

"Yes, and between your behavior and yesterday's market report, we thought that a conversation with your loving friends might be warranted."

"Oh, Taylor." Jill moaned at the thought.

"And yes, there's Taylor. What's with this sudden engagement, for God's sake?" Charlene demanded. "Just after telling us how suspicious you were getting about her?"

They stared, mystified, as Jill began to laugh, then in concern as her laughter became slightly hysterical and turned into tears.

"Oh, God. Okay, I admit it, I'm a little drunk," she finally said, wiping her eyes. "My life is such a clusterfuck these days." She paused as her voice wavered, and Vivian took her hand again. Charlene took the other one.

"So tell us, baby, what's going on?" Charlene said gently.

"Let me," Vivian said as Jill continued to pause. She filled Charlene in quickly on the information she had gathered and the meeting she and Jill had attended in DC with Taylor's other victims, as well as Jill's wedding trap. Charlene sat back, silent and wide-eyed, as the narrative continued, then turned to Jill.

"Well, that's one thing. What about your money?" Charlene asked, casting an inquiring glance to Vivian as well. "Viv, you used to be in big bank investing. What do you think?"

"I think our girl here has sort of lost her financial marbles," Vivian said bluntly. "Jill, it's not just the market downturn that's damaged you, it's what you've been doing. I'll just ask it outright: are you a gambling addict?"

Jill stared at her, started to answer harshly, and then stopped. Silence reigned at the table for several minutes as Charlene and Vivian patiently waited. They watched Jill's face change as she stared at the table, from defensive outrage, to introspection, and finally to utter sadness. "I don't know," she whispered, looking up at them with moist eyes.

"I just don't know," she repeated. "I know I've done some boneheaded investments lately—"

"Boneheaded?"

"Okay, crazy," Jill admitted with a small, apologetic smile. "Like that company I was banking on to win the lawsuit and return megabucks."

"And Harrah's," Charlene added.

"Yes, there's the casinos, brick-and-mortar and online," Jill said, shaking her head. "I just don't know. It's such a high when I win that I just can't stop. It's the same with the market."

She paused. "Oh. I guess that's the definition of an addict, isn't it?" she said, voice wavering again.

Charlene and Vivian nodded and took her hands again. "When did this start? Do you remember?" Vivian asked.

"Oh, yes, I do," Jill answered promptly. "When I retired. I just suddenly didn't have anything to do. I educated myself on the stock market so I could handle my investments myself instead of paying so much to the money managers. Huh, don't get me started on the money managers. Bunch of thieves!

"So that did it for a while. I read, of course. I hung out with my friends as much as their schedule would allow, and made new ones. And I always had my causes to raise money for. But it wasn't the same. More and more, I'd wake up in the morning and think 'I should get up,' and then I'd think 'What for?' and roll back over. I was sleeping my life away.

"Then one day, on a lark, I went with one of my Commerce Club buddies on an outing to Cherokee Casino in North Carolina. It was fall and the drive was beautiful. It was so much fun we stayed an extra day. So I started taking those junkets by myself and then I thought, 'Why travel?' and just started gambling online."

"You've severely drained your accounts," Vivian said gravely.

"I know," Jill said. "When my broker, Bill, called with a market call earlier today, I almost freaked, and it's never been a concern before. There was always plenty, no worries. God, I've become one of those profligate trust fund brats and it shames me to say it. And I guess that's why I've been so moody and unsettled lately. I just don't recognize myself anymore. I'm really ashamed of myself."

At that, her voice broke completely and she fell silent, staring down at the table.

The waiter took this inopportune time to come ask for their orders, and Vivian took over.

"Steaks, three, medium rare. Three house salads, house dressing. Roasted potatoes all around. Water, and a big pot of coffee. Leave both. Got it?"

"Yes, ma'am." He nodded and hastily withdrew.

Charlene leaned across the table and pressed Jill's hand in hers. "Darling girl. You know I love you. We all do, and we've been watching with increasing alarm as you've teetered closer to the rails. We're not going to let you go over, and that's that. The good part is, you have a good head on your shoulders."

Jill stifled a sob and shook her head in misery, dabbing at her eyes, and reached for her martini.

"Huh-uh," said Vivian firmly, pulling it away and pushing the glass of ice water toward her. "That's enough of that."

"Yes, it certainly is," Charlene agreed. "Time for some tough love, girlfriend. I'll start with the good part. You *do* have a good head on your shoulders. I can tell you've been thinking about this for a while, or you would have blistered us with an immediate defense the minute you got the drift of this conversation."

Jill nodded reluctantly. "Yes, I have," she said. "It just made me feel worse and worse, more of a failure every time I looked at my life. I even thought about needing to get real about my investments and actually did a little research before buying yesterday."

"Yes, I saw that," Vivian said. "And I think you did all right in your judgments. I'm just not sure about the amounts you allocated. It might be time to be a little more conservative in your actions."

"So, you've already started, you see?" Charlene said encouragingly. "You didn't get here in a minute and you won't get out in a minute, either, but you're on your way and you started all by yourself. And to tell you the truth, I wonder if this finding out about Taylor didn't help you on your way back. There's nothing like anger, sometimes, to sharpen the senses.

"Which brings me to my next point. You needn't feel ashamed, Jill. Everyone makes mistakes. But the one thing I do wish you'd done differently was to not hold all this within yourself. Once the spiral begins, it often takes an outside perspective to help you step away from it and regain your equilibrium. You didn't do that. You completely ignored your safety net—us. And for that, I really *am* pissed off at you. How could you think so little of us that you didn't think of how we could help?"

"I thought I could win," Jill whispered. "I thought I could get it all back and no one would ever have to know what a fool I'd been. Except it just got worse and worse. And then I met Taylor and got all embroiled in that mess, which skewed my thinking even more. Well, not that I was doing much thinking."

She looked so embarrassed that they all had to burst out laughing, even harder than the comment deserved, the relief was so great.

"Oh, yeah," said Charlene, wiping her eyes. "Well, there is that, isn't there? But sweetie, I do want to talk to you seriously about your addiction. Maybe it's not a chronic thing, but it has affected your life, and very seriously. Jill, I think you should consider joining Gamblers Anonymous, at least for a while. See where you fit into all that. No matter what the outcome, I don't think it can do anything but help."

Jill frowned and eyed her discarded martini, which Vivian whisked away to the bus table.

"There," she said, sitting again. "That takes care of that. You don't need it, Jill. One of the things that attracted me to you from the beginning was your clear strength of will. You remind me of your oil wildcatter ancestors. You're nobody's fool, at least not for long. So you've been foolish for a while. You had a major life change when you retired, and the impact of that shouldn't be underestimated. You happened to have had enough disposable cash to ignore the psychological implications and fall into some bad habits.

"But that's not you. You are a businesswoman and philanthropist, a very intelligent person. Passionate, but on the whole, balanced. That's who you are. And that's who you'll get back to being. And you'll stop feeling sorry for yourself, dammit!"

"Yes, a thousand times yes!" cried Charlene. "Now, straighten up and fly right, Jill. The time has come. We're not getting any younger, and you're past the time for being a mewling helpless little thing."

"Ouch," said Jill, wincing.

"Well, yes, ouch," Charlene said firmly. "You have it coming, you know? 'To whom much is given, much is expected,' remember? And you've been given a lot. So grow up and use it."

"And now, here's your steak," added Vivian calmly as the waiter arrived. "Intervention over. Let's eat."

Jill stared at her two friends for a moment as the plates were delivered, then picked up her knife and fork.

She put them down again.

"I love you guys," she said, looking both in the eye. "Thank you. You and Robby and Dory are my greatest treasures. I will look into GA. I promise."

"Good." Charlene nodded.

"Best news I've had all day," said Vivian. "Now,

bon appetite!"

And, smiling, they all dug in.

A few miles away, Robby and Dory were strolling in companionable silence as they walked Killer along the tree-shaded sidewalks of Virginia-Highland. Greeting the occasional neighbor and their pets, they ambled along admiring the stately new houses and comfortable old cottages that defined the neighborhood. Killer paused often, seeming to find a new and fascinating bulletin from the neighborhood dogs on every blade of grass.

At one stop, Robby announced, "Well, I've decided."

"Decided what, sweetie?" Dory absently asked as they moved along.

"Your punishment. No chocolate for a month."

Killer looked back in puzzlement as Dory stopped dead in her tracks. "Oh!" she wailed. "A *month*?" She looked at Robby in dismay.

"Don't tell me you think that's too harsh. I know your sweet tooth will make that hard, Dory, but it hardly even matches the infraction. You really shook up our relationship, to its foundation. "

"Yes, I know." Dory sighed. "You're right, of course. But oh, no chocolate. For a whole month! I know it seems silly, but that's harsh. I've never even gone a couple of days without some chocolate. It's my major jones." She brightened on reflection. "At least I might lose a little weight."

Robby had to laugh as they moved on. "You make lemonade out of lemons better than anyone I know, girl. And if it makes you feel any better, don't forget I'm depriving myself, too. You know how I adore your German chocolate cake."

"Oh, that reminds me, I'm making it for the neighborhood meeting next week. Well, at least you won't be completely deprived. But seriously, darling," she said, stopping again. "You know how I feel. I'd make you chocolate cakes every single day if I thought that would help erase the pain and trouble I caused."

"Don't tempt me, but no need, baby," Robby replied, nodding to a passing neighbor. "Water under the bridge. We're good." She gestured to a creamy brick, two-story traditional house with shamrocks carved in the gleaming white bargeboard of the eaves. "Oh, look, they're doing some work on the wedding cake house. I guess that porte-cochere did need a little work."

"Well, thank goodness," Dory joked, putting her arm in Robby's. "Heaven knows we can't have tacky porte-cocheres in our 'hood. How do you even know that term?"

"Hey, I might've been a cop, but I've got years of home improvement shows under my belt, too. A little respect, here, okay?"

Dory smiled up at her lover as they turned the corner. "Abso-tively. You got it, love," she said, and they wandered back toward home in absolute contentment.

Chapter Twenty-five

The Capitol City Club was resplendent in its full summer bloom, grass militarily cut, fine topiaries carefully groomed, fountains splashing, and brilliant blooms crowding the beds. Uniformed valets received the top-of-the-line cars in the curving driveway and whisked them away to their safe resting place.

The crème de la crème of Atlanta society was present. Designer dresses and suits ruled the day. Each hair was cut to the millimeter of perfection. The best Charles Heidsiek champagne bubbled and glowed in crystal glasses soundlessly delivered by the almost invisible servers. The guests settled into their chairs, low-voiced conversations providing a whispering background to the scene as hushed footsteps carried late arrivers to their seats. Classical music played softly as the afternoon sun bathed the floral arrangements at the front of the room.

"Oh, quit fussing," Jill said as Taylor readjusted her orchid corsage for the tenth time. "You know you look beautiful, as usual."

"Well, you know, it's not every day a girl gets married," Taylor replied archly. Since she had accepted Jill's proposal, her manner of speaking to her had relaxed considerably. She was less deferential and much more assured, Jill thought grimly to herself, then suppressed a smile.

"I know," she said. "You don't have to tell me that. I never imagined that I'd be walking down the aisle, personally. So, who's that guy you seemed to recognize out there?"

"Oh, that's Cisco," Taylor said, frowning. "I'm kind of annoyed he's here, actually. I didn't invite him, just mentioned we were getting married and he must have gotten the details from the newspaper announcement. He's just an old business acquaintance from LA. Don't know the guy next to him. But I'd be surprised if he hung around after today. Well, it's another present, right?"

"I suppose," Jill replied smoothly. "Long as he's not a crasher, honey."

"No, no one to worry about." Taylor turned to admire herself in the mirror again. She had chosen a creamy silk Vera Wang gown, cinched tightly with an enormous silk rose just off-center to her tiny waist below a gathered strapless top. Its billowing skirt was complemented in front by an overlaid, v-split voile skirt, below a similarly split silk one. Diamonds sparkled at her throat and demurely twinkled on her ears through her luxurious mane of thick hair. Her strikingly blue eyes were subtly adorned with dark liner, with a faintly lavender shadow on her lids and a dusky gray in the lid crease. Her naturally high cheekbones were highlighted by a slightly darker blush below them. She looked like a queen and, head held high, she proudly carried herself like one.

"By the way, speaking of LA, you haven't mentioned the movie in a while. What's going on?" Jill idly asked.

"Oh, not much," Taylor replied. "I forgot to tell you. Sorry, baby, but the investment window closed and my part of it is over. We'll just be watching for returns now, but it'll be a couple of years, of course, until production is wrapped. I'm sure Paolo will keep us apprised."

"Oh, I see," Jill said. *Yeah. Better the equal partner in the bank accounts than a quick hit-and-run, huh? Oh, Taylor, how your lying eyes do deceive. But they are beautiful eyes, no one can contest that.*

The string quartet finished Handel's *Water Music*, the entry cue, and Taylor gathered herself for the march down the aisle. Jill opened the door and held out her arm. "My dear," she said, soberly.

Taylor seemed to come to the moment suddenly, a little taken aback at Jill's demeanor. "Goodness, darling." She laughed. "You needn't be so grim. This is a happy day, right?"

"Unforgettable, for sure." Jill smiled, placing Taylor's hand on her arm and guiding her through the foyer toward the aisle. The quartet segued into Pachelbel's *Canon in D* when the two appeared at the door. Taylor quickly shifted from modestly downcast eyes to a triumphantly broad smile, clearly enjoying the admiring glances as she passed.

"Lord, there's just no way around it," Dory hissed bitterly to Robby. "The woman is simply gorgeous. I just can't believe that this is happening, though. And so fast! I can't help thinking that Jill is making a huge mistake."

Robby nodded soberly. "Well, nothing we can do about it now," she murmured back. "We'll just have to be there for her if it all comes tumbling down."

"And who's that attractive woman with Charlene, and the other one?" asked Dory, craning her neck as inconspicuously as possible.

"Oh, I think she's a friend of Wallace's," Robby whispered back, smiling. "Her name's Vivian. I don't know the other person."

"Oh, *that's* Vivian?" Dory said, wide-eyed. "Oh, my. Well. Hmm. No wonder Jill's been a little distracted lately and less enamored of Taylor. Which is why I'm just so bloody confounded right now. What on earth is Jill doing marrying Taylor when she's been admiring Vivian for weeks?"

"You're right," Robby said thoughtfully. "I know, it all makes zero sense. But I have a feeling that something's going on. Look how placid Charlene looks. Maybe she knows something we don't."

Dory suddenly looked sharply at her beloved, whose lips were twitching into a smile. "Robby, is there something you're not telling me?" she demanded in a whisper. "Why are you smiling? You do, you *know* something! Out with it."

"Hush, too late, baby. They're about to begin. Just watch and enjoy the show."

Thunderstruck, Dory sat back in her chair and turned her eyes to the front.

The Justice of the Peace looked like he came straight out of Central Casting, dark hair with a touch of gray at the temples and dark eyes that echoed his smile.

"Dearly beloved," he began. "We are gathered here to witness the joining of these two people in the celebration of marriage."

Taylor stared at him raptly as he continued with the time-honored ceremony. He described the characteristics of a happy union and enjoined the couple to work toward those ends before inviting anyone with an objection to the union to "speak now or forever hold their peace."

Silence reigned as a few heads turned with bemused smiles. Everyone looked back to the officiant who cleared his throat to continue, when a voice startled everyone.

"Ah, yes, I have a word or two to say." Vivian rose and moved down the aisle with the companion Dory had spotted. Mouths gaped as they approached the couple.

Taylor whirled around, furious, her eyes flashing at this arrogant intruder.

"What the hell do you mean? Who are you? How dare you disrupt my wedding?"

Vivian smiled. "Well, ma'am, my name is Vivian Rhodes and I am a private investigator. I have a client who has some questions about your integrity."

"And I'm Ramona Phipps," added another voice as a woman stood. "Remember me, Catherine? Surely you haven't forgotten our time in Provincetown?"

"Oh, but you must remember me, Olivia," came another voice as an elegant, older woman rose. "We so enjoyed our trip to Hawaii. I'm sure it was just a coincidence that my bank account was short ten thousand dollars after you disappeared."

Taylor's angry expression evaporated as her face blanched, and she stepped back slightly as she looked about wildly. Jill supported her arm in an ever-tightening embrace. But she stood erect to make her last stand.

"You have no right to come in here and make such wild accusations, any of you! I have nothing to hide and, even if I did, this is not the time or place to raise such complaints."

Vivian and her companion had reached the front

of the room. Taylor tossed her head and dismissed Vivian with a contemptuous look, but then looked questioningly at her companion.

"Well, ma'am, I'm sorry to dispute that, but I'm afraid the time really is now. I am Special Agent Deborah Foster, Federal Bureau of Investigations, Fraud Division." Her right hand reached under her jacket. "It is my painful duty, Ms. Smith—or should I say Ms. Harris? Or perhaps Ms. Robbins is more to your liking?—to arrest you for violation of the Securities Act of 1933 and the Securities Exchange Act of 1934. I have some colleagues in other agencies who are mightily interested in talking with you, too."

The audience gasped and Taylor stared at her, motionless. Shaking herself, she turned to Jill, stark terror in her eyes. "Jill?" she said pleadingly.

Jill held her arm even more tightly as Agent Foster reached for her arm, and Taylor quailed under the sheer fury in Jill's eyes.

"Oh, Taylor," she said icily. "Did you think it would be this easy? Do I look like a fool? Did you not think that I wouldn't have you checked out when you started trying to fleece me and, worse, my friends in your phony investments? Oh, please. Your time is over, darlin', and you can take that to the bank. Pardon the pun."

As she turned away, Taylor uttered a single strangled cry as Agent Foster pulled her hands behind her back. Her eyes swept the room, stopping as two men stood. Only then did she notice that one was handcuffed as well, his arm held by the official-looking gentleman next to him.

"Cisco?" she said, hardly breathing.

"Sorry, doll," he replied. "But a plea bargain is a

plea bargain."

Taylor looked desperately around for help, but the faces she saw reflected only confusion that was changing, in some cases, to outrage. The agent guided her, pale as death, back down the aisle, but she halted abruptly as a big vision in a white tuxedo stepped into the aisle before her. Bear folded her strong arms across her chest and smiled broadly at Taylor.

In an instant, her fury returned.

"You," Taylor shouted loathingly as Bear smiled in delight.

"Yes, ma'am," Bear chortled. "Why, it purely tickled me to death to be able to help prove you were present the night of the Buckhead burglary. Not that you could have had anything to do with it, of course."

Taylor stared at her, transfixed, and Bear's grin spread even broader.

"Oh, sorry, darlin', I know it's hard for a skinny little white uptown bitch like you to wrap her mind around someone like me having any effect at all on your privileged life. But trust me, if I can't whup that sorry ass for your spoiled-brat, racist, classist attitude, I'll take this as a second-best consolation prize. Have fun in the slammer, bitch."

Taylor continued to stare back at Bear in disbelief as Agent Foster hustled her back down the aisle in a much different fashion than she had imagined.

Dory sat, still stunned, until the sound of Robby's soft chuckle brought her back to her senses.

"Robby Martin, you knew about this, didn't you?" she whispered accusingly. "And it must've been in the works for quite some time to have all the arrangements in place. Oh, my gosh, arrangements! Jill must've spent a fortune on this, and all for nothing?"

Robby nodded as she watched Taylor's exit, big designer rose all askew, still craning her neck at Bear.

"Yes, but I didn't know until recently. And I wouldn't say it was all for nothing, either. Look at Jill. I think she's having a very good day."

Dory looked to the front of the room and beheld a triumphant Jill, surrounded by her friends and acquaintances and smiling broadly. Nor did it miss her notice that Vivian was close by her side, helping her field the questions being peppered at them.

"Good grief," Dory said. "It's going to take me a while to comprehend all of this. And *you*," she said accusingly. "Are going to help me do it, you little rat."

"Understood," Robby answered, laughing. "Now, shall we go to Jill's wedding-reception-turned-victory party? She called me this morning to let me know that this was all a 'go,' and that we should be ready to party hearty. And I, for one, am ready to do that. Shall we?"

"Yes, ma'am." Dory smiled, taking her hand. "Well, if this don't just beat all, though," she said, shaking her head. "Good God, what a day. What could happen next? Oh, I know, don't ever ask that, you find out. Well, okay, onward. I think I could use a drink as I process all this."

Chapter Twenty-six

The after-work crowd at Two Urban Licks had not yet begun drifting in as the friends gathered for their leisurely catch-up dinner. Charlene had arrived first and raised her wine glass in salute, then gestured grandly to the appetizers awaiting her friends.

"Welcome, ladies. Hope you don't mind my going ahead," she said. "I got the salmon chips and roasted artichoke to get us started." As Robby, Dory, and Jill settled into the booth, the waiter hustled over to take their drink orders.

"Good evening, ladies, welcome back. The usual?" he asked.

Robby nodded. "Yup, a Blue Stripe beer, please."

Dory got her vodka gimlet. And Jill, smiling, shocked everyone by ordering a seltzer and lime. That stopped the action immediately.

"Jill?" Dory asked, peering at her friend. "Since when is the martini queen not drinking? I know you're not pregnant. Are you all right, honey?"

Jill laughed at the mystified looks surrounding her, except for Charlene, who smiled in approval.

"No, no worries, my friends. I'm fine. Better than fine, actually. Boy, have I got a lot to tell you."

"What? More?" exclaimed Dory, eyebrows raised. "What more could you possibly have to tell after the incredible wedding-that-wasn't?"

"Oh, lord, where to begin? Well, okay, the wedding. It was a gas, wasn't it?"

"A gas? A *gas*?" Dory laughed. "Are you kidding? It was the event of the century. It'll be ages before Atlanta society stops talking about it. My God, it was better than any movie thriller I've ever seen. So help me, I'll never forget the look of loathing and rage on Taylor's face as she was dragged back down the aisle, big bow all askew. Good lord."

Jill smiled. "I know. I feel a little small, I have to confess, at the lack of pity I feel for her. And I mean none. Real *schadenfreude*. Oh, and one more detail I found out from Vivian: turns out Taylor took out a big life insurance policy on me. Geez, that made me shiver, I have to say. No telling how far that girl would go."

"Oh, my God." Charlene breathed in sharply. "That's downright sinister."

"Yeah," Robby soberly agreed. "Gee, so sorry you've had such a boring life lately, Jill. So what's with the non-alcoholic beverage?"

"Oy. Okay, I have something to tell you," she said. "Charlene knows already. Well, you might have noticed I've been a little, uh, flighty lately."

Robby choked and she mock-glared at her.

"Okay, okay, maybe flighty is not the word. More like 'crazed' might be more appropriate," she admitted.

"Well, now that you mention it, yeah," Robby said sympathetically. "I noticed every now and then and wanted to help with whatever it was, but it seems like we've all been running in circles lately."

"Boy, ain't that the truth," Dory said. "Every single one of us. Whatever happened to our peaceful lives? But anyway, hon, what's been wrong? Well, other than Taylor, of course."

"Boy howdy, and wasn't that just enough?" Jill said. "But no, this predates even Taylor, although her free-spending ways and sort of chaotic approach to life didn't help much."

"Yes, we noticed in New Orleans," Robby said. "She never did stint on the cost, did she?"

"No, that's for sure. Anyway," Jill continued. "Since I retired I've sort of been at sixes and sevens. It's like I lost my center of gravity when I left my work. I didn't realize what an organizing principle in my life that was. And I got—hmm, what's the word—well, sloppy, I guess. I lost my discipline completely, and it's affected everything. Like, my own self-image, and lately, my finances."

"Oh, dear," Dory said. "We were wondering if you were okay after the downturn, but you seemed to brush it off."

"Yes, well, I brushed off everything. But here's the thing: the less I paid attention to actually running my own life, the more I drifted and the less I liked myself. And the less I liked myself, the more self-destructive I became. I think I was desperate to be distracted from the me I was coming to despise, so I looked for distractions like Taylor and sex and drinking."

"Oh, yeah," Dory said, rolling her eyes. "Those are the big ones."

"Anyway, so Vivian had access to my financial accounts to monitor and keep them from Taylor's greedy little fingers, and she could see what I was doing. Like, incredibly dumb investments, which is bad enough, but also no protection for my accounts from any downturn, like a stop-loss order."

"Uh-oh," said Robby. "How bad were you hit?"

"Oh, you don't want to know," Jill said, shaking

her head. "Daddy must be rolling over in his grave. Well, enough to make some back, for sure, and pay for the 'wedding,' but I'm seriously depleted overall. Funny, money doesn't mean much when you have it, but it sure rises in importance when you don't, huh? Relatively speaking."

"Amen," said Dory emphatically.

"Oh, yes, that's right, Dory," Jill said. "I forgot! Can't wait to hear your report. Well, I'm just about done.

"So, it turns out that Charlene had been watching me pretty closely." She looked at Charlene, who smiled at her. "And she and Vivian got their heads together and staged an intervention. I couldn't believe it. But it just so happened that they did it the very day I almost got broadsided coming out of the Women's Commerce Club, probably because of the two or three martinis I'd had before getting behind the wheel. I was pretty shaken. So I was vulnerable to their confronting me, or I would've just gotten mad and read them the riot act, and not listened to a word."

"Oh, Jill." Dory whispered.

Robby, who had remained silent, had a face like a thundercloud. Abruptly, she leaned forward and spat out, "Dammit, Jill! You know I'm not one to go on, but I swear, I could just kill you right now. What the hell were you thinking? You of all people could afford to call a service to take you wherever you wanted to go. Or call one of us. And not just for a ride, either, lady. How dare you suffer in silence when you have a posse at your beck and call, ready to listen and help twenty-four seven? I thought we were friends."

Jill hung her head. "I know, I know. I'm sorry, really. Not only because I agree it was sort of insulting to you, but also because my pride didn't do me any good at all. I just sank further and further into the abyss. But Charlene and Vivian's come-to-Jesus talk came at the right time. And that's why I'm not drinking right now, I'm just taking a little vacation until it's just a pleasurable experience again, and not a crutch or a habit. And I'm paying close attention to the market and my investments, to battle back. If I don't, I do believe Daddy'll haunt me!"

"Please don't be so hard on Jill, darling," Dory said gently, putting her hand on Robby's clenched fists. "I know how a person can spiral down into a situation and lose her way out."

"Right. Well. Just don't do it again." Robby huffed, barely mollified.

"You have my heartfelt promise," Jill said sincerely.

The waiter arrived and took their orders, and they looked at each other expectantly. Dory sighed and said "Okay, I guess I'll go next."

"So, you know about the book. I met with Robert, my publisher, and he was just as unhappy as you might imagine. Partly because I did just what you did, Jill—I didn't share my problem with him, the person I probably most needed to talk to, professionally speaking. I stayed silent for a solid year. Poor guy. If we weren't old friends, it would've been much, much worse, I'm sure.

"So, I told him about a strategy I'd developed with my publicist, Annabelle, and my meeting with Gwen Fanning, the writer who made me come out with the truth. Which, I have to tell you, was such a relief.

"After a while I finally heard from Robert. He was still royally pissed off, as you can imagine. I'm sad to think that our relationship probably will never be the same. But he's a businessman and he liked my new book a lot, so he's not going to fire me or sue me. He agreed to gamble on publishing me once more. I'm glad and grateful. And I'll spend the rest of my career trying to make it up to him.

"So, part of the strategy was to go on *Perspective*..."

"I know," Charlene said. "You did great! We all watched, of course."

"And that turned out pretty well, thank God. Some were ugly, but the audience in general gave me credit for being honest, if late, about it. The panel, too. I got off easy.

"Now, the second and third and probably into-infinity steps are to respond to as much of the email and social media posts that as I humanly can. Boy, is that ever a challenge. Social media never stops. But I figure I'll give it a month or two and then gradually taper off some, when I'm old news. Maybe longer, I'll see.

"The biggest thing is my new book offer, which seems to be working. Annabelle pointed out that it could increase my mailing list, and it has, immensely, which can only be good. So I'll make much less from this book, at half off, but I'll get some, and Robert will still do well. He's been encouraged by the public response and the sales of *Quitting*, even, since the TV show. So I'll potentially have a lot more people buying the new book, so it might wash. And, this is the best book I've written yet, so hopefully that'll help even more.

"Whew. Well, that was exhausting, but most of my life is, these days. There's just one area that's not and I want to acknowledge that publicly." She turned to Robby. "I want to say for the record how much I love my soulmate, and how much beyond grateful I am to her for forgiving me and helping me through this awful mess. I'll be making it up to you for the rest of my life too, Robby Martin. I love you."

"Hear, hear," said Charlene.

There was a moment of silence as they sipped their drinks and the dinner was served. Cutlery scraped on plates and appreciative "Mmms" echoed around the table, until Charlene cleared her throat. Eyes turned expectantly to her as she took another sip of her wine.

"Well, I suppose I've been in drama, too, as you know," she said. "But it turned out fine in the end. Connie did, in fact, have a daughter, who's a pretty neat human being, too. Danielle's a nursing student at UC Santa Barbara, and a good one. And Connie, once her defenses crumbled, turned out to be the okay person I remembered. She was just desperate for her daughter and made the mistake of turning to blackmail to try to rescue her future."

"Despite being perhaps the most miserable failure at blackmail ever," commented Robby.

"Yes," Charlene smiled. "My valiant warriors, Robby and Jessie, found out all about her and I confronted her. It only took a little bit of a challenge for her bravado to fall apart completely."

"Oh, good, so you're done, then?" asked Dory.

"Well, not exactly," Charlene answered. "In fact, my involvement with them will continue for a little while. I'm going to pay for Danielle's schooling."

"What?" Dory exclaimed. "I swear, y'all, you're going to give me a heart attack. What on earth for, Charlene? She's no responsibility of yours. And her mother tried to blackmail you."

"Well, I thought about it," Charlene said softly.

"A lot, actually. It occurred to me that, although I've done some things to contribute to society—at least, I hope I have—I never had the opportunity to know for sure I'd made an impact on an individual person. And I have been blessed with a lot, a lot that I can share. So once I learned about her, I picked her as sort of my personal charity. Kind of a foster, if you will. And I'll tell you all about her. She's eminently worth the support. She's a terrific kid. The world will be better for her being in it."

"Well, I'll be," Dory said. "Char, you are one good human being. Good for you. But I'll reserve my opinion until time tells us more, if you don't mind. And if I get even a hint that you're being taken advantage of..."

Charlene smiled. "I hear ya, Dory, and thank you for caring for me. And I mean that to all of you, you know."

Robby picked up her beer and raised it in a toast. "To us," she said.

"Yes," Dory exclaimed, raising her glass. "May we all be in heaven a half hour before the devil knows we're dead!"

"Good Irish toast, but, I'll do you one better, the Texas way. Here's to our foursome," said Jill. "'I would rather be with the people in this room than with the finest people I know.'"

"Oh, you rat," cried Dory, laughing. "Say something nice."

"Oh, okay, I'll change it." Jill grinned. Here's another: 'Burn old wood, read old books, drink old wine, and keep old friends.' You're stuck with me forever, you guys."

"Hear, hear," said Charlene, and they all took a

sip.

"Right," said Dory. "Now, what else is going on, ladies? Jill, how's Vivian? Oh, a blush, now there's a story! And Charlene, how about an update on Lee?"

Charlene smiled. "Well, she'll be visiting again soon," she said. "And who knows? Maybe even stay."

A chorus of "Oohs" greeted that. "Gee, you know, I have to say I'm kind of amazed. After so many years of having such a quiet and relatively solitary life—well, except for you guys—I'm actually interested in a special woman. Not that you're not special. But will wonders ever cease?"

"Well, honey, you deserve all the happiness possible," Dory said. "I think we all do. And while I think of it, I have something else to toast. I got this in New Orleans and have been waiting until we were all together, just us four. It's a miracle I didn't forget it."

"Imagine that," Jill said.

Dory rolled her eyes at her and pushed on. "No, really. It's a new tradition for us. Look!"

She pulled a small box out of her purse and put it on the table, her friends' eyes fixed on it as she opened it.

"Oh, it's a puzzle," Charlene said.

"Not just a puzzle," Dory said. "Look closer."

Robby grinned. "Well, look at that."

Dory smiled triumphantly. "It's a friendship necklace. Each one of you gets a piece of it, which is why each one has an initial. I figure when we get together to update each other, we can reassemble the whole necklace into the complete heart with each report."

"Oh, I like it," Jill said. "We are all for one, after all."

"And one for all."

Raising their glasses, the four warmly toasted to their good fortune.

"To friendship," said Charlene.

"To our logical family!" cried Dory.

"To happy endings," added Robby

"To the love we share," finished Jill. "The Four Musketeers, a toast to us!"

The candlelight reflected the glow of their glasses and the gleaming silver heart as the four friends resumed their conjoined lives, to whatever new adventures awaited.

About The Author

One day in the mid-1990s, Josette answered a newspaper ad (remember them?) and found her favorite and only freelance client: the Centers for Disease Control and Prevention. She spent more than twenty-five years in a dream career, being her own boss and actually being paid to listen to and report on the most fascinating conversations.

She has been politically active, serving as Chair of Georgia's GAPAC ("gay'pac: How It Sounds Is What We Are"), the forerunner of the political powerhouse that is now Georgia Equality. During her tenure she served as chief cook and bottle washer for the GAPAC News, a LGBT newspaper, and along the way she had articles published in the Atlanta Journal-Constitution and Creative Loafing. Now, she gives small but regular donations to the causes she holds dear and of course writes letters and emails to people who really should be doing better.

Josette likes to make a point in her books, and this one is all about community. It's her first with the Sapphire Publishing family, a community that she's thrilled to join.

Other books by Sapphire Authors

Twisted Deception - ISBN - 978-1-939062-47-5

There are two types of people who can't look you in the eyes: someone trying to hide a lie and someone trying to hide their love.

Addie Blake's life isn't black and white—more like a series of short bursts of color that sustain her until the next eruption. She isn't a ladder-climber in the corporate world. Instead, she works long hours at the office and even at home, something her mechanic girlfriend, Drake Hogan, can't stand. If Addie can't focus on Drake, then Drake finds arm candy that will. After a long week of late nights and a series of text-messaged demands, each one a bigger bomb than the last, Addie has had enough of her Motor Girl.

Greyson Hollister inhabits a world where everything is either black and white, or money green. She's a polished, certified workaholic. As head of Integrated Financial, she has built the ladder others want to climb. Now she intends to attend a business mixer to confront a rumormonger and kill merger rumors involving her company.

Detective Nancy Hill, the lead detective on the Elevator Rapist task force, has just been called in to investigate an attack at Integrated Financial. She can't quite put her finger on it, but something doesn't add up with this latest assault, and Greyson Hollister isn't exactly lending a helping hand.

A storm's brewing on the horizon. Can Addie and Greyson weather it, or will it blow them over?

Highland Dew – ISBN – 978-1-948232-11-1

Bryce Andrews, west coast sales director for Global Distillers and Distribution, is tired of the corporate hamster wheel. She needs a change.

A craft whisky trade show offers her inspiration and a chance to revisit Scotland and the majestic scenery of the Speyside region—best known for the "Whisky Trail." Bryce and her coworker, Reggie Ballard, need to find a wholly original whisky for their international distribution division by visiting a number of small distillers.

A blind curve, a dangling sign, and weed-choked driveway draw Bryce directly into a truly unique opportunity. She discovers a struggling family, a shuttered distillery, and a spitfire of a daughter called home to care for her confused father.

Fiona McDougall—the only child and heir to the MacDougall & Son legacy, had her career teaching in Edinburgh curtailed by fate…or serendipity.

When the stars finally align, the two women work together to resurrect a dream for themselves and the family business—if they can weather the storms of unscrupulous business practices in the competitive whisky market.

CPSIA information can be obtained
at www.ICGtesting.com
Printed in the USA
LVHW112303280119
605607LV00002B/269/P